Published by:
Famous Seamus L.T.D.
London

U.K.

©2018 Mick O' Shea

Illustrations courtesy of Eamonn Byrne

All rights reserved.

No part of this book may be reproduced in any form, or by any means, electronic or mechanical, without prior written permission from the publisher.

9781999910228

First edition printed in London.
www.thefamousseamus.com

Anarchy In The, UK

Mick O'Shea

In Remembrance:

Malcolm McLaren (1946 – 2009)

Sid Vicious (1957 – 1979)

Joe Strummer (1952 – 2002)

Johnny Thunders (1952 – 1991)

Jerry "Niggs" Nolan (1946 - 1992)

Rolf "Nils" Stevenson (1953 – 2002)

Dave Goodman (1951 - 2005)

Tracie O'Keefe (1960 - 1978)

Leee Black Childers (1945 - 2014)

And not forgetting the man without whom none of the following tale would be possible . . .

Bill Grundy (1923 – 1993)

Professional thanks to: Sam Vitale, Simon Maree, Gary Huggins, and everyone at Famous Seamus Publishing, Bernard Rhodes, and Leee Black Childers

Special mention to: Tasha "Bush" Cowen, Shannon "Mini B" Stanley, Matt Whapshott Lisa "T-bag" Bird, Paul Young (not the singer), Sean Young, Roop & Deb, Joel & Aggie from The Old House at Dorking, Ziggy P & Mel King, Gemma and Donna (a.k.a The Girls), Boo & Alex, Zoe Meadows, Dan, Jeannie & "Pinks", Luke & Áine, Tony Makin & Pads, Kat & Jordan, James "Spunky" Willment, "Scouse Mark" Rudge, Chris
"Hammy" Hamilton, Johnny Diamond, Charlotte Belmont, Jack & Kat, Steve & Julie Pyke

Introduction *Anarchy In The UK* is the long-awaited sequel to *Only Anarchists Are Pretty*, which was published by Helter Skelter in October 2004. The idea was always there to pen a sequel at some point but owing to the untimely death of Helter Skelter's CEO, Sean Body in 2008, the manuscript was left simmering on the backburner whilst I got on with other things.

Having been picked up and then dropped again by two other publishers I'd begun to doubt whether the book would ever see the light of day, but my faith was eventually rewarded. Sean's belief was also rewarded when *NME* and *Mojo* both gave *Anarchists* glowing reviews, while Tommy Udo at *Classic Rock* went so far as to hail it as 'Classic New English Library British pulp fiction.' Whilst lamenting that the text wasn't printed on brittle yellow paper bound in a lurid cover, he declared the idea alone to be 'genius' before ending by saying: 'there are eight million great rock 'n' roll stories to be told this way, and so far this has been the best of them.' Lofty praise indeed . . .

It wasn't only the media who lauded my creative conjecture, however, as Glen Matlock and Malcolm McLaren were both very complimentary in their respective appraisals. Glen had been aware of the book from the beginning, so though being extremely pleased; I wasn't too surprised to find a copy of the book nestled on his bookshelf. Hearing Malcolm say he'd bought – yes, *bought* - his copy whilst in New York on a business trip left me literally at a loss for words. And whilst all this didn't prove enough to put me in the running for the 2004 Booker Prize, to my mind it wasn't a bad return for my first literary effort.

Of course, the sequel everyone assumed I'd write would cover the 'Sid-era' Sex Pistols when mayhem replaced the music and disharmony was the resonant chord. But whilst I certainly intended to cover the eventful eleven-month period from Sid's clandestine rehearsals with the group in Glen's absence during February 1977 through to the group's dying horse demise at Winterland Ballroom in San Francisco the following January, I felt the chaos and media feeding frenzy surrounding the Anarchy In The UK Tour of December 1976 was worthy of committing to paper.

As with *Only Anarchists Are Pretty*, from a historical point all the dates, places, and faces, within *Anarchy In The UK* are just as you'll find them in any non-fictional Sex Pistols tomes relating to that frenetic five-week period. And so if you're still sitting comfortably, then we'll continue . . .

Mick O'Shea
Still Living The Dream
April 2017

The Anarchy In The UK Tour

Fri 3 December Norwich East Anglia University Cancelled

Sat 4 December Derby King's Hall Cancelled

Sun 5 December Newcastle City Hall Cancelled

Mon 6 December Leeds Polytechnic Played

Tue 7 December Bournemouth Village Bowl Cancelled

""""Sheffield *University Fell Through*

Thu 9 December Manchester Electric Circus Played Fri 10 December Lancaster University Cancelled

"""""Preston *Charter Fell Through*

Sat 11 December Liverpool Stadium Cancelled

"""""The *Cavern Fell Through*

Mon 13 December Bristol Colston Hall Cancelled

"""""Bristol *University Fell Through*

Tue 14 December Cardiff Top Rank Cancelled

"""""Caerphilly *Castle Cinema Played*

Wed 15 December Glasgow Apollo Cancelled

"""""Wolverhampton *Lafayette's Fell Through*

Thu 16 December Dundee Caird Hall Cancelled

Fri 17 December Sheffield City Hall Cancelled

"""""Carlisle *Market Hall Fell Through*

Sat 18 December Southend Kursaal Cancelled

"""""Maidenhead *Skindles Fell Through*

Sun 19 December Guildford Civic Hall Cancelled

"""""Manchester *Electric Circus Played*

Mon 20 December Birmingham Town Hall Cancelled

"""""Bingley *Hall Fell Through*

"""""Cleethorpes *Winter Gardens Played*

Tue 21 December Plymouth Woods Centre Played

Wed 22 December Torquay 400 Ballroom

Cancelled """"Paignton *Penelope's Ballroom*

Fell Through

""""Plymouth *Woods Centre Played*

Sun 26 December London Roxy Theatre Cancelled

The original 19 venues in bold, with alternate venues in italics

Prologue
Heathrow Airport: Saturday, 8 January 1977

Unlike his fellow Sex Pistols, Steve and Paul, Glen had no intention of posing with Suzi Sue Ballion and the other herberts that Vivienne Westwood had hurriedly rounded up to welcome them home. Vivienne might have been Malcolm's girlfriend stroke business partner, as well as being responsible for designing the majority of the clothes on sale at the shop, but she had no influence or input regarding the group. He also ignored Ray Stevenson's impassioned plea for him to get into the picture. As far as he was concerned it was people like Suzi that were making a mockery of everything the Sex Pistols had achieved.

Following the Pistols' fateful appearance on the Today show at the beginning of December the tabloids were portraying punk rock as being played by people with no musical talent. Yet whilst that might apply to Suzi and her Banshees, who'd made their shameless debut at the so-called 100 Club Punk Festival back in September, he, Steve, and Paul had been together for two years before John had even joined the band. And they'd had to put plenty of legwork into that eighteen-month period to get to where they were. The jumped-up Banshees were getting their name splashed about the papers because Suzi had flashed her tits - well, what tits she had - on stage at the Screen On the Green back when the Pistols played there at the end of August. The memory of the Banshees' pitiful performance at the 100 Club Festival still made him grimace. It could hardly be called a "debut" as they'd only got the gig because Malcolm had needed another band to shore up the festival bill.

Suzi and her boyfriend Steve had recruited John's mate Sid to play drums, and a guy that hung around Malcolm's shop called Marco on guitar. Marco could actually play a bit, but the fact that Steve didn't know one of a bass from the other, and that Sid had never played drums before was neither here nor there. Their "performance" was intended to be a one-off - a "Warholian 15 minutes" kinda thing. They'd tortured the crowd with what could best be described as a meandering twenty-odd minute, nondescript Velvet Undergroundorientated dirge over which Suzi had warbled snatches from Bob Dylan's "Knockin' On Heaven's Door", and The Beatles' "Twist And Shout", with snippets from "Deutschland Uber Alles" and *The Lord's Prayer* thrown in for the hell of it. Continuing to ignore Stevenson's pleas, he walked across the tarmac and grabbed the flight case housing his Fender Precision bass guitar from the baggage trolley holding their equipment. The airport police – on realising it was the Sex Pistols - were beginning to sniff around now, and one of them was giving Stevenson some grief about his taking photographs at an airport. They were behaving themselves, and their carnet was all in order, but you could see the sods were itching for the chance to do something.

The Pistols had just returned from a four-day promotional trip to Holland where they'd played two dates in Amsterdam and another in Rotterdam, with the Heartbreakers acting as support, as well as performing "Anarchy In The UK" on a Dutch TV show called *Disco Circus* to help promote the single which had recently been released on EMI Holland.

The three shows had gone well enough – particularly the first of their two appearances at the legendary Club Paradiso in Amsterdam. The Paradiso was a converted church. The Pistols had played the Notre Dame Hall a few weeks back, but that had been in a room beneath the church. The Paradiso still had all the original stain-glassed windows so it was a surreal experience. Their television appearance had also been something of an eyeopener. They were sharing the *Rock Circus* bill with an Afro-rock outfit called Osibisa, the Three Degrees, Diana Ross, and the Dutch band Golden Earring. Golden Earring had been playing for something like fifteen years yet they were only really known for their song "Radar Love", which had been a big hit in the UK two or three years ago. He'd really liked the song - especially the catchy bass riff, which to his mind made the song. While awaiting their turn to go on he'd got chatting with the band's bass player, Rene? . . . Rinus? . . . Well, it definitely began with an "R". He'd complemented the guy on his playing style. Rene/Rinus had seemed really chuffed and had asked which songs. Well, the obvious one was "Radar Love", but no sooner had he offered as much the guy walked off.

If playing inside a real circus tent wasn't surreal enough, some bright spark connected with the show had actually thought it a good idea to have plate-spinning dwarves join the Pistols on stage. Thankfully, Graham Fletcher from EMI International, who'd accompanied them on the trip, had made the producers see the potential error of their ways by pointing out that one of the dwarves being impaled upon Steve's Les Paul might not make for good family entertainment.

They'd long since passed through Heathrow's passport control, but were forced to wait for the cabs Malcolm had supposedly booked to take them home. But owing to their tightfisted manager's refusal to also hire a van to ferry the gear back to their rehearsal place on Denmark Street poor old Nils was going to have to hump it all the way back to the West End on the bus. Their one-time road manager was now managing Suzi's band full time, and he'd heard a rumour that Nils had cheekily sneaked the Banshees into Denmark Street to rehearse in the Pistols' absence. There was no way of substantiating the rumour of course, as Nils was hardly likely to admit it. Whatever the case, his bass was coming home with him. Besides, he had a few song ideas he wanted to work on.

After the shows John, Steve, and Paul had headed off into the red-light district. They'd taken the rip out of him for not going with them, because he was "frightened of Celia finding out." It wasn't so much the fear of Sonia finding out, but rather the risk of giving her a dose when he got home. Besides, he'd had his eye on a girl he'd spotted in the crowd at the first Paradiso show on the Wednesday night. He'd been hoping to see her in there on the second night, but she hadn't showed.

Malcolm had also had a pop at him; said he wasn't being "out there" enough onstage. He hadn't even bothered to dignify that with a response. John was "out there" enough for anyone. And what was Steve doing onstage that was so great? The moves he did make onstage he'd nicked from either Pete Townshend or Johnny Thunders. Malcolm had had to put Steve right about that, and not before time.

They were always on at him for not being "anarchic" enough; that he should be coming up with suggestions to create a bit of a buzz. Yet when he'd suggested their going out during the night and daubing "Sex Pistols" on the door of the Anne Frank House, or the walls of Centraal Station, John, Steve, and Paul didn't want to know.

So while they'd gone off to ogle the tarts in the windows, They'd gone back to their digs to work on some new song ideas.

Even that wasn't without incident. The old couple that ran the "brown", as the café cum rooming houses were known in Amsterdam, were used to having visiting bands under their roof as the Paradiso and Melkweg were within walking distance. Because of the bollocks the *Evening News* had printed about John supposedly throwing up on the plane on the way over, the couple had been besieged with calls from *Daily Mirror* and the other bleedin' UK tabloids. He felt sorry for them having to field calls all day, and he'd literally just walked through the door when the phone had started again. He'd quickly shock his head at the old boy to indicate he wouldn't be taking the call before heading for the stairs.

Out of the ideas he'd been mucking around with of late, he'd come up with three really strong melodies. He was really pleased with one in the key of A that he'd tentatively named "Rich Kids". He was desperate to get back to Greenford so he could start working it into a proper arrangement - if he ever got back to Chiswick, that is. Where were these bleeding cabs anyway?

Of course, it was the *Evening News'* bullshit story about John puking on the plane that had finally pushed EMI into dropping the bombshell that they were dropping the band from its roster. And so whether their appearance on *Rock Circus* had captivated Holland's disenfranchised youth was now something of a moot point.

Malcolm had expected the announcement that the naughty Sex Pistols were being thrown off EMI would have had have of Fleet Street staking out Heathrow's arrivals lounge. Malcolm had called Vivienne from Schiphol airport to have her round up the usual suspects to come and greet them like conquering heroes at the gate. And Malcolm needn't have bothered any road. Although the tabloids had descended upon Amsterdam on hearing the news of the sacking, Nils' brother Ray was the only photographer that had bothered to show his face on this side of the Channel. Malcolm and Vivienne had long-since fucked off back to Clapham in her mini, but at least Nils would now have some unexpected help with the gear.

If truth be told he hadn't been all that surprised at EMI's decision as
relations between the band and the label had been steadily deteriorating ever since their teatime tête-à-tête with Bill Grundy on *Today*. And whilst certain high-jinx during the recent UK tour hadn't served to further endear them to the stuffed shirts over at Manchester Square, it was ironic that the label should elect to tear up the band's contract over an incident that didn't actually happen.

He'd yet to see the *Evening News'* article of course, but from what Celia had told him when he'd spoken to her on the phone, the band had caused some sort of "rumpus" at Heathrow, and had "vomited and spat their way to an Amsterdam flight." Without mentioning any names, the *News'* Johnny-on-the-spot claimed that one of the band members had thrown up in the corridor leading to the aeroplane. That was utter bollocks, because the closest anyone had come to being sick was when they were actually on the plane and John started mucking about and spitting the chewed-up peel of the orange he'd been eating into the sick bag. Childish it may have been, but it certainly didn't merit spreading across the front page.

Fletcher had been with them the whole time they were at Heathrow. He knew the story was a total fabrication. They didn't learn about the latest shit-storm till they'd come off stage at the Paradiso. The following morning Fletcher had called the office at Manchester Square. He'd told his boss, Hilary Walker, that the *Evening News*'s story was total bullshit.

He also called Brian Southall, EMI's head of press, telling him to call the *Evening News*' offices at Carmelite House and demand they put a retraction in the next edition. Fletcher said that Walker and Southall had been sympathetic, and had believed his version of events. But he'd sensed from their demeanour that the dye had already been cast.

Poor Fletch had literally found himself between punk rock and a hard place. He'd been championing the Pistols since catching the band headlining the first night of the 100 Club Punk Festival. And unlike most of the EMI wallahs he'd met, Fletch was happy to muck in and lend a helping hand. He hadn't even objected when Malcolm had put him in charge of the stage-lighting at the first Paradiso show, despite his later admitting that his knowledge of stage-lighting didn't extend beyond changing a light bulb.

Fletch, of course, had also found himself in the unenviable position of having to play intermediary between Malcolm and Leslie Hill when the shit hit the fan back in London. Hill was the head honcho of EMI's Music Division. Fletch had been with Malcolm when Hill had called to break the news to Malcolm that the band were off the label. He'd braced himself for the verbal backlash, but Malcolm was most likely too shocked to react.

Glen had only met Hill on a couple of occasions. He seemed an alright enough sort, but was definitely a company man. So he'd been taken aback when Hill flew out to Amsterdam soon after speaking with Malcolm. To Malcolm's surprise, and everyone else's surprise for that matter, Hill had said that he knew for a fact that the *Evening News*' story was a total fabrication. He'd even tried arguing as much with EMI's chairman, Sir John Read. Hill's petitions had fallen on deaf ears, however. EMI's Music Division might account for over 50 per cent of EMI's total sales for the previous tax year, but the corporation wasn't about to let a pop group threaten its rating on the London Stock Exchange.

He thought back to the time of the signing; how EMI had shouted from the rooftops that they had signed the "new Beatles". Ironically, Bill Grundy had been the first TV presenter to introduce the Fab Four on camera back in October 1962. They hadn't been "Fab" at the time of course, as EMI had only just released their debut single "Love Me Do". Grundy had apparently thought it beneath him to introduce a band he'd never heard of. What was that about history repeating itself . . .?

Chapter One
Denmark Street: Friday, 3 December 1976

**THE FILTH
AND THE
FURY!
Uproar as viewers jam phones**

A POP group shocked millions of viewers last night with the filthiest language heard on British television.

The Sex Pistols, leaders of the new "punk rock" cult, hurled a string of four-letter obscenities at interviewer Bill Grundy on Thames TV's family teatime programme, "Today".

The Thames switchboard was flooded with protests. Nearly 200 angry viewers telephoned the Mirror. One man was so furious that he kicked in the screen of his £380 colour TV.

Grundy was immediately carpeted by his boss and will apologise in tonight's programme. Daily Mirror, Thursday, 2 December 1976.

Glen had been bubbling with excitement when he'd set off for Denmark Street that cold, crisp Friday morning to meet up with the rest of the band, as well as guys from The Clash and The Heartbreakers. That night they were playing the University of East Anglia in Norwich; the opening show of a 19-date UK headline tour to promote their debut single, "Anarchy In The UK", which had been released the previous Friday. The Damned were also on the bill, but Glen knew that owing to Malcolm's ongoing spat with the Croydonbased quartet's new manager, Jake Riviera, who also co-owned Stiff Records, The Damned would be travelling separately. Upon his arrival at the band's rehearsal space a half hour or so later, however, his exhilaration quickly evaporated into stale tobacco-tinged ether. It seemed there was a problem with that evening's show at Norwich, while several other dates had been cancelled, or were in danger of being cancelled. A show being cancelled at the eleventh hour was all part and parcel of being in a band. Back in October they'd been set to play shows in Torquay and Plymouth at the same venues that were included on the tour, with a third show in Penzance the following night. The contracts had been signed back in August, only for all three shows to fall through the day before the Torquay date He remembered being pissed off at the time, but the band's signing to EMI on the Friday had more than made up for it.

Malcolm never really offered much by way explanation whenever a show fell through, but there was no need for anyone to explain what was going on with the tour dates. Two days ago – was it really only two day ago? – they had appeared on *Today*, Thames TV's early evening regional news magazine programme.

They were holed up at the Roxy over in Harlesden with the guys from The Clash and The Damned running through their respective sets, working out the timings and changeovers and what have you, when Nils had called to tell them about the interview, and that Thames were sending a Daimler to pick them up and ferry them to the studio. They hadn't wanted to go, but Malcolm was still fretting about putting enough bums on seats to make the tour a success. Stiff might have been picking up the tab for The Damned, but The Clash and Heartbreakers weren't signed to a label so their expenses were coming directly out of their EMI advance. Malcolm said they were doing the interview whether they wanted to or not, as the show's producers had promised to play a 30-second clip of the "Anarchy" promo video at the start of the interview. The main incentive for their agreeing to do it, of course, was Malcolm's threat to hold their wages. What should have an inconsequential two-minute chat tagged onto the end of a two-bob TV show was now front-page news thanks to the grouchy Grundy wilfully baiting Steve to "say something outrageous" on camera.

Glen had since learnt that the band had only been offered the *Today* slot on account of some cock-up with the Musicians' Union over the promo video for Queen's latest single "Somebody To Love". Whoever had thought to close that night's show with the Queen video hadn't thought to get clearance to broadcast the single by the all-important MU. It seemed EMI had a 50 per cent stake in Thames Television, and so when *Today*'s producers discovered the cock up over the video, they'd hurriedly put a call into Manchester Square to enquire if any other EMI acts might be available. He'd also heard that the producers had specifically asked for the Pistols. Whichever way the invitation came about, one would have thought that whoever took the call at Manchester Square would have given the show's producers fair warning that it might be prudent to insist the group mind their language as the show was broadcast live to a teatime audience.

Ever the opportunist, Malcolm had somehow managed to round up Simon and Simone from the shop, along with Suzi Ballion and her fella, over to the TV studio on Marylebone Road. Simon and Simone helped out at the shop, and he could only assume Suzie and Steve just happened to be in there when Malcolm had made the call. Needless to say, Simon and Simone had both been decked out in SEX attire.

On arriving at the studio they'd been escorted through to the green room and given free reign to help themselves to whatever was on offer. There hadn't been all that much in the way of "alcoholic hospitality": a few half-pint cans of Heineken and a bottle of Blue Nun, which Steve had sneakily commandeered for himself. Suzi and the others were already in there waiting for them, so had obviously gotten first dibs. But he and the rest of the band had been drinking steadily all day during rehearsals, so the Heinekens had topped them up nicely.

After about 20 minutes or so they'd been taken through to a corner of the studio where Grundy, of course, was already sat waiting. He'd been amazed at how naff it all looked seeing it for real. Whoever said television was all smoke and mirrors knew what they were on about. What looked like a proper enclosed studio on the telly, were really just a couple of painted plywood sheets embossed with the *Today* logo forming an L-shaped screen propped up with a few bits of 3" by 2". They'd taken their places in the chairs lined up alongside Grundy in front boards and facing the cameras, while Suzi and the others had taken up position directly behind the band.

♪♪♪

Paul had sat directly next to Grundy, but getting two words from their drummer was hard work at the best of times so Glen had ended up doing most of the talking . . . initially, at least. Glen quickly realised that Grundy was pissed as a fart; going so far as to brag about it on air. He'd also prattled on about punk rock being the new craze, and something about the Sex Pistols being the new Rolling Stones. It was obvious from the get-go that the old soak had no intention of plugging the tour or the single – he'd sat prattling away to himself during the promo video clip. When the clip finished he'd tried to bait them about the "antimaterialistic" £40,000 advance they'd received from EMI. At one point early in the interview Grundy had asked what they'd done with the advance. The Blue Nun had obviously kicked in by then as Steve blurted out "we've fuckin' spent it!" loud enough for everyone in the studio to hear, yet no one said a word. Grundy hadn't even batted an eyelid! It was the same when John had mumbled something about it "tough shit". John had given Grundy the perfect opportunity to gain the upper hand. Yet instead of giving John a ticking off by reminding him the show was going out live, Grundy had got John to repeat the "rude word". To be fair, John's face had gone as red as a helmet. But Grundy's adopting the headmaster at school assembly act was never gonna work.

With the clock running down Grundy had turned his attentions to Suzi and Simone. Suzi clearly hadn't expected to find herself thrust into the spotlight. All she could come up with was some cheesy comment about her having always wanted to meet Grundy. The old letch must have got a boner. He actually suggested he and Suzi meet up backstage afterwards. Steve had called Grundy a "dirty bastard". And that, of course, was when the shit had hit the fan. Grundy had been in the TV game long enough to know that you don't encourage someone whose obviously had a few sherbets to "say something outrageous" on-air. That was the "outrageous" thing in all of this! Throughout the remainder of the evening a Thames TV announcer had apparently issued on-air apologies for the foul language used during the interview. According to the reports in the papers, there'd been so many viewers calling in to complain that the station's switchboard was lit up like Oxford Street at Christmas. Of course, the tabloids had had a field day targeting the band, and the revolting new "punk cult" they were supposedly spearheading. There's been no mention of Grundy's deliberating setting out to antagonise them during the interview, but at least Thames had the decency to suspend him.

Glen had to hand it to Malcolm. As part of the deal to get the band to go on the show, Malcolm had got Thames to agree to let him have the use of the Daimler. So while they they'd been in the green room waiting their turn to go on, the chauffeur had schlepped out to Heathrow to pick up The Heartbreakers and deliver them to their digs in Earl's Court. The guy was oblivious as to what had happened on the show, and had dutifully delivered them back to Harlesden. On arriving back at the Roxy they had regaled the guys in The Clash and The Damned about Steve having given Grundy a good coating off before getting back to rehearsing. Glen had also given his flatmate Mark a run through of events when he got home, but when he'd woken up the following morning Bill Grundy had been the last thing on his mind. Indeed, his only concern was that Johnny Thunders and the other Heartbreakers would have shaken off their jet-lag by the time everyone met up at the Roxy later in the day. But it had only taken a phone call from his mum to shatter that illusion.

Going on *Today* had been so last-minute that there wasn't time to let anyone know about it. He wasn't sure whether his mum and dad even bothered with the show, but as luck would have it one of their neighbours had caught the announcement about the Sex Pistols at the beginning of the show and had popped round to give them the heads up. So while he'd been knocking back the lagers in the green room, his mum had been frantically ringing round the relatives to ensure that every possible member of the Matlock clan would be poised in front of their television sets at the appointed time. He'd honestly had to stifle a chuckle imagining the look on his mum's face when Steve called Grundy a "dirty fucker" and a "fucking rotter". He doubted his dad would have gone as far as putting his foot through the TV screen like that idiotic lorry driver from Waltham Abbey or wherever, but the tone in his mum's voice had left him under no illusions that the repercussions would be reverberating well into the coming year.

The tabloids had soon found out about the band having a rehearsal place on Denmark Street. Paul had stayed over with Steve rather than schlep back to his mum and dad's place in Shepherd's Bush. They'd got the shock of their lives on finding a posse of reporters camped out on the doorstep. He'd had been lucky in that respect, but the *Daily Mirror*'s "Filth and Fury" headline staring out from the placard outside the local newsagents had proved a stark warning that life wasn't quite going to be the same again. Things had only got worse as people were now openly staring at him as they passed him on the street. And the woman that ran the corner shop that always had time for a quick chat about how the band was doing had made him feel as welcome as a turd in a teacup.

More worrying, of course, was the reaction over at Manchester Square. Nick Mobbs, who was head of A&R at EMI, and was responsible for signing the Pistols, said how the office had been inundated with calls from people within the industry congratulating them on what they all perceived to be one of the greatest publicity stunts ever seen on the eve of a make or break promotional tour. The suits that operated from the label's hallowed sixth floor who were responsible for EMI's defence, electronics, and medical divisions, however, had taken a dim view at having the corporation's prestigious name and reputation sullied by a mere pop group. On top of that, the packers at EMI's packing plant in Hayes had refused to handle the "Anarchy" single. Malcolm had been revelling in the publicity, but the thought of the record being unavailable in any of the towns and cities they were set to play during the tour had wiped the smile from his face.

Leslie Hill placated Malcolm by volunteering to drive down to the packing plant to sort things out and get the single's production back on track in time for the tour. Fleet Street had also laid siege to Manchester Square, of course. With the throng of reporters showing no sign of dissipating until they'd got a corporate quote or two, Hill had also suggested to Malcolm that the best course of action might be to stage an impromptu press conference. By presenting the band's version of events, they might be able to play down the incident.

The band had done quite a few interviews with the music press, but the conference had been their first experience of what the gutter press was capable of; how they twisted a situation to get a story. One photographer had tried bribing them with a couple of cans of lager to get them to sit closer together. They'd readily accepted the beers, but Steve had refused to get closer to John because of his smelly armpits. It was obviously meant as a joke, if only to break the tension. He'd burped while taking a swig from one of the cans. He'd said "pardon", and thought nothing more of it. Yet the journo's twisted account read: "Pistols refused to sit together on account of Johnny Rotten's stinking armpits and, when the bass player was asked a question, he just belched." It really was just too ludicrous for words.

Hill had made all the right noises about how EMI was a bastion of British decorum, and that there would be no repeat of what everyone agreed was an unsavoury episode. Hill had no doubt been hoping the band would appear remorseful for the reporters, but there was sod all chance of that happening. Grundy had obviously thought his having to interview a band he'd never heard of was beneath him. He'd looked to exact his revenge in belittling the band on camera, and Steve had shot him down in technicolour flames.

They'd been late arriving at the Roxy after the conference owing to Terry Slater, the head of EMI Publishing, having taken them for a pint at one of the pubs on Tottenham Court Road. Slater had been the first within EMI to recognise the Pistols' worth by offering them a publishing deal.

In an attempt to diffuse the ongoing situation he'd suggested changing the copyright line on "Anarchy In The UK" from EMI Music Publishing to Sex Pistols Music Publishing. Unlike EMI Records, EMI Publishing was a separate entity, housed in offices on Oxford Street. Slater's idea, however, had been brusquely rejected out of hand by his superiors.

♫♫♫

The Sex Pistols had been rehearsing at Denmark Street for around fifteen months. Glen, had never been one to brag, but it was down to his bringing Malcolm's attention to the ad in the *Melody Maker* classifieds that they got the place – that and the £1,000 Malcolm agreed to put down as a deposit of course. The two-storey space was actually situated to the rear of Denmark Street, and only accessible from the street via a narrow passageway. They'd still soundproofed the downstairs room so as to avoid complaints from the shopkeepers. The upstairs room was meant to serve as the band's HQ, but Steve had moved a bed in there the first chance he got. Up until recently, Glen had shared the modest living space with Steve. He'd found it amusing having a W1 address while living a squat-like existence. It had been a right shithole when they'd moved in, and while hygiene didn't feature too high on Steve's list of priorities, he had at least pitched in with making the place liveable. Steve had claimed the bed, of course, which had meant he'd had to settle for a mattress by the window. But again, given Steve's fondness for wearing the same clothes for days on end . . .

The funny thing was he and Steve had actually gotten closer from their living cheek by jowl. But he'd recognised it was perhaps time to move on when Steve tried tempting him with a liver sandwich that he'd used as a makeshift fanny. He'd even gone into detail about his technique! Nils had claimed his spot while his mattress was still warm. That was another reason why he couldn't understand Nils' absence? Or maybe Steve's sandwich recipe had something to with it . . .?

Glen hadn't long been there himself when Malcolm came swanning through the door sporting the silver-flecked fur coat that Vivienne had bought him for him to take on the tour. Bernard Rhodes, The Clash's manager, following close behind. The mole-like Rhodes would fly into a rage whenever anyone called him "Bernie". "Bernie is a cab driver! My name is '*Bernard*!'" Of course, he'd been "Bernie" from that day on.

He knew from what Paul had told him about the possibility of that night's show in Norwich being cancelled that Malcolm had been on the phone with the vice chancellor at Norwich University. Malcolm had been happy to put a grand down as a deposit, but had refused to have a telephone installed. He worried about the bills Steve might ring up calling the sex chat lines. And not without reason, either. The nearest public phone box was a fiveminute walk away on Upper St. Martin's Lane.

Malcolm and Bernard were huddled together in the corner, but the room was just about big enough to swing the proverbial cat so he had no trouble eavesdropping on their conspiratorial mutterings. It seemed a guy called Frank Thistlewaite, whom he presumed to be the vice chancellor at Norwich University, was standing by his decision to cancel that evening's show. His decision, however, wasn't because of the band's behaviour on the *Today* show per se, but rather over concerns about the show proceeding peacefully in light of the adverse publicity surrounding the Sex Pistols. In response to Bernie's saying something about a "student sit-in", Malcolm explained that fifty or so students were threatening to stage a sit-in in the university's administration block to protest over what they perceived as a direct attack to the Students Union autonomy. Thistlewaite, however, had insisted that a sit-in, or indeed any other such radical actions taken by the students, would not bring about a reversal of his decision. He was even willing to offer the Students Union money from UEA funds to cover any losses the Union incurred over the show being cancelled.

Malcolm, of course, tried to make light of the unexpected last-minute change to the tour's itinerary by insisting the student protest would provide them with far more exposure than they could have hoped to generate had the show gone ahead.

The silence that had descended upon the room while everyone digested the news was soon shattered with Malcolm's seemingly throwaway comment to Bernie about hoping to get a similar reaction from the students at Lancaster University. But Glen knew from the uneasy look that had passed between Malcolm and Bernie that the two university dates weren't the only cancellations. It seemed that the shows in Newcastle, Bournemouth, and Glasgow were also definitely off, while Liverpool was in doubt – and that was only the opening half of the tour.

Glen suspected Malcolm was still holding back about the severity of the situation. His bombshell about the cancellations had understandably brought on a slew of questions, but Malcolm had waved away their petitions saying he needed to speak with Leslie Hill before plotting a course of action. He also needed to get confirmation from Hill that the situation with the packers at EMI's pressing plant in Hayes had been straightened out as Hill had promised. Despite the depressing state of affairs, Glen couldn't help smile at the thought of the packers – predominantly local housewives working part-time to earn some extra pin money – being happy to work for a corporation that was raking in millions of pounds from its weapons systems and electronics arms that were killing people by the thousands, but were refusing to handle their single because of a bit of swearing on TV?

Malcolm's insistence that "Anarchy" be issued in a plain black sleeve rather than EMI's standard red/orange company sleeve had made it difficult enough for anyone looking to buy the single. But if Hill didn't get his finger out sharpish, then there was more chance of finding Lord Lucan hiding in the record bins. Malcolm said he'd already tried Hill's office several times but without success. Malcolm had at least made the decision to have Sophie Richmond, his assistant cum general dogsbody, call the Derby Crest and alert the hotel's manager that they would now be requiring rooms for that coming night as well.

Malcolm had recruited Sophie to help him put together the 100 Club Punk Festival, and she'd been serving as his PA ever since. She was going out with Malcolm's old Croydon College chum Jamie Reid. Reid was of the same political mind-set as Malcolm. They'd been at Croydon at the time of the Paris riots, and Malcolm and Reid had organised a 300-strong, student sit-in, barricading themselves within the college's South Norwood annexe in support of their Parisian counterparts. The students in Paris had come uncomfortably close to bringing down the French government, whereas Croydon's "les enrages" had set fire to a desk.

Reid had co-founded *Suburban Press*, which was a radical community printing press collective or something. Malcolm was so impressed by what his old friend was doing that he brought him on board to design the ripped-up Union Jack Flag promo poster for the "Anarchy" single. He'd also designed the tour poster.

It wasn't until Malcolm mentioned his annoyance at Nils' absence that Glen remembered their one-time road manager had agreed to a temporary return to his former duties after falling for Malcolm's spiel that this was going to be the greatest tour in rock'n'roll history.

Glen still thought that Nils had been a tad hasty over his decision to quit as their road manager. He still didn't know all the ins and outs of it. Nils was claiming that Malcolm had reneged on a promise to give him a bigger slice of the Sex Pistols pie following the band's signing to EMI. Malcolm, of course, was denying having made any such promises. Nils had been with them since March or early April, and he'd honestly expected him to come crawling back cap in hand within a day or two asking Malcolm for his job back. This proved not to be the case, however, and he'd since heard that Nils was managing Suzi's band.

It had been the same with Bernie, of course. While Malcolm was in New York trying to keep the New York Dolls from falling apart, he'd entrusted the care of the band to Bernie. Bernie believed that his doing so had earned him the right to co-manage the band. He even had a letter that Malcolm had sent from New York stating as much. Glen had felt sorry for Bernie because his input had been vital to the band's development. And it was Bernie that had alerted them to John, after spotting him and his mates making a nuisance of themselves on the King's Road. Bernie had told him on more than one occasion that he and Malcolm had known each other for ten years or more, since first meeting at the Scene Club in Ham Yard. That was all well and good, but he could have told Bernie that he'd stood about as much chance as the Memphis Mafia being offered to co-manage Elvis by Colonel Parker.

Glen had known Malcolm for four years or so. Looking back, it was funny to think where his yearning for a pair of brothel creepers had brought him. His first port of call that fateful afternoon had been the Beaufort Street Market, and from there he'd idled his way further up the King's Road to World's End. Malcolm and Vivienne's shop, which was trading as "Let It Rock" at the time, was like no other shop he'd ever seen. If anything it was like stepping back in time to the late-fifties. Aside from the Teddy boy gear, the décor was of the period right down to the wallpaper. More importantly, they sold authentic brothel creepers specially imported from America. He'd gotten into a conversation with Malcolm, and came away with a Saturday job to add to his new pair of creepers. In that time, he'd come to recognise Malcolm's modus operandi; his skill at ensuring the carrots he dangled in front of those he needed to further his own ambitions remained tantalisingly out of reach. Then again, Suzi might have offered her own carrot for Nils to nibble on?

Glen suspected the real motivation behind Nils' temporary return to duties lay in cajoling Malcolm into allowing the Banshees to support the Pistols on a subsequent tour. Well if that was the case, Nils was pissing on his chips by failing to be here at the appointed hour. His brother Ray had also been welcomed back to the fold to serve as the tour's official photographer, but he seemed as mystified as everyone else at Nil's no show.

♪♪♪

Malcolm and Bernie had headed off for the phone box on Upper St. Martin's Lane. Paul was downstairs in the rehearsal room cleaning his kit, while Steve was making tea for everyone. John was sat on Steve's bed, staring about sullenly while sucking on a fag. Glen could sense their singer was in another of his moods, and he had no interest in starting a conversation that was sure to end in yet another argument or slanging match. Reaching into his travel bag, he fished out his dog-eared copy of the previous week's NME that he'd brought along to read on the coach. Continuing to avoid making eye contact with John he absent-mindedly leafed through the pages until arriving at the full-page advert for the tour.

Glen knew Malcolm had first begun plotting the tour two months earlier while the band was holed up inside Lansdowne Studios recording "Anarchy". He might have delegated the mundane day-to-day managerial tasks to Nils, but he was astute enough to recognise that the Pistols – having only played around sixty shows to date - were still relatively unknown outside of the major cities such as London, Manchester, and Birmingham. This, of course, was before the Grundy fiasco, and though "Anarchy" would be out in the shops, Malcolm didn't feel they had sufficient pulling power to undertake a national tour on their name alone. Glen knew that although Malcolm wouldn't want to risk their ending up with egg on their faces playing to half-filled venues, his anxiety stemmed from the tour funding coming out of their EMI advance; cash that was accruing interest in the Glitterbest coffers. Should they fail to put enough bums on seats, then . . . well, there was probably no need to worry about that. If yesterday's scenes at Manchester Square were anything to go by, they could probably fill some of the venues with reporters alone. Malcolm could have eased the financial strain by inviting another of EMI's up-and-coming bands - or even a band signed to another label - onto the tour and have their label pick up a portion of the tab.

Chapter Two

The Sex Pistols, the leading exponents of the Punk rock cult, who used obscene language on television earlier this week, are being banned from appearing at concerts on their nationwide tour.

At least seven engagements have been withdrawn, there are doubts about others, and women packers at EMI's record factory have refused to handle their latest single "Anarchy In The UK."
The Daily Telegraph, Saturday, 4 December 1976.

Paul was preoccupied with conducting a last-minute check of his kit when he heard footsteps descending the stairwell. He glanced across to find the Heartbreaker's affable drummer, Jerry Nolan, standing in the open doorway. As with Thunders, Nolan had undergone a radical punk makeover and looked totally different from his time with the Dolls. His Dolly trousseau having been replaced with a sharp suit; his once-trademark feathered bouffant now a mass of peroxide-blond spikes. Yet again, Nolan was munching on an apple. On each occasion he'd seen Nolan, he'd had an apple in his hand. It was like he had a constant supply. He remembered Malcolm having said something about Nolan's fixation with apples around the time he was arranging to bring the Heartbreakers onto the tour. Thunders' preferred daily fix was a tube of Smarties. He'd yet to discover if Walter Lure and Billy Rath had any non-toxic vices.

John had despised the New York Dolls, and was making no effort to hide his contempt towards Thunders and Nolan. Indeed, John's lyric to their song "New York" was a blatant putdown of the Dolls. Paul and Steve, however, had been huge fans of the band, and Paul couldn't help feeling a bit anxious as to what Thunders and Nolan's reactions might be to the song during the tour. Nolan, of course, wasn't an original Doll. He'd been brought in to replace Billy Murcia who died in somewhat mysterious circumstances in November 1972 during the Dolls' first visit to London.

Ironically, the Dolls had been on the cusp of signing a major record deal when Murcia had died. Murcia had accidentally overdosed on Mandrax while at a party somewhere on the Cromwell Road in Kensington. Instead of calling for an a mbulance, whoever was with Murcia at the party dumped him the bath and h ad poured coffee down his throat in an attempt to revive him. Poor Billy had choked to death as a result. He was just 21-years-old.

Steve had been in the audience when the Dolls played the second night of the Wembley Festival of Music at the Empire Pool alongside the Pink Fairies and The Faces towards the end of October 1972. Billy had been behind the drums that night of course; most likely dreaming of headlining such events when in reality he'd less then ten days to live. Paul's first experience of the Dolls came the following November when the band had made their one and only UK TV appearance on *The Old Grey Whistle Test*. The show's presenter, "Whispering Bob" Harris had churlishly dismissed the Dolls as "mock rock", but what the fuck did that cunt know!

Malcolm had actually met the Dolls whilst he and Vivienne were in New York on some trade fair or other. The band had visited the shop during their visits to London in 1972 and '73. On the latter visit, Malcolm had slavishly followed the band to Paris like a love-struck groupie.

Malcolm's infatuation with the Dolls was such that on hearing they had been dropped by their management company he'd headed for New York leaving a less-than-pleased Vivienne behind to run the shop and raise their kids single-handed. He'd received criticism in some quarters for supposedly having brought about the Dolls' demise by having them dress up in patent red-leather stage outfits, while playing in front of a hammer and sickle backdrop. By the time of Malcolm's involvement, however, the Dolls were broken beyond repair. Their second album, the aptly-titled *Too Much Too Soon*, said everything about the Dolls' plight: too much drinking, and way too many drugs.

Against all the odds, Malcolm managed to keep the Dolls' bandwagon rolling for several months before the wheels finally fell off in a Florida trailer park with Johnny and Jerry serving notice by flying back to New York and reacquainting themselves with their heroin dealer.

The Dolls had enjoyed being the dandies of the New York underworld, but the scene had moved on in their absence. By the spring of 1975 new bands like The Ramones, Blondie, and Television were now making waves at a new club on the Bowery called CBGBs. Johnny and Jerry were quick to get in on the act by forming The Heartbreakers with Richard Hell, the aspiring poet and one-time-Television bassist that Malcolm had tried to lure across to London

to front the nascent Sex Pistols; guitarist Walter Lure was shamelessly poached from fellow New York outfit, The Demons.
Hell's tenure with The Heartbreakers had also proved fleeting owing to his demands for a more prominent role within the band. Johnny, however, had had more than his fill of under-the-spotlight jostling with Dolls' frontman David Johansen, and had no intention of reliving the experience. Hell's replacement, Billy Rath, had only recently returned to New York from Florida where he'd been eking out a living hiring himself out as a male escort to the resort's wealthy female holidaymakers.
"Now, that's what I like to see," Nolan chuckled from the doorway. "A drummer who's got his shit together to know it never hurts to check through his skins one last time before hitting the road."
"Thanks," Paul nodded, resting his snare-cymbal across one knee whilst giving it a cursory wipe with an old Watney's beer towel. Aside from serving a keepsake from his time working as an apprentice electrician at the brewery, the towel was brilliant for cleaning cymbals. "Shouldn't you be doing the same, Jerry?"
"Already taken care of," Nolan chuckled again, playfully extending his open palm to reveal two packets of Rizla cigarette papers. "Took some doin', I might add. You see, back in the states we call these 'Elephant papers'. The guy in the shop by our hotel didn't know what the fuck I was talking about! So, this is where you guys rehearse, huh?" he nodded to
himself, stepping further into the room. "It's not too big, is it?"
"Well, it suits our purposes," Paul shrugged, sliding the cymbal back inside a brandnew leather case that had come courtesy of their EMI advance. "Well, it is from my point of view seeing as I tend to stay put."
Nolan paused to pocket both the papers and the partially eaten apple. "Ain't that the truth? You can keep all that strutting about the stage with a guitar. I mean, Johnny was born to play guitar, whereas I'm happy to make music sitting on my ass . . . Though I have been known to fall off of my stool on occasion." He grinned.
"You and me both,' Paul grinned; the memory of his tumbling off his stool midway through a gig at Chelmsford Maximum Security Prison back in September flashing through his mind's eye. It had been his last day working at the brewery, and – as tradition warranted - his workmates had wanted to give him a proper send-off – especially as he was escaping the 9 - 5 drudgery. Of course, the solitary drink he'd promised himself had turned into a bucketful. Malcolm had been waiting for them at the prison gates. Paul was picturing Malcolm's face as he staggered towards him when he was distracted

from his reverie by approaching footsteps outside. He and Nolan both glanced over to the doorway as the Heartbreakers' roadie/guitar tech cum soundman Keeth Paul appeared in the doorway.

"Do you need anything from the store, Niggs?" he asked, calling Nolan by his nickname. He paused, giving Paul a quick nod of acknowledgement before returning his attention to Nolan. "Johnny's run out of smokes."

"Might as well get me a pack while you're there," Nolan nodded. "And see about getting' me some more apples," he shouted after the retreating Paul. "Have you met Keeth yet? He asked Paul; his eyes still fixed on the open doorway. "He's a good kid; used to help us out back in the Dolls. He fished a crumpled pack of cigarettes from the inside pocket of his jacket, flipping the lip while extending the packet towards Paul. "Shame about tonight's gig," he said wistfully.

"Yeah, bit of a sickener," Paul shrugged, waving away the proffered cigarette.

"And this is all because you guys swore on some crummy TV show?" Nolan struck a match against the wall and turned away briefly to light his cigarette.

"Well, it's one way of getting your name in the papers, I suppose." He took a long draw on his cigarette before continuing. "How long is it that you guys been together, anyway?"

"About two and a half years all told. But about eighteen months with John in the band.

"He's an interesting character," Nolan nodded. "Johnny, I mean." "It's been said before," Paul nodded.

Jerry took another long drag; savouring the nicotine. "You ever hear of a guy called Richard Hell?"

Paul nodded, sensing immediately where the conversation was heading. "What about him?" he asked.

"Richard was in a band called Television –"

"Yeah, Malcolm's told us about all that," Paul cut in. "That he wrote a song called 'Blank Generation'."

"Not a bad song as it goes," Nolan nodded. "Richard was also in the Heartbreakers for a while, but that's a story for another time. I guess the point I'm trying to make here is that a lot people back in New York think that Malcolm maybe kinda . . . let's say 'borrowed' some of Richard's ideas, and that he passed them onto Johnny."

"Such as?"

"Well, the spiky hair for one."

"John had his hair like that before he even joined the band," Paul countered. "And what about Bowie . . . or Iggy; they've both–"

"Okay, okay," Nolan conceded. "But the whole safety-pins thing. Now that *was* definitely Richard's idea. I know that for a fact 'cos he was wearing ripped-up clothes held together with pins when he was in Television. And that has to be . . . like two years ago now." He took a last draw on his cigarette while glancing about the room.

"Use the floor, Jerry; John and Steve do."

Nolan crushed the butt against the doorframe before flicking it over his shoulder. He opened his jacket and fished a fresh cigarette from the packet, and popped it into the corner of his mouth before continuing. "What I find amusing about the while thing is that Richard only got his look 'cos some girlfriend of his got so pissed at him that she cut up all of his clothes. And as Richard had a gig that night, but didn't have any money for new clothes, he used safety-pins to hold the ripped ones together."

"Well, they do say that necessity is the mother of invention," Paul smiled, walking back towards his kit.

"True, enough," Nolan nodded. "But guess who just happened to be at Richard's show that night? Malcolm, that's who!" he added when Paul failed to respond. "From what I hear, Malcolm jumped on the next plane back to London – with Syl's guitar, I might add – and he starts managing you guys. And just for the record, Malcolm never managed the Dolls. He got us some shows, and he helped in other ways. But he was never our manager."

Paul grabbed up the case housing his bass drum and started back towards the doorway. "I'm not gonna argue that Malcolm was impressed with Richard Hell. Christ, he talked about him enough when he got back from New York! But John was definitely wearing torn clothes before he joined the band. I mean, that's what made him stand out. And I definitely remember him wearing a ripped T-shirt when he auditioned at the shop."

"Sure, but-"

"Alright, here's one for you," Paul interrupted, grabbing up another case. "When me and Steve were at school, there was this kid in our class called Johnny Eslin. Johnny would turn up to school with one of the legs of his pants held together with safety-pins.

He also had ginger hair as it goes."

"You're saying Johnny auditioned at the shop?"

"Johnny Eslin?"

"No, no," Nolan shook his head irritably, grabbing up another of the cases and following after Paul. "I don't know who the fuck this Eslin guy is. I'm talking about John!" he jerked his chin towards the ceiling for emphasis.

Paul had to bite his bottom lip to stop himself from sniggering. "I'm just messing with you, Jerry. Yeah, John auditioned at the shop. He sang along to

Alice Cooper's 'I'm Eighteen' on the jukebox; it's one of Malcolm's favourites as it goes."
With the cases stacked against the wall Paul set off up the stairwell, but paused on seeing Thunders in muted discussion at the top of the stairs with the Heartbreakers' manager, Leee Black Childers. "Don't worry," Nolan smiled, pushing past Paul. "They can't be talkin' about nothin' important, or else I'd be up there with them," he shouted, loud enough for Thunders and Childers to hear. "Johnny's probably just bustin' Leee's ass over somethin' he ain't done," he added, continuing up stairwell." And knowin' Johnny, it'll be somethin' Leee didn't know he was supposed to do, anyhow." "Got it in one, Jerry," Childers sighed wearily.

♪♪♪

The Kentucky-born Childers had only been looking after The Heartbreakers' affairs since October, but had been involved in the music business in one form or another since 1971. He'd started out as the stage director on *Pork*, Andy Warhol's outrageous play, which was based on conversations recorded at "The Factory", the enigmatic artist's studio on 47th Street. Since then, he'd briefly managed Iggy Pop, and served as the official photographer for David Bowie's MainMan management company before gravitating towards the New York Dolls.
Upon taking the Heartbreakers' reins, Childers had pleaded with his MainMan colleague, Tony "Ze" Zanetti, to co-manage the band with him. Zanetti had himself been approached separately by both Thunders and Nolan whilst they in turn were sounding out Childers.
Thunders and Nolan were regarded as rock'n'roll royalty on the Lower East Side, but their reputation was such that Childers' varied attempts to secure The Heartbreakers a record deal had come to nothing. With nothing other than occasional dates at CBGBs and Max's Kansas City on the calendar, Malcolm's invitation onto the Anarchy Tour had proved something of a welcome distraction. Despite Malcolm's having only booked them one-way tickets to London, the Americans had headed for JFK with a renewed spring in their step.
Nolan wrapped his arm around Thunders. "So where have you guys been hidin', huh?" "What are you, my mother?" Thunders quipped.
"Don't you go playin' the tough guy, Johnny boy," Nolan grinned, while mussing Thunders' hair. "I'd hate to have to teach you some manners in front of Paul here."

"I might ask you what you was doin' down there?" Thunders retorted while smoothing his hair back into place. "You weren't tryin' to corrupt our friend here now, were you, Niggs? It's way too early in the tour for that," he added, tipping Paul a sly wink.

"Me an' Paul were just shootin' the breeze," Nolan grinned. "Us drummers gotta stick together."

"Did Niggs tell you we took Waldo and Billy over to the King's Road yesterday?" Thunders asked Paul.

During his Dolls heyday, Thunders' face was usually hidden behind his backcombed bouffant. Had Paul already not met him the previous afternoon, he would surely have passed Thunders in the street without recognising him. He still looked as though a stiff breeze would knock him over, but there was an air of menace about him; a brooding countenance that was typical of all American-Italians. In fact, Thunders wouldn't have looked out of place in *The Godfather* films. From what Malcolm had said about Nolan, Paul knew his fellow drummer had the walk to match the talk as the saying went. Lure and Rath also had an intimidating aura about them; each looking capable of breaking bones and well as hearts. The cherub-faced Childers was sporting a black biker jacket, yet looked anything but menacing.

"They, ah . . . they wanted to see the 'birthplace' of the London punk rock scene," Thunders continued, pulling back the flap of his jacket to reveal the You're Gonna Wake Up One Morning . . . T-shirt that he'd obviously purchased during his visit.

Printed beneath the slogan, "You're Gonna Wake Up One Morning And Know Which Side Of The Bed You've Been Sleeping On', the shirt comprised of two lists: one list laying waste to those pop stars, artists, playwrights, publications, and institutions that Malcolm and Bernie had deemed passé, while the other extolled the virtues of countercultural icons and working-class heroes.

Hidden within the "loves" was the first printed mention of "Kutie Jones and his SEX PISTOLS"; the name Malcolm had thought up for the band long before he'd given any serious consideration to managing them.

"They couldn't believe how fucking small the place was, man," Nolan chuckled.

"Neither could I on my first visit. My old man's garage back in Queens is bigger."

"If we're being critical, Jerry; no one would ever get themselves lost inside CBGBs either," Childers countered.

"Hey Paul, what's the name of the weird-looking chick who works there?" Thunders asked. "You know; the blonde chick with the crazy make-up and beehive."

"That would be Jordan," said Paul. "Her real name's Pamela, but she calls herself 'Jordan'."

"She looks as though she might be a bit of a handful," Nolan offered, holding the cigarette packet out to Thunders.

"More like two handfuls I would have thought," Thunders grinned, mock-cupping his hands to his chest.

"And we also met Sid," Childers beamed. "Such a nice young man; even if he wasn't exactly what I was expecting."

"Yeah," Nolan nodded. "The guy did look kinda scrawny to me."

"He wouldn't have been no match for you, huh, Niggs, that's for sure," Thunders said, suddenly ducking into a boxing stance and playfully shadow-punching his friend.

"Sid told us how upset he was about missing out on being on television the other night," Childers smiled. "I obviously didn't see the show, but he would have looked good on camera; so photogen-"

Childers fell silent as Malcolm suddenly appeared at the bottom of the stairs.

"Come on, boy," he snapped at Paul as he bounded up the steps. "Get your drums on the bus. We'll be leaving in five minutes."

"Hello Malcolm," Childers said, taking a step back to all Malcolm to pass. "Did you manage to sort things out about tonight's show at Nor-witch University?"

"Nor what?" Malcolm frowned. "Oh, you mean *Norwich*? No, the damn vice chancellor isn't for budging. No matter. Bernard's right, the cancellations will give us more publicity than the tour ever could."

"Did you say 'cancellations'? Childers frowned, emphasising the plural.

"Nothing to worry about, Leee," Malcolm smiled. "You and your boys can rest assured that everything is under control."

"What about Nils?" Paul asked.

"What about Nils?"

"Well, we can hardly go out on the road without a road manager, can we?"

"Nils is on his way," Malcolm retorted irritably. But if he's not here by the time we're ready to leave . . ."

"Where was he?"

"Apparently he was with some Japanese girl that he met last night," Malcolm sighed wearily.

"Steve'll have a right go at him when he finds out," Paul chuckled
"Well, he'll have to get in line!" Malcolm snapped. "Putting this damn tour together has been a bloody nightmare . . . no offence, Leee," he added for Childers benefit.
"None taken," Childers shrugged.
"Do me a favour and get everyone moving," Malcolm told Paul before setting off back down the stairs.
"I meant Steve'll have a go at Nils because he didn't bring the Jap girl back here last night for a threesome," Paul shouted after Malcolm.
"Is he always like this?" Childers asked Paul.
"Pretty much," Paul smiled
"You ain't seen nothin' yet, Leee," Thunders chuckled dryly.

Chapter Three

Pistols to open new Roxy venue

RAMONES OUT - DAMNED, CLASH IN

The Ramones have pulled out of the big punk-rock package tour, in which they were to have co-headlined with the Sex Pistols. As a result the whole tour has now been completely revamped.

It will be going ahead from the beginning of next month with the Pistols as sole billtoppers - supported by two other fast-rising British punk bands, The Damned and The Clash, plus American outfit Heartbreakers, fronted by former New York Doll Johnny Thunders.
New Musical Express, Saturday, 4 December 1976.

The coach Malcolm had hired for the tour could hardly be described as state-of-the art, but it was certainly a cut above the decrepit transit-vans he'd provided for the Sex Pistols' previous forays out of the capital. It's being equipped with a reliable heating system was appreciated by all on board – especially the guys from The Heartbreakers and The Clash. Aside from providing a welcome sanctuary from the biting December wind, the coach was also serving to provide a sense of unity. The media's backlash against the Pistols seemed to be extending to any band daring to show solidarity with the Pistols. So much so, in fact, the tour had become an "Us against Them" mentality. Whether The Damned would have shown solidarity with the Pistols was something of a moot point as Malcolm remained unmoved in his insistence that Stiff Records shoulder their act's costs.

Stiff Records had been set up by Jake Riviera – a.k.a. Andrew Jakeman – and his business partner Dave Robinson. The two budding entrepreneurs were already both wellknown on the London music circuit having between them managed pub rock combos Brinsley Schwarz, Chilli Willie & The Red Hot Peppers, and Dr. Feelgood. Indeed, the label had been incorporated thanks to a £400 loan courtesy of the Feelgood's frontman, Lee Brilleaux. However, the fledgling label's shoestring budget meant The Damned would have to settle for B&B accommodation rather than the salubrious five-star hotels the Pistols, Clash, and Heartbreakers would be enjoying.

Had the Sex Pistols been an ordinary pop group, McLaren could have eased the financial strain by inviting another of EMI's up-and-coming bands - or even a group signed to another label - onto the tour and have their label pick up a portion of the tab. But of course, therein lay the problem because the Sex Pistols were far from being a run-of-themill pop group.

They were the leaders of what the UK music press was hailing as the most exciting scene to come out of Britain in the last decade. As yet, of course, The Damned was the only other act within the new scene to have secured a recording contract. Inviting The Damned onto the tour was the most viable option as they'd accrued a sizeable following, but McLaren was loath to deal with Riviera. Instead, he'd turned his attention to New York.

The obvious choice from the groups making a noise at CBGBs were, of course, The Ramones, whose eponymous album had served as a clarion call for many of the groups that had sprung up in the Sex Pistols wake – including many of the musicians that were sitting on the coach. The Ramones had played two London dates back in July at The Roundhouse and Dingwalls. When the news was announced, McLaren had approached renowned London promoter John Curd at the latter's home to see about getting the Sex Pistols onto the Roundhouse bill. Legend had it that Curd responded by bodily ejecting McLaren out into the street, so it must have come as something of a surprise – if only to the UK music press - when McLaren subsequently announced that The Ramones would be co-headlining the Anarchy Tour with the Pistols.
Aside from The Ramones, McLaren also invited Talking Heads – whose punk style came with a more sophisticated, syncopated beat - to share support duties with The Vibrators. The Vibrators had supported the Sex Pistols at the 100 Club back in August, and had also appeared alongside The Damned on the second night's bill at the 100 Club Punk Festival. They had recently signed with Mickie Most's RAK Records.

McLaren's efforts, however, would come to nought and he was forced into a major rethink when all three bands announced they were withdrawing from the tour.
Despite having suffered the indignation of having had his transatlantic advances spurned not once but twice, Malcolm was still keen to add a little Lower East Side allure to the forthcoming tour. Following several desperate late-night telephone conversations The Heartbreakers were added to the bill.

♪♪♪

Glen woke with a start. Someone or something had bumped his elbow from the armrest; the sudden and unsolicited jolt knocking him out of sync. It took several bleary-eyed moments of mental readjustment for him to realise where he was and indeed why he was there in the first place. Even in his disorientated state he remembered his manners, and instinctively placed the back of his hand against his mouth to stifle his jaw-wrenching yawn while taking stock of his surroundings. He remembered he'd been reading the *Daily Mail*'s scathing editorial: "Never Mind Morals or Standards, the only Notes that Matter Come in Wads". The editorial was an open attack on record companies that "specialise, and capitalise in peddling out the same old three-chord product which can be sold and resold over and over again just as long as the packaging changes". It had gone on to lambaste the record companies for cashing in on each generation's desire to shock and outrage the one that had gone before.
What the editorial had failed to mention, however, was that neither EMI, nor McLaren for that matter, had initially desired publicity.
Everyone knew that nothing sells newspapers quite like a good scandal, but the dynamic of said scandal is such that it needs to feed on the public's fear and panic. McLaren's supposed show of insolence was only to be expected, but EMI's refusal to react accordingly had obviously incensed Fleet Street's powers-that-be. So much so, in fact, that the newspaper had seen Leslie Hill's apparent lack of contrition as an excuse to publish an exposé on him which contained a photograph of his Buckinghamshire home, and a canvassing of his neighbours.
Glen remembered Bernie telling him about a quote some politician or other had made recently. He couldn't remember the quote word for word, but it was something about the "truth being halfway around the world before the truth had got out of bed." He'd lost count of how many times Malcolm had said how they would be vindicated in the coming week's music press as several editors and journalists had apparently called him offering their support. That was all well and good, but with the music papers going to press on a Wednesday, the new editions wouldn't be out until next Thursday. If Queen's promo video had been slated for the Monday evening edition of *Today*, instead of Wednesday, they'd at least have had a fighting chance.
There were those on the scene that thought Bernie an acquired taste, but Glen had a lot of time for him. He didn't say much, but what he did say was always worth listening to. Malcolm and Bernie had known each other for years. At

the time Malcolm and Viv took over the lease at 430 King's Road, Bernie had been running a Saturday stall on the nearby Antiquarius Antiques Market selling T-shirts and second-hand leather jackets. That, of course, had been just one of his money-making ventures. Bernie's main source of income - at least from what Glen could gather - was a share in a Renault dealership/garage housed within one of the old railway storage sheds over by Camden Lock. The Clash were now using the shed's upstairs room as a rehearsal space. They had christened it "Rehearsal Rehearsals". It was an in-joke: they were rehearsing to be good enough to rehearse.

Bernie used to meet up with Malcolm and Viv at The Roebuck at the end of the day. They would discuss ideas for T-shirts that Malcolm and Vivienne would sell in the shop. The most notable shirt, of course, was the "You're Gonna Wake Up One Morning" shirt, that Johnny Thunders was wearing. As he was working at the shop he'd been one of the first to get hold of the shirt. Steve had since "borrowed" it and painted his bleeding name on it. Cheek! Little could Malcolm and Bernie have known how relevant the shirt's meaning would become? The *Today* show might only have gone out within the London area, but because of the headlines many a teenager would now be pondering which side of the bed they'd been sleeping on

The shirt had also played a part in The Clash coming together. Their guitarist, Mick, who was sat fast asleep next to him, had been wearing the shirt the night he and his mate Tony had gone along to the Nashville Rooms in West Kensington to checkout a band called Deaf School. Bernie had been there that night, and also happened to be wearing one of the shirts. It was because of this that they'd started a conversation.

According to what Mick had told him about the encounter, Tony had, albeit halfjokingly, told Bernie to "piss off out of it" as he was cramping their style. Quick as a flash, Bernie had told them they should be the ones doing the "pissing off" as he'd designed the shirt. .

At the time, Mick and Tony had a band of sorts going called "London SS". Mick had since said that the name stood for "London Social Security", but he wasn't fooling anyone. Bernie, however, had been intrigued enough by the name to agree to a meeting and see them rehearse. On agreeing to act as their manager, he'd called a meeting at some pub or other in Shepherd's Bush where he'd dumped a shit-load of Nazi paraphernalia – swastikas, Iron Crosses, an SS dagger, and what-have-you on the table in full view of the other punters. Bernie told them that if they wanted to call themselves "London SS", then they had to be prepared to deal with everything the name entailed. In the end, nothing had come of it as Mick and Tony could never keep a line-up long enough to do a show. But Bernie had stayed in touch with Mick.

Before being rudely wrenched back to reality, Glen had been enjoying a fantasy involving himself, his girlfriend, Celia, and a tub of whipped cream. He closed his eyes again in the hope of drifting off again and catching up with Celia, but it was no use. He contemplated waking Mick, before deciding against it and reaching for the Mail which had slid from his lap while he was dozing. He'd no idea as to how long he'd been dozing, but catching sight of the signpost for Luton that flashed past the window he knew it couldn't have been all that long. He was surprised that Mick had succumbed to travel-weariness so soon into the journey - particularly seeing how he had been jabbering away like an overwound Kewpie-doll from the moment the coach had pulled away from Denmark Street. To those that didn't know Mick, his excitement might have seemed a touch naïve, but Glen knew this would be his friend's first experience of staying in a hotel.

Glen opened out the *Mail*, idly flicking through its dog-eared pages until arriving at the page featuring Bill Grundy's riposte to his two-week suspension. Here they were, with the tour in danger of turning into a Monty Python farce, and yet Grundy was about to sod off on holiday with the wife for a fortnight. Thanks to the Steve, Grundy was the most famous TV presenter in the country. He wouldn't be surprised if the old soak wasn't surreptitiously enjoying being in the spotlight. It was hard to believe Grundy was only 52. Well, that was his age according to the *Mail*. Speaking from his home in Cheshire, Grundy was insisting he knew nothing about his two-week suspension, yet was bemoaning his having been cast as the "scapegoat" of the whole saga. *Make your mind up, Billy boy!*

Grundy went on to explain how he hadn't been involved in the decision to invite the Sex Pistols into the studio as such decisions were apparently made at the morning conference which he wasn't required to attend. Again, despite denying he'd been suspended, Grundy confirmed that he'd received a call late Wednesday evening from Jeremy Isaacs, the Controller of Thames Programmes, informing him that he wouldn't be doing the following Wednesday's show. The interview had ended with Grundy boldly declaring that he would be most surprised if he were to lose his job over what had happened, and that he believed the Pistols had deliberately set out to swear on the show in order to guarantee maximum publicity for themselves and their new single.

The *Mail* had also spoken with Grundy's wife, Jane, as well as one of his daughters. Unsurprisingly, both had leapt to his defence claiming that it was

"completely out of character" for Grundy to have encouraged bad language when he knew young children could be watching the show.
The page opposite the article was carrying a quarter-page ad for John Collier, the clothing manufacturer. The annoying jingle from the company's TV ads automatically popped into his head. To exorcise the inane ditty just as quickly again, he started humming the bass line to The Faces' "Three Button Hand Me Down". It was the song that he'd chosen to play during his audition for the band. It had a really intricate bass line that had taken him a couple of weeks to master. And while he wouldn't claim to be in the same league as Ronnie Lane, he known from Steve and Paul's slack-jawed expressions that he'd got the gig. With it's opening couplet about not needing anyone's opinion about what clothes you wore", he'd thought "Three Button Hand Me Down" would be a great song to cover. He'd gone as far as suggesting as much shortly after John's arrival. John, however, had dismissed this idea out of hand before calling him a "cunt".
Glen was the first to admit that his and John's relationship had never been what anyone might call close. They were chalk and cheese personality-wise. Indeed, had it not been for their being in a band together, there would be no reason for them to pass the time of day. They'd actually gotten along alright in the beginning, but John's negative attitude to anything and everything around him had eventually begun to grate. Ironically, he'd been considering taking Steve and Paul to one side and asking them to choose between himself and John. It wouldn't have been an ultimatum as such, more of a "we were doing this for two years before John arrived on the scene," and we can always find someone else. Steve and Paul had often grumbled about John in the past. And there'd been occasions when he'd sensed Malcolm had been itching for any excuse to show John the door. Of course, John was now the centre of attention – "King of the Punks" according to one of the tabloids – and guitarists, bassists, and drummers were two a penny.
He was distracted from his introspection on seeing Bernie making his way down the aisle towards where John and Paul Simonon, his opposite number in The Clash, were poring over that morning's *Daily Express*, with its front-page banner headline: "PUNK? CALL IT FILTHY LUCRE".
Glen was already familiar with the contents of the *Express*' rant about how EMI was set to cash in on the band's appearance on *Today*. Poor old Leslie Hill had again found himself in the firing line for his having defended the band while blaming Grundy for being "foolish enough" to inviting the band to be outrageous. Hill was also insisting there was no question of EMI dropping the Pistols. The *Express* had found an EMI insider – of the "I wish to remain

anonymous" variety, needless to say. According to the *Express*' mole, EMI would make a huge profit from the band's appearance on *Today*. The mole had gone on to explain that owing to the mounting publicity, it was anyone's guess just how big the Pistols might become. If the single were to reach the UK Top 10, it would be selling somewhere in the region of 10,000 copies per day and grossing £30,000 a week for the label.

♪♪♪

Glen watched Bernie slide in beside John. He could see Bernie was anxious to question John and Paul about the *Express*' headline story. He'd spent many an hour in Rhodes' company, and yet he knew hardly anything about his past. The little he did know was that his mum had fled Russia at the end of the war, and that after somehow managing to get her hands on a forged birth certificate on the black market she'd come over to England and settled in the East End of London. Bernie had apparently been born not too long after this. His mother had subsequently married, but the marriage hadn't lasted. His mum had ended up working for one of the leading tailors on Savile Row making suits for the likes of Cary Grant. He remembered Bernie once saying that there wasn't a note or riff that he couldn't identify owing to his having been schooled in the story of the blues by the lovelorn American servicemen calling on the Soho street prostitutes that had kept an eye on him while his mother worked all hours to make ends meet. It was a great story, but Glen wasn't sure as to its veracity as he also remembered Malcolm telling him that Bernie had spent several years at the South Norwood Orphanage.

Glen looked up to the front where Malcolm was regaling their driver Andy with some fanciful tale or other; all the while gesticulating wildly like an overexcitable orang-utan. The more he thought about it, the more he'd come to view Malcolm more of a raconteur than a manager. He couldn't help wondering whether it was his Jewish genes that gave him his gift for theatrical embellishment. Bernie, of course, was also of Jewish descent. Yet while Bernie was happy to stretch the truth to suit his needs, there was no arguing that he was suited to managing a band.

It was obvious from John's expression that he knew what Bernie was up to, but he purposely took his time reading the *Express*' back page article in which the former Arsenal captain, Frank McLintock - who was now plying his trade with Queen's Park Rangers - expressed his belief that the current Arsenal team were capable of emulating the Gunners' team of five seasons ago in doing the "Double" and lifting both the League Division One title and the FA Cup.

Being an avid Gooner, he kept Bernie waiting a few minutes longer perusing his one-time hero's opinions before finally returning his attention to the *Express*' front page. "I wouldn't trust a single fucking word of what's written in here,' he sneered, casually tossing the paper onto the table. "Don't know why people bother readin' these rags. Fuckin' journalists make it all up as they go along. Isn't it funny how the '*Daily Snail*' was interested in speaking with Grundy's nearest and dearest!" he spat. "I didn't see them coming to speak to my mum and dad to get their viewpoint on what's going on. Or me, for that matter!"

"That's because the journalists that work for the *Mail* are too lazy to get arses over to Finsbury Park," Simonon quipped.

"I don't live in Finsbury Park, Paul," John retorted. "I happen to live in a squat in Hampstead with Sid."

"And very commendable that is, John," Rhodes nodded. "The more we show the Greater London Council that they can't expect people to live on the street when there is adequate housing in the capital the better things will be for the common man."

"What do you mean '*we*'? Mick Jones shouted across. "I don't see you slumming it down Davis Road with the rest of us, Bernie."

Rhodes glanced over at Mick, but chose to ignore him. "The *Mail* isn't being totally biased in its coverage," he continued. "There's an article in today's edition saying how the Thames switchboard was jammed all Wednesday evening owing to the number of irate viewers that were calling in. According to the *Mail*, the majority of these people were calling in to demand that Grundy be sacked!"

"Then Joe Public ain't as fuckin' stupid as I thought," John shrugged.

"And *The Evening News* is siding with us," Rhodes nodded, getting into his stride. Last night's edition carried Leslie Hill's quote about Grundy having wilfully goaded you boys. Steve only said what he did because Grundy practically begged him to. You could have put any teenager in the country in front of a television camera, plied them with free booze, told him to say something outrageous, and they'd have done exactly the same as Steve."

"Yeah, it wasn't as if Grundy didn't know we had a few drinks prior to going on air,"

Glen offered. "I mean, he'd popped into the Green Room while we were in there."

That morning's *Daily Mirror* and the *Sun* had again both devoted their respective front pages to the events of Wednesday evening, while that coming Sunday's *News Of The World* was promising a shocking report on 'pop's new heroes'. Not wanting to be left out of the feeding frenzy, London's flagship paper, the *Evening Standard,* had also joined in the Fleet Street feeding frenzy by declaring the Sex Pistols to be nothing more than "Foul-Mouth Yobs".

"I still don't see what all the fuss is about, anyway," John sneered. "It's not as if it's the first time that anyone's sworn on British television, is it?" "No, that particular honour goes to Kenny Tynan,' Rhodes nodded.

"What band's he in then?" Mick quipped.

"Not everyone who uses four-letter words on television is necessarily in a pop group, Michael," Rhodes sighed. "If memory serves, this was back in 1965. Isn't that right, Malcolm?" he asked, glancing up as McLaren appeared at his shoulder.

"Is what right, Bernard?" McLaren asked.

"I was just explaining about Kenny Tynan and when he-"

"Ah, Kenny," Malcolm smiled. "Kenny's a highly respected film, theatre critic, and-" "Like Barry Norman?" Mick asked.

"Yes, Michael; like Barry Norman," Malcolm nodded. "But Kenny is also a lauded writer, of course. Always does things with a touch of elegance. When he married his second wife over in New York a few years back, he had Marlene Dietrich acting as a witness. The Justice of the Peace actually interrupted the service to warn Marlene to step away from the open door for fear of someone slapping her on the arse. Kenny has dined out often on that tale, I can tell you."

Malcolm fell silent for a few moments, as if picturing the aging Hollywood diva hurriedly shuffling away from the door. "In regard to the incident I suspect you're referring to, Bernard," he said, turning to Rhodes, "then Kenny was participating in a late-night live television debate on theatre censorship. He was asked if he would allow a play to be staged in the West End in which sexual intercourse was represented on the stage. He told the interviewer, Robert Robinson - who you might know from his fronting the television quiz show thingy, *Ask The Family* - that he doubted that there were any rational people around who would find the word 'fuck' offensive. As you can imagine, the public outcry was massive. The BBC were forced to issue a formal apology."

"Who says history doesn't repeat itself," Rhodes beamed.

"Kenny basked in the notoriety – especially after Mary Whitehouse wrote a letter to the queen suggesting that Kenny should be given a good spanking. You must remember Kenny?" he asked John. "He was always popping into the shop." "Vaguely," John shrugged.

"Kenny had a thing for Jordan," Malcolm chuckled. "What, with Kenny and the ITN newsreader, Reggie Bosanquet, poor Jords hardly got a moment's peace."

Chapter Four

<u>AUTHORITIES ACT OVER CAMPUS SAFTEY FEARS</u>

UEA shoots down Sex Pistols concert

The University of East Anglia today put an end to tonight's planned concert by punk rock group Sex Pistols because of fears of violence on the campus.

Vice-Chancellor Dr. Frank Thistlewaite, acting with executive authority on behalf of the University's Council, has cancelled the concert because of publicity surrounding the group and its reported attitude to violence.

A storm blew up around the group earlier this week after they used four-letter words in a television interview.

"The university cannot be satisfied this concert would go off peaceably and for this reason the university has cancelled," said Mr. Frank Albrighton, the university's information officer, today.
Eastern Evening News, Friday, 3 December 1976.

Glen was still thinking about Malcolm's flair for the theatrical as he watched his manager make his unsteady way back up to the front and retake his seat. There were still those within the music media that believed it was Malcolm's love of showmanship that had proved the motive behind his staging the "punk festival" at the 100 Club. There was no arguing that Malcolm had had his nose put out of joint when the organisers of the so-called "First European Punk Festival", that was staged in Mont de Marsan in southwest France back in August, had dropped the Sex Pistols from the bill on account of their supposedly demanding top billing, but the true purpose behind the 100 Club festival had been a showcase to secure the Pistols a recording contract.

The 100 Club shindig was actually Malcolm's second attempt to woo the record companies. The first showcase came at the Screen on the Green cinema in Islington at the end of August; the Bank Holiday "Midnite Special" with The Clash and Manchester's Buzzcocks providing support. Malcolm had opted to stage the showcase at the Screen on the Green simply because he knew the manager and could get the place for free. But being a cinema, of course, it was wholly unsuited for staging live music. Those A&R reps that had stove off sleep to catch the Pistols' performance had gone away again convinced the Pistols were a busted flush, and that punk would be a fading memory by Christmas.

The Pistols had put in a far more competent performance at the 100 Club, but Glen couldn't be certain whether the festival had played any part in landing the band a recording contract with EMI. Several companies had expressed an interest in the demo tape Malcolm was touting, the frontrunner being Polydor Records. Polydor's A&R chief, Chris Parry, had considered signing the Pistols as far back as May, only to subsequently cool his ardour upon discovering that someone within the Pistols' entourage – namely Steve - had rifled the pockets of Doctors of Madness when the Pistols had played support to the then up-andcoming Polydor act at a show in Middlesbrough.

Malcolm, of course, had kept the band in the dark over Polydor's renewed interest, but from what he'd since learned Parry had tabled a £20,000 deal, with an additional £20,000 to be set aside for recording costs and other sundries. Knowing how Malcolm's mind worked, Glen knew that Parry would have only seen the cards Malcolm chose to lay down, but Parry had been so sure it was a done deal that he booked the Pistols session time at Polydor's DeLane Lea Studios in Soho to begin working on "Anarchy" as the debut single. Of course, the card that Malcolm had kept closest to his chest during his negotiations with Parry was that he had entered talks with EMI. It probably wasn't of much consolation to Parry, but the Pistols themselves had only found out they would be going with EMI rather than Polydor on the actual day of the signing.

EMI's offer hadn't been all that different to the one Parry had tabled. EMI had offered a £40,000 advance on a two-year deal: £20,000 upon signing the contract, with the remaining £20,000 payable in October 1977. What's more, while the contract stated that EMI would provide funding for "reasonable recording costs", there was some clause or other tucked away in the small print that apparently enabled the label to recoup those same costs from the band's future royalties. The only reason Malcolm had gone with EMI was because of the corporation's standing; it's being the home of The Beatles and Cliff Richard.

Glen still didn't know whether Polydor's tabled offer had played any part in EMI's decision, but the contract had been signed, sealed, and delivered within a day, making it the fastest-ever signing in EMI's history.

Since signing with EMI, Glen had done a little research into the label – not only to satisfy his own curiosity, but so he'd have the answers to his parents' never-ending questions. He couldn't blame them really. And he'd have been pissed off if they hadn't have shown any interest.

EMI, or the Electric & Musical Industries to give the corporate giant its proper title, had formed in March 1931 following the merger of the Gramophone Company (made famous, of course, by its "His Masters Voice" label, and the Columbia Gramophone Company; that same year the newly-incorporated company had opened its now-legendary recording studios at Abbey Road. Aside from its music division, EMI had fingers in other highly-lucrative pies, such as developing radar equipment and guided missiles at their Laboratories in Hayes, Middlesex, and its heavy investment in the radical CAT brain scanner which would supposedly enable doctors to examine the inner workings of the human brain without resorting to surgery. The corporation also owned a chain of restaurants, cinemas, and hotels.

With EMI already gearing up for the impending Christmas sales rush, the band had barely had time to celebrate the signing before heading into Lansdowne Studios in Holland Park to record "Anarchy".

Glen was still a bit peeved that Malcolm had used the "artistic license" clause he'd had written into the contract to veto EMI's wish to release "Pretty Vacant" as the Pistols' debut single. And it wasn't only because it was his song. EMI had simply felt that "Vacant" would be the more radio-friendly of the two songs and therefore more likely to generate sales. Without conferring with Malcolm, the suits at EMI's Group Repertoire Division had decided amongst themselves to release "Anarchy" through its subsidiary label, Harvest. Malcolm, to his credit, had put the kybosh on that one. It said EMI on the contract, and it was going to say EMI on the record. There had been further fun and games with Malcolm's insisting that "Anarchy" be issued in a plain black sleeve. EMI's marketing department had demanded to know how anybody was supposed to find the single. That had played right up Malcolm's street, of course. He told them that he didn't want "anybody" to happen upon the record by chance; he only wanted those that were aware of the band to go into their local record store and ask for the single by name.

Malcolm had resumed his position at Andy's shoulder, one hand gripping the headrest of the latter's chair. Glen could well imagine Malcolm bragging to Andy how he'd masterminded the whole *Today* saga in order to boost sales of "Anarchy" and whip up publicity for the tour. He'd been saying as much to anyone willing to listen since the previous afternoon. Yet nothing could be further from the truth. Malcolm had sat with his head in his hands during the drive back to Harlesden, bemoaning how the band had ruined all his hard work. What was most surprising was the music press buying into his bullshit. You'd think someone might have challenged Malcolm's claims by enquiring how much input he'd had in *Today*'s programme schedulers selecting to end that particular show with Queen's "Somebody To Love".

A sudden commotion from further along the coach distracted Glen from his musings. He glanced over his shoulder in time to see Billy Rath wrestling a bottle of some description from The Heartbreakers' flunky. He watched the two Americans clowning around for a few moments before turning his gaze towards John. There might be precious little that he and John could agree on these days, but he suspected John shared his dissatisfaction over Malcolm's inviting The Heartbreakers onto the tour.

Glen's reservations had nothing to do with The Heartbreakers' musical abilities. It was obvious from watching them going through their paces the previous afternoon at the Roxy that they could play. His objections stemmed from the Americans' offstage activities. Thunders and Nolan were both renowned heroin addicts, and he suspected Lure and Rath were no strangers to the drug. The tour was in enough trouble as it was without their having to pander to a bunch of druggies. Malcolm had played it all down, of course, but his fears had soon been justified. As The Heartbreakers were coming offstage after completing their half-hour set, he'd mentioned to Nolan how much he'd enjoyed their song "Chinese Rocks". As he hadn't been able to decipher much of Thunders' vocals, he'd been unaware that "Chinese rocks" was New York street slang for heroin. That was until Nolan plucked an empty syringe from his pocket, while demanding to know whether he was "a man or a mouse".

♪♪♪

At that moment Nolan was sat gazing into space; seemingly lost in thought. "I don't know 'bout you, Johnny; but I'm still struggling to get a handle on this," he said, glancing briefly at Thunders sitting next to him before focusing on Steve and Paul opposite. "You guys went on some crummy TV show, said 'fuck' a couple of times, and you made the front page of every newspaper in the country? C'mon; what the fuck? What. The. Fuck!" "Yeah, but this is England we're talking about here, Jerry," Paul chuckled.
Thunders looked as equally bemused as Nolan. "What did this Grundy do to provoke you guys?" he asked.
"He just wasn't interested in what we were about; the tour, or anything," Paul shrugged.
"He was just trying to take the piss out of us, like."
"The cunt was more pissed than we were!" Steve grinned. "I coated him off good an' proper."
"You did what?" Nolan asked.
"I coated him off," Steve repeated for Nolan's benefit. "You know, put the cunt to bed."
Thunders dug Nolan in the ribs. "Somethin's getting' lost in translation here, Niggs," he chuckled. "They used to speak English here at one time. I remember readin' it someplace."
"Ha-ha," Paul grinned. "But the dirty old sod was coming on to Suzi something proper. For all Grundy knew her mum and dad could have been watching." "Who's Suzi?" Thunders asked.
"She's a Banshee."
"Sounds like a Japanese motorcycle," Thunders chuckled.
"Suzi's the lead singer in the Banshees," Paul explained. "The 'Banshees' are a band."
"Yeah, you must have seen her boat in the papers?" said Steve. "You know her 'boat'," he continued on seeing Thunders and Nolan's blank expressions, "boat-race . . . face."
Thunders turned to Nolan. "You know, Niggs," he deadpanned, "if only we'd have said 'fuck' on that Limey whistle-stop show a coupla years back we'd have made the front pages."

"Wouldn't you have needed one of mics to be switched on for that?" Steve countered with a sly smile.

Thunders and Nolan exchanged a knowing glance. "But they were switched on, Steve," Thunders said.

"Yea, sure they were," Steve grinned. "We've played live in a TV studio," he said, glancing sideways at Paul. "When we watched on the telly a few days later, every time I moved away from the mic the sound dropped. There was none of that when you were on the *Whistle Test*. And I was at the Spastics charity gig at the Empire Pool, remember?"

"We've been busted, Niggs."

"You been busted, Johnny," Nolan retorted. "I didn't fuckin' mime. Drummers can't fuckin' mime! Ain't that right, Paul?"

"I'm just messin'," Steve smiled, taking another swig from the can of Tartan Ale he was nursing. "You would have got on the front pages if you'd have run across the floor and given 'whisperin', bucktooth baldie fuckin' Harris a slap for callin' you 'mock rock'!"

"And I fuckin' would have done if I'd have heard him," Nolan snarled. "But we were a . . . we'd been partying a little."

"Probably why they had you mime then, innit?" Roadent, the Clash's factotum quipped suddenly rearing up from the seats behind.

Roadent's actual name was Steve Connelly, but he'd been rechristened by Paul Simonon shortly after taking up his roadying duties with the Clash. The happy-go-lucky, 18-year-old originally hailed from Coventry, but had made for the bright lights of London upon his being released from prison having spent three months at Her Majesty's pleasure for non-payment of fines. Connelly had been working with The Clash since their show at the ICA in October. After the show he'd offered to help them load up their gear in return for a bed for the night. The Clash's frontman, Joe Strummer, loved the idea of having an ex-con on the Clash team, believing it gave the band certain kudos. And Roadent certainly wasn't above celebrating his time behind bars as he'd attended the Pistols' recent show at the Notre Dame Hall sporting a white shirt his prison number emblazoned across the back.

"You're a funny guy," Nolan said, his fixed on Connelly.

"I try to be," Connelly grinned, meeting Nolan's gaze.

For a heartbeat Paul and Steve weren't sure which way this was going to go. They liked Roadent well enough, but neither was going to stand in Nolan's way.

"Relax, Jerry," Thunders said at last. "I'm sure our friend here didn't mean anything by that . . . did you?"

"No, of course not," Connelly replied.

At that moment Rhodes appeared at Paul's shoulder. "What are you doing, Stephen?" Rhodes asked Connelly.

"Nothing, Bernie," Connelly grinned again. "Where did you come from? He's like the shop assistant from *Mr. Ben*, isn't he?" he asked no one in particular.

"Call me 'Bernie' once more, and you'll be disappearing from this bus soon enough!" Rhodes retorted.

"Alright, keep your hair on," Connelly said, rolling his eyes at Paul before brushing past Rhodes and moving up the aisle.

"What can we do for you, Bernie?" Steve asked.

"Don't you start!" Rhodes snapped. "I've enough with that idiot!" he said, jerking a thumb over his shoulder at the retreating Connelly. "I just wanted to ask Johnny and Jerry for their opinion on this," he added, leaning across Paul and placing a copy of that morning's *Sun* on the table.

Thunders and Nolan exchanged yet another puzzling glance. "Uh, no thanks," Thunders said, glancing from the paper to Rhodes. "We've been discussing what happened the other night for the past like forty minutes . . ."

Now it was Rhodes' turn to look perplexed. "I'm not referring to the headline," he smiled as the realisation dawned. "I was referring to the article that accompanies this photograph," he said, jabbing a finger at the photograph of Cindy Breakspeare, the newlycrowned Miss World, signing autographs outside a London bingo hall.

Thunders picked up the paper and cast an eye over the article in question. "Ah, when it says 'Miss Jamaica' . . . I think they're referring to the country and not the neighbourhood in Queens."

"What . . .? No," Rhodes chuckled. "I just wanted your opinion on the scandal that has erupted over South Africa's decision to enter two candidates - one girl being white and the other black - in the recent Miss World contest. Their doing so led to nine other counties boycotting the pageant."

"And where does our opinion fit in exactly?" Nolan asked.

"Well, America's long-standing troubles over civil rights are well-documented . . ."

"Yeah," Thunders mused. "But we've never really gotten involved with political issues like race or religion. Our music focuses on street politics. Ain't that right, Niggs?"

"Fuckin' A," Nolan nodded

Steve took the paper from Thunders. "I don't know what the fuck you're bangin' on about, Bernie," he said, eyeing the photo of Breakspeare. "But I wouldn't mind breakin' my fuckin' spear on her."

"Is that all you think about, Steve?"

"Pretty much, yeah," Steve grinned.

"But can't you see what the *Sun* is doing here?" Rhodes asked. "They've chosen to print this photo of Cindy posing with two black women in a subtle attempt to play down the political scandal that has marred the contest. It's all about 'action versus reaction'."

Paul covered his ears in mock protest. "Oh no, here we go again!"

"Action versus what . . .?" Thunders asked

"Don't fuckin' encourage him," Paul grinned.

"'Action versus reaction' comes from Newton's third law of motion." Rhodes was forced to grab hold of Paul's headrest to steady himself as the coach suddenly lurched on the motorway. "When one body exerts a force on a second body, the second body simultaneously exerts a force equal in magnitude and opposite in direction on the first body."

"And in English . . . please" Thunders grinned.

"In layman's terms, it basically means that every day-to-day event - no matter how small or inconsequential it may seem - is an '*action*'. This 'action' then automatically produces a '*reaction*'. And what happened with the Miss World pageant is a classic example of this."

"How so?" Thunders asked, playfully ignoring Steve's and Paul's pained expressions.

"Well, the first 'action'," Rhodes continued, drawing an imaginary line in the air with his finger, "was South Africa's decision to enter two contestants in the pageant. This then brought about a 'reaction' when those nine other countries I mentioned earlier withdrew their own contestants. The second 'action' was the Jamaican government's decision to deny Miss Breakspeare a homecoming parade to celebrate her victory."

Rhodes paused while pushing his spectacles up the bridge of his nose so that he could massage the indents caused by the frame. "By definition, the Miss World pageant is an international event, but unlike the Eurovision Song Contest the pageant is always staged in London regardless of the nationality of the previous year's winner."

"Man, you lost me back at the lights," Nolan groaned. He slipped a cigarette into the corner of his mouth while fumbling in his jacket pocket for his lighter with his other hand. 'Isn't she the same chick that's going out with Bob Marley? You guys know Marley?" he asked Steve and Paul after pocketing the lighter. "His latest album, *Rastaman Vibration*, is his best yet."

"Yeah, I've got a copy," Paul nodded.

Nolan leaned into the table. "What do you think of the Carlton Barrett's drumming style on 'Johnny Was'? Johnny loves that song, don'tcha, Johnny?" he asked, glancing sideways at Thunders.

Rhodes retreated a few steps up the aisle, sensing there was little point in continuing now that music had been brought into the conversation. "Cindy became romantically involved with Marley when she moved into an apartment on the road where he was living." "Why don't you just say Bob's fuckin' her?" Steve shouted after him.

Chapter Five

AS YOU will no doubt have noticed Fleet Street went absolutely bananas over the Sex Pistols last Thursday.

Ignition point for the biggest press ballyhoo over a rock group since the Stones relieved themselves against a garage wall almost a decade ago was the Sex Pistols' appearance on London Weekend's "Today" programme, a teatime magazine-format show dealing principally in local news and personalities.

The furore began when the group delivered a series of four-letter words after being baited by interviewer Bill Grundy, man of fifty-two summers, six offspring and no little wit.
Needless to say the TV station's switchboard was jammed with hysterical calls from the moment John Rotten uttered his first muted ruderie.
Sounds, Saturday, 11 December 1976.

Glen made his across the motorway services car park; his step somewhat lighter now that he'd emptied his bladder. He, as indeed had several others onboard, had been in desperate need of the loo for some time and it had taken the near-threat of mutiny before Malcolm had finally relented. His carefree air rapidly disappeared into the ether, however, on nearing the bus and seeing Malcolm and Bernie huddled together in a conspiratorial conference.

"What's going on out there?" he asked Mick on retaking his seat.

"Why what's happenin'?" Mick asked.

"Malcolm and Bernie are looking pretty anxious about something," Glen explained, jabbing a thumb towards the door. "From the look on Malcolm's face you'd think the Inland Revenue had finally caught up with him."

"Ain't got a Scooby Do, mate, Mick shrugged, following Glen's gaze. "You don't think it's cos more dates have been cancelled, do you?"

Glen had been about to respond when Simonon came bursting back onto the coach closely followed by Roadent. The two rogues had formed a tight bond on account of their sharing the upstairs room at The Clash's rehearsal space. They'd plotted a commando raid on the service station's shop, and judging from their boisterous step their thieving raid had proved successful. Glen was astounded that someone who'd spent time inside would be foolish enough to risk his liberty for the sake of a few chocolate bars.

Glen knew that Mick had been against hiring Roadent, but had acquiesced to Joe and Paul's petitions. From the icy stare Mick gave Roadent as he came past, the ice appeared no nearer to thawing.

Simonon and Roadent hadn't been alone on the raid as Steve was skipping across the car park playfully plucking chocolate bars from his pockets and juggling them in the air.

"Steve don't wanna give up his day job," Mick grinned on seeing his namesake make a hash of it.

"That used to be his day job," Glen said dryly as they watched Steve grabbing up the bars and stuffing them back into his pockets. "Nicking that is."

Glen knew all about Steve having done a stint in a remand home a few years back, yet it still amazed him that he'd avoided serious jail time. He'd a criminal record as long as his arm, with offences ranging from breaking and entering, stealing cars, and driving without either insurance or a license. That was nothing compared to the stuff he'd gotten away with, of course. In fact, the majority of the band's equipment came courtesy of Steve's "five fingered discount".

Needless to say, Steve's living in the heart of Tin Pan Ally had proved irresistible to him. His preferred method was to hurl a brick through the window of one or the music shops on Denmark Street, grab a guitar, and have the guitar stashed under his bed before anyone was the wiser. Once he'd tired of the guitar he'd unload it at one of the other shops.

Glen had even allowed himself to act as Steve's fence. He'd readily suspected the guitar Steve had given him was hooky, but he'd naively thought his agreeing to do the deed would give him a few brownie points. How wrong he was there! He'd taken the guitar into Macari's on Charing Cross Road. He should have known the game was up when the owner kept making excuses to keep him in the shop. Sure enough, the boys in blue had come through the door, and he'd been bundled off to West End Central.

He'd given the cops some cock and bull story about having bought the guitar from some bloke in the Roebuck. They bought it hook, line, and sinker, but said they were still charging him with handling stolen goods. They'd left him to stew in one of the custody cells, only to return a half-hour or so later to say they'd decided to charge him with theft. He'd shit himself, but it turned out theft was actually the lesser charge. Something about that if there weren't people handling stolen goods, thieves wouldn't bother nicking stuff in the first place. He'd gone up in front of the beak at Great Marlborough Street Magistrates Court the following week, and been given a year's conditional discharge.

"It's like the bleedin' Bash Street Kids' Christmas outing," Mick said, rolling his eyes as Simonon and Roadent playfully squabbled over their cache of stolen goodies. "If only he was as good at roadyin' as he seems to be at thievin'."

"You're not a fan, are you?"

"Let's just say he's on probation," said Mick, his eyes still fixed on the unsuspecting Roadent. "I'm certainly not happy about him livin' at Rehearsals. He's distractin' Paul from practicin' his bass."

"But you can't argue that Paul's playing has come on leaps and bounds recently," Glen offered. "I mean, he was all over the place when you made your debut with us up in Sheffield in July. But he was solid enough when we played Lanchester Poly the other week."

"Yeah," Mick nodded. "But he needs to learn to make do without having the notes drawn onto the neck of his bass. And I can't keep nippin' across the stage to tune it for him midway through a show, either. It's fuckin' embarrassin'!" "I can imagine," Glen nodded.

"Havin' said that, I couldn't imagine Paul not being in the band. He's really come into his own on stage since we told Keith to sling his hook,"

"What's Keith up to these days?" Glen asked. "I used to see him knocking about, but haven't seen him in ages."

"Last I heard, he was muckin' about with Sid an' Viv in the band they've got goin'. They're calling themselves the 'Flowers of Romance'. I've taught Viv a few chords, but she ain't that great yet. Joe's girlfriend is playin drums for 'em, but she ain't really a drummer."

"I still can't believe John gave it to 'em, the name I mean," said Glen. "I still think we could have worked it up into a proper song. But I was outvoted as usual. What's the latest with you and Viv, anyway?" he asked hurriedly, in the hope of steering the conversation away from his ongoing troubles with John.

"It's on and off like a bleedin' light bulb."

"You better ask Viv, 'cos I don't have a fuckin' clue."

"You say Paul's come into his own with Keith gone," Glen said, swiftly changing subject again. "But it hasn't done you any harm either, has it?"

"Well, you know what they say about 'too many chefs'," Mick grinned. "And besides, it was me an' Joe that was writing all the songs anyway. Keith only came up with 'What's My Name?' the whole time he was with us."

Glen glanced down the aisle to where Strummer was sat. "How come he's bleached his hair?"

"He's done it for the tour," Mick shrugged. "Looks good, don't it?"

Glen didn't respond. He suspected this was the latest stage in Strummer's metamorphism. Prior to his joining forces with Mick and Paul, Strummer had fronted The 101ers; a pub rock outfit that he'd put together from amongst his fellow squatters at 101 Walterton Road. He said he was 22, but there were rumours floating about that he was at least two years older. Was it Bernie that had got him to lie about his age? To be fair to Strummer, it was a brave move on his part as The 101ers had been making something of a name for themselves on the circuit. They'd even released a single, "Keys To Your Heart", through the independent Chiswick Records. In all likelihood, The 101ers would have advanced another couple of rungs up the ladder by now had Strummer not recognised a wind of change was in the air when the Pistols had supported his band at the Nashville at the beginning of April. Strummer wasn't the only one in The Clash to undergo a sartorial makeover. When Glen had first met Mick his hair had been halfway down his arse. He'd also been wearing hideous leopard-print bellbottom flares and platform shoes.

Glen remembered the encounter coming about around the time the Pistols had been looking for a second guitarist. Paul had been wavering about committing himself fully to the band, as he hadn't thought Steve was good enough on guitar. Malcolm had placed an ad in the *Melody Maker* classifieds for a "whizz kid guitarist, no older than 20, and no worse looking than Johnny Thunders." None of the hopefuls that had responded were any better than Steve. Well, there was that 15-year-old kid called Steve New. He could play alright, but Malcolm had thought 15 a bit too young.

Mick and his mate Tony had been really put out on seeing the ad, as they'd thought they were the only ones in London that knew who Johnny Thunders was. Bernie was had taken London SS under his wing by then, and had brought them round to Denmark Street. He, Steve, and Paul had been shocked that Bernie was bothering with a bunch of throwbacks. He couldn't remember much about the other two, other than they were Norwegian. There'd been something about Mick, however. So much so, they'd invited him to stay behind and jam with them. He couldn't remember why John wasn't there that night. It was a mid-week night, so he could have been off watching Arsenal.

They'd been impressed enough to consider offering Mick the gig as second guitarist, in the band. He and Malcolm had subsequently tried to track him down, but as they were going behind Bernie's back, they could hardly ask for Mick's phone number. They succeeded in getting an address where Mick might be found. That was a surreal experience in itself, as they'd had to conduct their enquiries with one of Norwegians through the letterbox as he refused to the open door.

It would have been great to have had Mick in the Pistols, but they'd decided to stick with Steve as the sole guitarist in the end.

Glen was so caught up in his reverie that he hadn't noticed Strummer was now occupying the seat in front of him. "I could feel me ears burnin'," he grinned.

"We were just sayin' how much Paul has improved on bass," said Mick.

"You're right there," Joe nodded, plucking a roll-up cigarette from behind his ear. "Got a light?" he asked Mick. He paused while lighting the roll-up. "Do you remember that night at the Mucky Duck in Sheffield" he asked Mick; his face momentarily wreathed in smoke.

"When Paul got stuck playin' the riff at the start of 'Listen'."

"Yeah, it wasn't the most auspicious of debuts, was it?" Mick chuckled.

"Ours wasn't without incident," said Glen, thinking back to the Pistols' own debut at St. Martin's College of Art. They'd opened for a rock'n'roll revival outfit called Bazooka Joe. He'd gotten them the slot on account of his being enrolled at St. Martin's and serving on the college's concert committee. "They pulled the plug on us after ten minutes or so after John called of the Bazooka Joe lot a 'cunt'."

"Nothin' new there then," Mick smiled, glancing over his shoulder to where John was now sat. "And Paul was just nervous, that's all."

"He wasn't on his fuckin' own, was he?" Joe chuckled.

Glen sat studying Joe. He knew from something Mick had let slip a while back that Joe had enjoyed a private education; some boarding school out in Surrey somewhere. Another skeleton Bernie was anxious to keep tucked away at the back of the Clash cupboard. Since then he'd found it amusing how Joe didn't always remember to drop his H's.

"But at least we'd been on stage before," said Mick. "Thinking about it now, maybe we rushed things a bit. For Paul, I mean."

Joe shook his head dismissively. "Chuck 'em in at the deep end and see if they can swim. That's what I always say. What do you think of me 'air?" he asked Glen.

"When you going back to get it finished?"

But it is finished, Sex Pistol," Joe whispered conspiratorially. "It's my disguise . . . to keep the press hounds off my scent."

Glen glanced at Mick before turning back to Joe. "No offence, Joe, but there's people on this bus that don't know who you are."

♪♪♪

Glen had expected Malcolm, or maybe even Bernie to make some sort of announcement when they came back on board, but to his dismay, the two merely settled back into their seats and continued their conspiratorial mutterings. He was fed-up with trying to secondguess what was going on, and was contemplating going up to the front of the coach to get some answers when Rhodes suddenly got up out of his seat and made his way down the aisle. Seizing his chance to finally get some answers, Glen grabbed hold of Bernie's arm. "Is Malcolm ever going to let us in on what's going on, or are we going to be kept in the dark until we get to Derby?"

"Kept in the dark?" Rhodes frowned, glancing from Glen to Mick. "I'd hardly call it that."

"Then what would you call it?" Glen pressed.

Rhodes paused momentarily; staring out of the window as if formulating a response. "This is going to be the most significant tour in the history of rock'n'roll, Glen," he said at last. "This is history in the making!"

"That may well be," Glen replied nonchalantly. "But it isn't going to be much of a tour if any more sodding dates are cancelled, is it?'

"Who said anything about more cancelled dates?"

"C'mon, Bernie," Mick sighed. "You don't have to be Sherlock bleedin' Holmes to see that something's goin' on."

"You and Malcolm weren't fretting about the weather back there, were you?" said Glen.

Rhodes glanced about him to see if anyone was eavesdropping. "I suppose there's no harm in telling you," he said at last. "But keep it under your hats until Malcolm makes his announcement." He glanced over his shoulder to satisfy himself that McLaren wasn't watching before continuing. "While we were at the services Malcolm called the office and spoke with Sophie. Sophie told him that Sunday night's show in Newcastle is now definitely off. Can you believe the city council have said the decision was made so as to 'protect their children'? The Rolling Stones would kill to get publicity like that!"

"But that's hardly-"

"And several other venues are now apparently also threatening to cancel," Rhodes interjected, cutting Glen off in mid-sentence. "I don't know the full ins and outs, but Guildford is one of the shows under threat. Don't look so despondent," he said to Glen.

"This is the Anarchy Tour after all."

"And there was me thinking the tour was supposed to be about us promoting our new single."

Rhodes appeared genuinely taken aback at this. "But the cancellations will give the single more publicity than the shows ever could," he said. "Can't you see what's happening here? Why even as we speak the students at Norwich University are staging a sit-in demonstration in protest at tonight's show being cancelled. And when kids up and down the country hear about the demonstration on the news they'll want to go out and buy the record. It's like the Paris riots all over again."

"Don't you think you're over-egging the pudding a bit there?" Glen said sourly.

"'Over-egging the pudding'?" Rhodes gasped. "We could throw all the eggs at Bernard Matthews' turkey farm into the mix, and we'd still need more! You're not seeing the bigger picture here. Those students in Norwich aren't simply demonstrating because of a cancelled rock'n'roll show. They're demonstrating because they're fed up with being told what they can and can't do by those in authority. And what's happening in East Anglia is just the start." Before either Mick or Glen could respond he turned on his heel and scurried back to his seat.

"Well, what did Leee have to say?" Malcolm asked without glancing up from his notebook.

"I haven't spoken with Leee yet," Rhodes said hesitantly.

This proved sufficient to grab McLaren's attention. "What do you mean?" he asked.

"There appears to be some dissention in the ranks," Rhodes told him. "Some of them are getting a bit edgy. They feel they have a right to know what's going on."

"Well, they'll just have to wait!" Malcolm snapped. He closed his notepad and slipped it back into the leather satchel he'd bought specially for the tour. "I don't mind admitting,
Bernard, at this moment I'm not even sure I know what the hell's going on."

"But surely you must have anticipated a reaction to-"

"Oh, do spare me your Newton's third law ramblings!" McLaren cut in. "Having one or two venues cancel would have been great for publicity," he said in a softer tone, "but I honestly didn't expect anything like this! It took me three months to put this tour together, Bernard. Three months of hard work, bloody hard work. I had to get the bands, sort out the fees, the contracts, the hotels . . . And all the while I had Viv nagging me about how I was leaving her to run the shop. I don't know how Larry Parnes put up with it all those years, I really don't."

"None of Parnes' acts ever swore on TV," Rhodes smiled. "Think what the reaction would have been back then if Tommy Steele had dared to say 'fuck' on *Sunday Night at the London Palladium*."

"Or dear Billy," McLaren chuckled to himself. "To paraphrase the *Mirror*'s line from yesterday we'd have had 'The Filth From Fury! To hell with the cancellations, Bernard! We'll fight fire with fire. When we get to Derby I'll have Sophie get onto EMI and tell them to have their lawyers threaten to sue any venue that cancel. Can you believe the management at the hotel in Norwich where we were meant to be staying tonight is refusing to refund the deposit? They're saying something about it being company policy." "Probably due to it being such short notice," Rhodes shrugged.

"Short notice! We only found out today!" McLaren seethed. "I'll have Sophie add that to EMI's list for their lawyers to sort out when we get to Derby."

"So the show in Derby is still on?"

"As far as I'm aware," McLaren nodded. "That's if we ever get to Derby," he said, looking over to the open door where Andy was stood smoking a cigarette. "Andrew, is there any reason why were still stuck here in the middle of nowhere?"

Andrew shrugged his shoulders whilst crushing the stub of his cigarette against the side of the coach. "Can't set off yet, Malcolm. Not everybody's back yet."

Malcolm got to his feet and scanned the coach. "Who the hell are we waiting for?" he demanded of no one in particular.

Childers got to his feet and advanced up the aisle. "Sorry Malcolm, my boys haven't got back yet. Did you happen to see Johnny and Jerry while you were in there?" he asked Steve, pointing in the general direction of the service station.

Steve crammed the last two chunks of a Yorkie Bar into his mouth before responding. "I think they-" He suddenly burst into a coughing fit, sending bits of semi-chewed chocolate and spittle over Paul.

"You fuckin' animal!" Paul shouted; ignoring Steve's coughing spasms.

"Does anyone on board know the Heimlich manoeuvre?" Ray Stevenson asked.

"Wasn't he the head of the Gestapo?" Roadent grinned.

"Here they come, Malcolm," Rhodes shouted. A heartbeat later a raucous cheer sounded as Thunders came up the step closely followed by the rest of the Heartbreakers.

McLaren watched in bemused silence as the glassy-eyed Americans came filing past and retook their seats. "They haven't, surely," he gasped. "Not even Johnny Thunders could score at a fucking motorway services."

"They ah, they brought provisions,' Childers smiled wearily. "I'm acting as a pharmaceutical dispensary as well as their manager."

♪♪♪

Nolan pulled a comb from his top pocket and started running it through his hair. "Hey you guys," he said to get Steve and Paul's attention. "When we were at the truck stop back there we saw the funniest thing, man."

"Yeah, what was that?" Paul asked.

"There was a poster on the wall advertising soup that comes in a fuckin' box. Soup in a fuckin' box! I thought I was seeing things, man."

"Oh, you mean the new Chef Square-Shaped Soups. They're new . . . Well, new-ish."

"Now, I gotta tell you," Nolen said, sliding the comb into his top pocket. I've seen some things in my time. But I ain't never seen soup that comes in a fuckin' box?" "Yeah, don't it leak out or nothing?" Thunders asked.

"It's powder, Johnny," Paul explained.

"Me and Niggs like our powder," Thunders smiled knowingly

"Well, I wouldn't go snortin' that stuff or you'll end up with a fuckin' pea stuck up your hooter,' Steve grinned.

"And what would you know about snorting powder, my friend?" Thunders asked him.

Steve looked about him before responding. "You guys aren't the only ones on board that have tried heroin."

"Don't look at me!" Paul interjected.

"But you have, Steve; that what you're saying here?" Nolan asked.

"It was when we were over in Paris playin' some new club a couple of months back. It was my twenty-first birthday, so I thought I'd celebrate in style."

"The stuff we tried in Paris wasn't bad," Thunders nodded. "Not as good as the stuff we get back home, but not bad."

"Did you go to Pere le Chaise while you were over there?" Nolan asked.

"Pearl who?"

"Pere le Chaise is a cemetery; the one where Jim Morrison is buried. Well, there's lots of famous people buried there, but Jim's grave is the one most people go to visit. Most Americans, anyways."

Steve grabbed a can of lager from the bag nestled between his feet and gave the ringpull a tug. "Nah, the only Doors I was interested in were the brothels," he said, taking a swig and wiping his mouth with the back of his hand. Malcolm paid for me to visit a Tom. He's good like that. 'Tom' is slang for prostitute over here," he added.

Nolan leaned across the table. "Getting back to the subject of powder, what are our chances of scoring some out on the road?"

"Dunno," Steve shrugged. "I've never gone looking for it. Mandies are more my thing. Shit. Sorry, Johnny, I didn't mean to . . ."

"It's alright, Steve," Thunders nodded. "I know you didn't mean nothin' by it. What happened with Billy was just one of those things, is all."

"When I got the news that one of the Dolls had died in London my first thought – and this is the God's honest truth here, guys - I thought it was Johnny that had died."

"Thanks for the vote of confidence, Niggs,"

"And it's worth pointing out here that Billy didn't die because he was a junkie," Nolan continued. "Sure he liked his Ludes, who doesn't? No, Billy died because some rich English bitches didn't have the guts to take the fuckin' rap! All those bitches needed to do was get Billy to a fuckin' hospital. The doctors would have pumped Billy's stomach and he'd still be alive."

"But then you'd have been out of a gig, Jerry," Paul said.

"True enough," Nolan shrugged. "But that would be a small price to pay to have Billy still around."

Thunders was sat staring into space, as though suddenly transported back to that fateful night of four years earlier. "And me and Niggs would have got together at some point," he said, snapping out of his trance. "Don't get me wrong, I loved Billy, but he was tight with Syl. When Niggs joined the Dolls, we became brothers. How you findin' the action on Syl's Les Paul by the way?" he asked Steve.

"It's fuckin' great! Tell him 'thanks' the next time you see him. That's something I've been dying to ask you guys. How did you find Malcolm? As a manager, I mean?" "Malcolm wasn't ever our manager, Steve," Nolan said dismissively.

"I guess you could say he was more like our haberdasher," Thunders smiled. "Has Malcolm told you about the costumes he had Vivienne make up for us . . . The red leather stuff?"

"Oh Christ, don't get me started on that!" Nolan chuckled. "We already had the song written – 'Red Patent Leather' – but those outfits were like somethin' off of *The Twilight Zone*!"

"And what's that we heard about Malcolm having you playing in front of a 'hammer and sickle' backdrop?" Paul asked.

"That was at the Little Hippodrome on East 56th Street," Nolan explained. "David's girlfriend, Cyrinda, sewed that Russian flag for us at her apartment. Lookin' back, it wasn't the smartest move we ever made. I mean, we was used to getting hassle from the straights over how we looked. But playin' in front of that flag made people think we was communists. If people think you're a fag in New York, you risk getting' a smack in the mouth. People think you're a communist you're likely to get fuckin' shot!"

"You'll see for yourselves when you guys come over to the states," Thunders nodded.

"Has Malcolm made any noises about that yet?"

"Not that I know of," Steve shrugged. "But then again, he never tells us nothin' about what he's plannin'. I can't wait to get over to America. Them Yank birds won't know what's hit 'em. God help the first one. She'll have a fanny like a wizard's sleeve by the time I'm through with her."

Chapter Six

PRESS IS A FIVE-LETTER WORD
'.WERE THE PISTOLS LOADED?' screamed the page one headline of Friday's 'Sun'
The story was the same for the rest of the popular National Press. Punk Rock hit Fleet Street. A few four-letter words on the small screen and they went bananas. It carried on into Sunday's Press, where Punk and the Pistols overtook other matters of national importance. The Media – Press, Radio and TV – have the power to make or break a cult. With their 'Shock Horror Filth' outrage, they have made sure that Punk Rock isn't going to leave us just yet. In fact, they have helped to establish the music industry's biggest money-spinner for 1977.
Record Mirror, Saturday, 11 December 1976.

As the crow flies, the sleepy village of Littleover lay some three miles to the southwest of Derby city centre. The tour party arrived at the elegant nineteenth century Crest Hotel to find its foyer teeming with reporters, all of whom were eagerly clutching their notepads in anticipation of another front-page story. McLaren had been hoping Fleet Street might have tired of extracting their pound of flesh from the Sex Pistols and would have moved onto the next kill. He was pondering how to get everyone inside with the minimum of fuss when he espied a bald-headed, bespectacled figure push his way through the throng and out onto the forecourt.

"No need for three guesses to figure out who this gentleman might be, is there?" he said to Rhodes while getting to his feet. "Nils, you come with me," he shouted over his shoulder. "The door if you please, Andrew. Oh, and Bernard," he said, glancing back to Rhodes, "makesure everybody stays on the coach till Nils and I have sorted out the reservations." He waited till the manager was almost at the coach before stepping off.

"Mr McLaren, I presume?" the manager said, his smile anything but welcoming.
Malcolm pointed beyond the manager's shoulder over towards the hotel. "How on earth did you convince that rabble to stay put?"

"The Chief Constable of Derby happens to be a personal friend of mine," the manager said without taking his eyes from Malcolm. "He sent one of his sergeants over. You've just missed him in fact. The sergeant told them that it would only take a phone call from myself and the lot of them would spend the weekend in the cells, and be charged with breach of the peace come Monday morning. "The warning doesn't only extend to reporters, Mr McLaren. Am I making myself clear?"

"As crystal," Malcolm nodded. "But I can assure you, you'll get no trouble from us. In fact, if you're happy to repeat your threat so that I can get everybody up to their rooms, I assure you that you won't hear a peep out of place from me and my boys. I'm guessing you got notification that we'll be needing the rooms for tonight as well as tomorrow night? And, I bet your takings at the bar have rocketed since they turned up, eh?" he said, gently manoeuvring the manager back towards his hotel.

"It's a bit posh here, ain't it?" Nils said, gazing about the foyer. "A cut above the fleapits you booked the band into the last time they played up this way. Or at least the last time I was with them."

Malcolm ignored him. "Do you know what time the 'Dumbed' are expected to arrive?" he asked.

"I take it you're referring to the Damned," Nils replied drolly. "I don't know, but they're hardly likely to show up here, are they?"

Nils, of course, had heard this line of rhetoric before. He knew that just inviting The Damned onto the tour had caused Malcolm great discomfort - primarily because he couldn't cope with having to deal with a punk-related group or project that wasn't under his direct control. Another reason was his dislike towards Jake Riviera, which was largely due to Riviera having had the audacity to establish his own record label. Although he continued to dismiss Stiff Records as nothing more than an outlet for third-rate pub rock merchants in public, he was nonetheless piqued that The Damned had pipped the Sex Pistols in being the first bona fide punk group to release a single. On top of that, they were apparently already making plans to record their debut album for Stiff.

Nils had first become acquainted with The Damned when they'd supported the Sex Pistols at the 100 Club back in August. He'd also been in attendance when they'd played the second night of the 100 Club Punk Festival in September. Indeed, he'd been standing within spitting distance from Rotten's pal Sid when he'd thrown a beer glass at the stage; the fallout from which had seen any group with punk rock affiliations banned from the club sine die. He knew that Malcolm would have liked nothing better than snub Riviera, but he'd been forced to invite The Damned onto the tour because with a single out their inclusion would add significant weight to the tour's overall package.

"I believe I got it right," Malcolm retorted, handing the last of the completed registration slips to the bemused receptionist. "I_can't for the life of me understand why they're not staying here tonight. Like you say, it's lovely. And it would have made things far less complicated," he added, handing several sets of keys to Nils.

"You know as well as I do why they're not staying here," Nils sighed wearily. "They're not staying here because Jake and Dave can't afford to put them in here. Rat told me that things were so tight at Stiff that they have to sell enough copies of the latest record to ensure the next one gets made."

"Oh it's 'Jake and Dave' now, is it?" Malcolm asked, raising an accusatory eyebrow.

"Hoping they'll sign the 'Bad Cheese' . . .?"

"I'm not biting, Malcolm."

"You nearly did," Malcolm smiled. "I saw it in your eyes. But getting back to the Dumbed. They could have at least followed behind us up here. I mean, how are we supposed to liaise if we have no idea where they are?"

"Rick said that he would ring me here at the hotel as soon as they arrived in Derby.".

"Who's Rick?"

"Rick Rogers," Nils replied. "Rick works for Stiff. He's acting as the Damned's road manager for the tour."

"And how's he getting here? On his horse, 'Trigger?'"

"I think you'll find that that was Roy Rogers."

"Well, I was half right, wasn't I," Malcolm said dryly. "I knew he'd have something to do with cowboys."

Nils offered Malcolm a wan smile. "I haven't got the energy, Malcolm. Who am I rooming with?" he asked, idly toying with one of the room keys.

"You're in with John."

"I thought you would have kept the groups together."

"How on earth could I possibly do that?" "Steve and Paul are joined at the hip. And could you honestly see John rooming with Glen?" He paused to pick up his satchel. "No, I've put John in with you so that you'll be able to keep an eye on him. Because" - he jerked his arm towards a small coterie of reporters that had drifted away from the main pack and were now loitering in the doorway in the hope that they might scoop their colleagues –
"this lot are becoming obsessed with him."
"What do you expect with a name like 'Johnny Rotten'?"
"Yes, but that's the whole point, isn't it?' Malcolm gasped. "I've spent the last twelve months creating an air of mystique around young Lydon. And I don't want him blurting out that he got the name 'Rotten' simply because of the state of his bloody teeth!"
Malcolm pocketed his own key and set off towards the lift. He was halfway across the foyer when Nils' shout brought him to a halt. "Tonight. What about tonight?"
"It's Friday," Nils sighed, taking a few steps towards Malcolm. "The boys are gonna want to go into Derby and have a few beers."
"That's out of the question."
"Then at least let them enjoy the bar here."
Malcolm glared at Nils as if he'd taken leave of his senses. "What, and let that lot loose on them?" he shouted, jabbing a finger towards the throng of reporters.
"You can't seriously expect them to stay in their rooms all night," Nils spluttered. "You gonna tell Johnny and Jerry they're to stay in their rooms, are you?"
"I don't have to, Nils," Malcolm smiled. "That's your job . . ."

♪♪♪

The frustration at being confined to their respective rooms was at least tempered with the availability of room service, and a party was soon underway in John and Nils' room.
"So what do you think, Nils?" Mick Jones asked, grabbing a couple of bottles from the serving trolley and handing one to Nils. "About the cancelled shows, I mean."
Nils took a long pull on the bottle, savouring its contents; his knowing he wouldn't be paying for it making the lager taste all the more sweeter. Before going outside to break the bad news, he'd had first enquired at reception

whether the Crest offered room service. He hadn't bothered going to Malcolm's room to run it past him first, and nor had he bothered to explain to John and the other Pistols that all sundry charges would most likely be coming out of their EMI advance. Nils had known Malcolm for several months by the time he'd accepted the latter's offer to serve as the Pistols' road manager. He'd often socialised with Malcolm and Vivienne, the three of them usually ending up at one of Andrew Logan's parties at Butler's Wharf on Shad Thames. Their last visit to the sculptor's studio cum warehouse was back in February when the Pistols and their entourage had conducted their own "St. Valentine's Day Massacre" in laying waste to many of Logan's prized works.

Despite their falling out he still respected Malcolm's gift of the gab, his ability to talk his way out of any situation . . . or at least most situations. While he couldn't claim to know all of what was going on, he knew that the unfolding events were way beyond Malcolm's control. It was no longer a case of how many venues might cancel, but rather how many of the nineteen shows would go ahead. In all likelihood, they'd all be back in London come Monday morning. And if Malcolm wanted to bill him for tonight's room service, then he could take out of the back pay he was still owed. £300 for eight months of babysitting the Pistols was an insult. He was still kicking himself for having taken the money, but he'd been skint at the time. And here was Mick Jones asking for his opinion on the cancellations. He took another pull on his bottle while formulating a response. "Well, Mick-"

"I'll tell you I fuckin' think," John interjected. "I think it's a fuckin' ludicrous state of affairs! This country is supposed to be a fuckin' democracy, right? Somewhere where everyone can supposedly say what the fuck he or she wants without fear of being thrown into prison. And yet here we are being denied that fundamental right. Is this England or Communist fuckin' Russia?"

"Is it right what I heard about the women workers at EMI's pressing plant refusing to handle the record?" Mick asked.

"That's what Malcolm's tellin' us," John replied sourly. "If my old man refused to do his job he'd get the fuckin' sack, wouldn't he? So why doesn't EMI threaten those silly bitches with the dole queue and see what happens then!"

"It's obviously-"

"If you ask me I think EMI are behind the whole fuckin' thing," John spat before Mick could finish. "I mean the record was definitely gonna be a number one, right? But how could like . . . how could Tony Blackburn sit there and go, 'And now boys and girls, here's the nation's new number one, "Anarchy

in the UK".' He'd look fuckin' stupid!" "That cunt always looks stupid," Joe sneered.
"What do you reckon to the chances of Bill Grundy coming to tomorrow night's gig?" Nils chuckled.
"He could be the guest of honour," John quipped. "That's if we could get him out of the bar, of course. I can't believe anyone would actually employ someone like that. He's a joke, and a bad one at that!"
"I don't think we'll be seeing him on the telly anytime soon," Joe grinned.
"You could dedicate 'No Future' to him," Mick chuckled.
"I might just do that," John cackled. "If we ever get to play the fuckin' song that is," he added wistfully.
"Bernie's making out like it was Malcolm who planned the whole thing," Joe said, helping himself to another beer.
"Well, that's Malcolm for you, isn't it," John shrugged; "always looking to take the credit whilst doing none of the fuckin' work! The only influence Malcolm had on what happened the other night was that he threatened to stop our wages if we didn't do the fuckin' interview."
There was a sudden knock at the door but nobody reacted. As Joe was happened to be nearest to the door, he begrudgingly got to his feet to let Dave Goodman, and his business partner Caruso Fuller. Goodman was the Pistols' resident sound engineer. Having recorded the demos that had proved pivotal in EMI signing the Sex Pistols, Goodman had been given the job of producing the "Anarchy" single at Lansdowne Studios in Holland Park.
Goodman was a capable enough engineer, but Lansdowne's state-of-the-art facilities were a huge step up from recording the Sex Pistols on a 4-track at Denmark Street, however, and the Pistols had spent seven weary days at Lansdowne repeatedly playing the song over and over again without having anything to show for their labours. Aside from the sessions taking a sizeable slice of EMI's £10,000 budget, Goodman's ongoing failure to wrap things up had forced EMI to put the original November 19 release date back another week. They'd eventually relocated to Wessex Studios in Highbury where Goodman once again wasted countless reels of two-inch tape vainly attempting to capture the Pistols' live energy. The normal recording process for a single took on average around three weeks. As the days continued to slip by with no sign of progress, Goodman was duly summoned to Manchester Square to be told he was off the project. The blow was softened somewhat with the label happy to use Goodman's version of "I Wanna Be Me" as the B-side.

Goodman's replacement, Chris Thomas, was Wessex's affiliate producer. Thomas had cut his teeth working on the Beatles' *White Album*, before going on to work with Procol Harum and Roxy Music, as well as oversee the mixing of Pink Floyd's *Dark Side Of The Moon*. He'd attended the "Midnite Special" showcase at the end of August. Though the Pistols' performance had left him unmoved, he'd been impressed with the chord changes on the "Anarchy" demo that EMI sent him.

Thomas' insistence that Rotten enunciate his lyrics had bruised a certain spiky ego, but within just five takes a finished version of "Anarchy" was in the can. EMI were understandably delighted, but in their haste to get the single out they erringly credited Thomas as producer on "I Wanna Be Me". EMI had of course apologised unreservedly for any embarrassment their oversight may have caused, but Goodman would nonetheless have to wait until the 15,000 copies already pressed had been sold before receiving his production credit.

Goodman and Fuller each grabbed a bottle from the trolley and settled themselves by the window. "What've we missed?" Goodman asked.

"Nothing much," Nils shrugged. "We were just discussing the *Today* thing . . . *Again*!"

"Well, it's big news whichever way you look at it," said Goodman. "What I can't understand is why they didn't just pull the plug when Steve swore near the beginning of the interview? I mean, I heard it plain as day."

"And you live over Dulwich way," John grinned. "Save my place, Mick," he said, jumping up from his bed. "I need a piss."

"Have one for me while you're there," Mick grinned.

John paused at the door while draining the last of his beer. "I still don't know what all the fuss is about. Let's face it; 'fuck' and 'shit' are words that people use every day." "Yeah, but not on *Crossroads*," Joe grinned.

The conversation had drifted by the time John returned. "We were talkin' about your mate Don from Acme Attractions," Goodman repeated for his benefit.

John eyed Goodman suspiciously. "What about Don?"

"I was just sayin' I'm surprised Don's taken such an interest in what the Pistols and the Clash are doing. He doesn't strike me as the punk type."

"Since when has there been a 'punk type'?" John snorted, grabbing up another beer from the tray before reclaiming his place on the bed. "And it just goes to show that you should never judge a book by its fuckin' cover, Dave! Don understands the connection between his culture and what we're doin'."

"Don brought Jeannette with him when he came to see us at the ICA," Simonon said. "Who's Jeannette?" Fuller asked.

"Jeannette's Don's girlfriend," Goodman explained. "She also works with Don at Acme Attractions."

"Yeah, well I wouldn't mind seeing her attractions," Simonon grinned. "She's fuckin' gorgeous. It's the main reason I go down there."

"You'll get no argument from me there, Paul," John nodded; his eyes suddenly lighting up on seeing Goodman reach into his pocket and pull out a golf-ball-sized lump of cannabis resin and a packet of cigarettes. From a second pocket he produced a packet of Rizla papers, a strip of cardboard, and a cigarette lighter and placed them on the carpet beside the resin.

"You constructin' one of your 'tour specials' there, Dave?" Simonon asked.

Goodman flashed Simonon a knowing smile while casually running the flame from his lighter under the resin. "I see my reputation precedes me. Oh, I forgot to mention it," he said, looking over to John, "I bumped into Sid the other day. He doesn't seem to have been affected too much by his stint inside for the glass-throwing thingy at the 100 Club."

"He's acting like it didn't affect him," John shrugged. "But I can't see how it couldn't have affected him."

"I got the impression he was pissed off that you didn't go and see him," Goodman said.

"I was gonna go visit him," John shrugged noncommittally. "But, well, you know how it is . . ." he said; his voice trailing off.

"Viv went to see him," Nils said.

"Jesus, wasn't his getting' a three-month sentence enough," John chuckled mirthlessly.

"Did he ever admit to throwing the glass?" Simonon asked John.

"Not to me he hasn't," John shrugged. "But I don't believe he did it anyway." "Me neither," Mick added.

"He did throw that glass,' Nils said flatly. "I was standing next to Sid at the time. Suzi and Steve were there as well."

"Well, if he did do it, at least there were mitigating circumstances," John mused.

"Such as?" Nils asked him.

"Well, the Damned were onstage."

"I don't think the girl that got a shard of glass in her eye found it all that funny though," Nils countered.

"That's only if it was true?" Mick sneered.

"I heard she was Vanian's girlfriend," Joe offered. "An' that she lost an eye."
"Absolute fuckin' nonsense!" John said.
"What, that she lost an eye?" Joe asked innocently.
"No," John replied, pausing for effect. "That Gravedigger Dave could possibly have a girlfriend."
"Was this how Sid got his 'Vicious' tag?" Fuller asked.
Goodman paused from rolling the spliff "No, no. He got that from beating up Nick Kent at the 100 Club.
"As in Nick Kent, the writer at the *NME*?
"The very same," Goodman nodded, while lighting the spliff. "I got a bird's eye view of it as well, as I was in the sound booth. And it wasn't only Sid that set upon him, because" he turned to look at John – "you're other pal Wobble joined in."
"Sid's about as 'vicious' as a fuckin' jelly baby; a half-chewed one at that," John chuckled. "But you wouldn't want to get on the wrong side of Wobble."
"I'll say somethin' for Sid; he ain't afraid to get stuck in," Mick offered, hungrily eyeing the spliff. "That night at the RCA, remember?" he said, turning to Joe. "Some hippie dickheads were chucking bottles at us on stage. The next thing you know, Sid comes running out of nowhere and does a kamikaze dive into the middle of 'em."
"Me and Joe downed tools and steamed in to help Sid out," Simonon nodded.
Goodman passed the spliff to Fuller. "And what were you doin' while all this was goin' down, Mick?"
"Mick stayed onstage," Joe cut in before Mick could respond.
"Someone had to stay in tune, didn't they?" Mick grinned.
Goodman was about to speak, but fell silent on hearing a muffled commotion coming from outside. A heartbeat later a loud pounding sounded on the door.
"Fuck me!" John exclaimed. "Sounds like a fuckin' SPG raid. Do the honours, Nils." "What did your last servant die of?" Nils asked, heading for the door.
"Devotion," John called after him. "What were we-?"
"Thanks for the fuckin' invite!" Steve sulked, pushing his way past Joe and settling on a corner of Nils' bed. Me an' Cookie have been sat in our room twiddlin' our fuckin' thumbs!"
"And you've drunk all the beer, you greedy cunts!" Paul chimed.
"Time for another trolley then," Nils smiled, reaching for the phone mounted on the wall between the beds
"You did time in Ashford, didn't you?" Goodman asked Steve. "The same gaff as Sid was in."

Chapter Seven

"The Sex Pistols disgusted and enraged viewers with their foul behaviour – Punk Rock? We say Punk Junk! – You'll be shocked by the report on Pop's new heroes. Only in the News Of The World this Sunday."World this Sunday."
News Of The World's TV trailer broadcast Saturday, 4 December 1976

"Yeah," Steve nodded. "It was nearly as bad as this fuckin' dump!"

"Ha-ha, hark at Alan fuckin' Whicker," John howled. "Why don't you write up a critique for the Michelin Guide?"

"Spin on this!" Steve spat, giving John the finger. "There are times when I wish Malcolm had got his fuckin' 'Johns' straight."

"What you on about?" Fuller asked.

"Viv had told Malcolm to keep an eye out for a guy called 'John' that she'd thought perfect for the Pistols," Goodman explained while chuckling to himself at John's pained expression on seeing Joe pass the spliff to Simonon. "This was back when the band was looking for a singer. Bernie Rhodes had also told Malcolm about a guy called 'John' that he'd thought fit the bill for frontman. The 'John' Viv was referring to was Sid. Sid's real name is John."

"Viv, in her infinite wisdom, decided that Sidney would be perfect for the Sex Pistols," John sneered. "But – and make sure I'm fuckin' next with that spliff, please Paul – fortunately for Steve, Paul, and Glen, she was too fuckin' late as Malcolm had already offered me the gig."

"It ain't too fuckin' late to bring Sid in, you know," Steve chuckled.

"I think we both know the answer to that, Steve," John winked at him.

McLaren, Rhodes, and Childers were seated at a table tucked way in the corner of the Crest's restaurant. "I distinctly told him to be here for ten-thirty!" Malcolm said irritably, glancing over at the clock mounted on the wall. "It's gone eleven!" he fell silent as the decidedly ragged-looking Nils appeared within the doorway. "Over here, boy!" he yelled, snapping his fingers loudly. Nils came trudging over and collapsed into a vacant chair. "Sorry, Malcolm, I fell back to sleep." he said, rubbing at his eyes. "Is there any coffee? I need a caffeine fix"

"You look as if you've slept in those clothes," Malcolm sighed, fixing Nils with a disapproving stare.

"Enjoyed a night on tiles have we, Sophie," Childers smiled. "It's our little joke," Childers explained, playfully patting Nils' hand. "When we met Nils at the airport the other night I thought he was he girl. Well, it had been a long flight . . ."

"Leee thought the Mohair I was wearing that night was a dress," Nils explained.

"Where's a fuckin' waitress when you need one?"

Malcolm appeared deep in thought. "Yes, I see why you would think the sweater was a dress, Leee. But I can't for the life of me see how you'd mistake Nils for a girl! Then again, there have been times when I've thought Sophie could pass for a boy . . ." "It was a simple misunderstanding," Childers smiled again. "I'd spoken with Sophie from JFK, so I assumed she'd be the one meeting us at Heathrow. Like I said, it was a long flight. And you were so sweet for not correcting me," he said turning to Nils. "You sat there the whole time we were in the restaurant."

Malcolm glared across at Nils. "What restaurant?"

"The Great American Disaster over on the Fulham Road," Nils told him. "So thoughtful," Childers nodded.

"And generous," Rhodes chipped in

"Yes, wasn't it," Malcolm said, eyeing Nils again.

"Don't worry," Nils said, stifling a yawn with the back of his hand. "I've got the receipt."

"And what's this Malcolm tells me about your having worked for the *Observer* newspaper?

"That's news to me," Rhodes smiled.

"I worked for Richard Buckle, the *Observer*'s ballet critic," Nils explained. "I'd had enough of art school, and was stuck for something to do. It was a right laugh. He had me dress up in this crazy purple Edwardian suit and high heels, and have me open the door for his friends. He liked to pretend I was his

'boy'. I helped Richard organise a ballet gala to raise the funds to buy Titian's Death of Actaeon. We got Rudolf Nureyev and Margot Fontaine involved."
"How interesting," Childers said. "Tell me more."
"There isn't all that much to tell, Leee."
"That's not strictly true, is it? Childers pressed. "What's this about your visit to Andy's studio while you were in New York?"
"Going over to New York was a spur of the moment thing really," Nils shrugged. "I can't remember how I ended up at the Factory now, but it was an eye-opener. I also saw the Dolls at Max's while I was out there." "Do you remember the date?"
"Sometime mid-April," Nils shrugged.
"I mustn't have been there that night," Childers smiled, resting his hand on Nils'. "I think I would have remembered you."

♪♪♪

Malcolm had called the meeting after spending the best part of an hour on the phone with Sophie that several other venues had cancelled. He'd only just come off the phone from Sophie when the local promoter called informing him that the local council had issued a press release sometime the previous evening. It seemed that while the council was content to allow The Damned, The Clash, and The Heartbreakers to appear at the Kings Hall, it would only allow the Sex Pistols to perform if the band was prepared to audition before the town's Leisure Committee at the venue at 3 p.m. that afternoon. Earlier that morning, a female reporter from the *News of the World* had approached him with an offer of £500 cash for an exclusive interview. He'd declined the offer thinking that the Derby show was going ahead. Upon learning of the council's eleventh-hour machinations he'd set off in search of the reporter, but she was nowhere to be seen.
"So, are you gonna tell us what Soph had to say, or do we play twenty questions?" Nils asked after draining the last of his coffee. "But from the look on your face I'm guessing it ain't good news."
Malcolm picked a bit of fluff from his turtleneck sweater before responding. "As you already know," he said, reading from the notes he'd made while speaking with Sophie, "tomorrow night's show in Newcastle and Tuesday night's show in Bournemouth are off, as is the one at Bristol Colston Hall. Sophie is looking into the possibility of switching that show to the local university. She has spoken with somebody at the university, but won't hear

anything back until Monday. However, she has been able to confirm that Monday night's show in Leeds is definitely proceeding as planned, as is the one at Manchester's Electric Circus on Thursday the ninth."

"Well, that's not too bad," Childers said.

Malcolm glanced up form his notes. "I haven't finished yet, Leee," he sighed. "Lancaster University is off, but I've got Sophie to look into switching this show to a venue in Preston. What's really annoying about this one is that the cancellation had nothing to do with the Grundy thing. Some of the female students at the university have apparently accused the Sex Pistols of being sexist. I mean, have you ever heard such nonsense?"

"Amazons," Rhodes chuckled. "I would say the Pistols are the least sexist band out there at the moment."

"*Sex* Pistols," Bernard," Malcolm said without looking up from his pad. He paused while making another alteration. "Sophie has already spoken with the local promoter for the Preston Charter, so we're just waiting to hear back. I'm also looking at booking a show in Croydon for the twelfth. I know this was originally scheduled as a rest day, but we've already got one or two more of those than anticipated," he smiled wanly. "The Sheffield City Hall date is touch and go, but from what Sophie tells me about what she's hearing from the promoter up there, I think that one will most likely still go ahead. Oh yes, that reminds me. We're looking at Sheffield University as an alternative for Bournemouth. I had hoped we'd found a suitable alternative for Southend in" – pausing to consult his itinerary – "at a place called 'Skindles' in Maidenhead. But as Sophie says the manager there is no longer taking her calls, I think we can put a line through that one as well. And it now looks as though we'll definitely have to look for an alternative venue for the show at the Cardiff Top Rank for Tuesday the fourteenth."

"Try 'Circles' in Swansea," Nils offered. "The Pistols played there in September a couple of nights after Cardiff. Got a good response that night as well, from what I remember.

"I'll bear it in mind," Malcolm nodded. We've already been offered The Castle in Caerphilly. Sophie has spoken with the owner, and she says she's happy to have us regardless of what the local council says."

"Wait while I tell my boys they'll be playing a medieval castle," Childers beamed.

"Caerphilly does indeed have a castle, Leee," Malcolm smiled. "But 'The Castle' is actually the local cinema

Nils plucked a folded tour flyer from his back pocket, opened it out, and placed it on the table in front of him. "What about next Saturday's show at Liverpool

Stadium?" he asked while pulling a crumpled cigarette packet from another pocket.

"That's another one hanging in the balance I'm sad to say," Malcolm replied, a weariness creeping into his tone. "We're looking at the possibility of booking an alternative at the Cavern Club-"

"Should have booked Eric's," Nils interjected, popping the last of his cigarette into his mouth. "Glen told me they got a great response-"

"You're not going to smoke in here, surely!" Malcolm snapped. "People are still eating."

"So?"

Malcolm leaned into the table. "We're lucky we're even being allowed to stay here for Christ's sake! So go outside!"

"It's fuckin' freezin' out there."

"Then go out into the foyer."

"Where were we?" Malcolm asked, watching Nils shuffle off towards the door. "Oh yes, Liverpool. I don't think we'll get much joy there as Sophie tells me a reporter called asking for a comment on a report in one of the local papers about Liverpool City Council trying to enforce a special one-day ban on punk rock groups."

"Can the councils over here do something like that?" Childers asked.

"It seems that they can do what they bloody well like where we're concerned!" Malcolm snapped, ignoring the disdainful looks his sudden outburst had brought from those sitting at a nearby table. "As things stand," he continued in a more measured tone, "there'll be a five-day break between the shows in Manchester and Caerphilly. So I think it would be prudent to return to London rather than continue running up expensive hotel bills."

"The boys are gonna love that," Rhodes sighed.

"Do you think I'm happy about it, Bernard?" Malcolm sighed. "In order to meet the running costs for the tour we need every show to be a sell-out. But if there's no show, then there's no money. And I can't see EMI agreeing to fund a nineteen day sightseeing tour.

So what choice do we have? I'm open to all suggestions."

"What about arranging some shows while we're back in London?" Childers asked hopefully.

"Well, there might be a possibility of booking the Notre Dame Hall again," Malcolm nodded. "I've also got Sophie to look into the possibility of booking the Rainbow Theatre, but I'm not going to hold my breath on that one."

"What about the Roxy?' Rhodes asked. "I know we're there on Boxing Day, but.

"I must really be losing the plot," Malcolm cut in. "I thought I'd told you about that fiasco. Terry Collins, the theatre's manager - who was more than happy to take my money last week – called Sophie yesterday to say he was cancelling the Boxing Day show because of the boys having graphitised his toilet walls."

"What about the Scottish dates?" Rhodes asked.

"From what I can gather, the Lord Provost of Scotland issued a statement yesterday saying how Scotland has enough hooligans of its own without importing them from across the border. He's even gone so far as to revoke the Glasgow Apollo's license for that particular night only. Can you believe that?"

"What's that you said about 'hooligans'?" Nils asked returning to the table.

"It doesn't matter, sit down," Malcolm said irritably. "What do you know about the toilets at the Roxy being vandalised?"

"'Vandalised' is a bit strong," Nils retorted. "There's a bit more graffiti than before, but that's-"

"You were supposed to be in charge!" Malcolm snapped.

"Alright, drop down a gear," Nils said testily. "What was I supposed to do, follow 'em in there every time someone went for a piss?"

"I'm just saying-"

"What about Dundee Caird Hall?" Rhodes cut in, hoping to diffuse the situation.

"What? Oh, yes, that one's still a possibility," Malcolm nodded.

"Oh, I do hope that one goes ahead," Childers said. "Johnny is really looking forward to playing in Scotland. He says he wants to play the bagpipes and eat haggis . . . whatever haggis is?"

"What's the plan for today?" Nils asked.

"Yes, today," Malcolm smiled. "I thought I'd save the latest bombshell till last.

"What are going to do?" Rhodes asked after Malcolm had finished explaining about Derby City Council's press statement.

"I have to admit to being at something of a loss with this one, Bernard. I mean, if we agree to perform for this Leisure Council then we run the risk of having to do matinee performances for every other council. And can you honestly see John and the others agreeing to perform in front of some 'leisure committee'? There's no way they're going to go along with it. Yet if we refuse to go along with the committee's request . . ."

"Well, there's no way my boys will play tonight," Childers said defiantly. "Not without the Sex Pistols."

"Nor will we," Bernard added solemnly.

Malcolm nodded his appreciation for the show of loyalty. "I'm just thinking out loud here, but what if we can show the local promoter that we were willing to perform in front of this committee', yet still be denied the chance to play this evening. If that were to happen, then the promoter would be contractually obligated to pay us half our agreed fee?" "I'm not following you," Childers frowned.

"What I'm saying is that we'll play these pompous arses at their own game. We'll agree to the council's demand. We'll get everything set up at the venue, and then once the committee members are there I want you" – he stabbed a finger towards Nils – "to call me here at the hotel."

"What then?" Nils asked.

"Then I'll phone the venue and inform whoever is in charge of the committee that the Sex Pistols will perform the private matinee show for them. But only," - he paused for effect - "if those same councillors are prepared to come along to the venue tonight to see the proper show."

"That just might work," Rhodes nodded approvingly.

"It's definitely worth a shot," Childers agreed.

Malcolm got to his feet to signal the meeting was at an end. "Go and see if everyone is up would you," he told Nils. "And make sure they know they're to stay in their rooms until I say different."

"What about breakfast?" Nils asked.

Malcolm fixed Nils with an icy stare. "I can't see how they'll be needing any breakfast after the feast they ordered through room service last night, can you? Oh, one more thing, he said grabbing up his satchel. "Tell your brother that if I see him taking any pictures today I'll break his camera."

Chapter Eight

"I have spoken to the manager of the group who tells me the Sex Pistols will not perform before the councillors unless we're prepared to come here this evening and see the whole of the show, which we are not prepared to do.

The Committee have decided that the concert of the Sex Pistols, they will not perform here tonight. But we are quite agreeable that the other three groups that have already been booked will go on."
Derby City Council's official statement: Saturday, 4 December 1976.

The Leisure Committee's private matinee was scheduled for 3 p.m. Malcolm had instructed Nils and Dave Goodman to head down to the Kings Hall and set up the PA system and the Sex Pistols' equipment to make it appear as though they were acquiescing to the council's ruling. He wasn't wholly convinced that his ruse would actually work, and so whilst preparations were underway at the venue he'd gone in search of Frank Brunger. Brunger was the manager of EMI's Harvest label, but was accompanying the tour from the comfort of his own car. The easiest and quickest solution to his immediate problems was to get EMI to settle the Derby Crest bill. Brunger lacked the authority to act, so Malcolm insisted that he call one of his superiors. Brunger had tried wheedling out saying it was a Saturday, but Malcolm wasn't taking no for an answer. Brunger had reluctantly called his immediate boss Mark Rye for advice on how best to proceed. Rye thankfully understood the situation and had called EMI's Group Repertoire Division General Manager, Paul Watts. Watts had initially proved reluctant to directly involve EMI in the day-to-day machinations of keeping a tour on the road, but had begrudgingly
agreed to contact the Crest and guarantee that EMI would cover the outstanding
bill.
With one set of problems sorted Malcolm had set off for the Kings Hall. He arrived at the venue in time to see Derby's mayor and mayoress, both bedecked in their
robes and chains of office, entering the venue flanked by the city's chief constable, and three other sombre-suited individuals that he assumed belonged to the Leisure Committee. Rather than introduce himself, he slipped in behind them and went i
n search of Nils and Dave Goodman while the committee members were ushered through into the auditorium. Malcolm found Nils having a cigarette by the stage door. "They're here," he said.
"Is everything set?"
"The boys could go on and actually play," Nils nodded. "The crew have even plugged in the amps and tuned the guitars."

agreed to contact the Crest and guarantee that EMI would cover the outstanding bill.

With one set of problems sorted Malcolm had set off for the Kings Hall. He arrived at the venue in time to see Derby's mayor and mayoress, both bedecked in their robes and chains of office, entering the venue flanked by the city's chief constable, and three other sombre-suited individuals that he assumed belonged to the Leisure Committee. Rather than introduce himself, he slipped in behind them and went in search of Nils and Dave Goodman while the committee members were ushered through into the auditorium.

Malcolm found Nils having a cigarette by the stage door. "They're here," he said.

"Is everything set?"

"The boys could go on and actually play," Nils nodded. "The crew have even plugged in the amps and tuned the guitars."

"It'll add to the fun," Malcolm smiled. "Where is Dave?"

"He's out the front with his mate Caruso. He says as no one'll know who they are, they can watch the fun without being hassled."

"I'm guessing the clock mounted above the stage is correct?"

"Dunno," Nils shrugged. "We came in the back way."

Malcolm started back towards the door. "Well, give it five minutes, then go out and switch the amps on."

"I haven't got a watch."

"Then count to three hundred!"

"Where will you be?"

"EMI have agreed to settle the bill so we're in the clear. But I want to see their pompous faces when they realise they've been had."

"But there might be press out there. If there are, you're sure to be recognised."

"They won't see me," Malcolm smiled.

The matinee performance was supposed to take place behind closed doors, but like Nils, Malcolm had anticipated someone on the council giving the local paper the heads up as to what was happening and grab the glory of capturing the foul-mouthed Sex Pistols being brought into line. When he stepped out into the wings, however he instantly recognised several faces from the swarm of reporters that had awaited their arrival at the hotel. He was going to enjoy this more than he could have imaged.

The committee were seated at a table directly facing the stage. Goodman and Fuller were stood some distance away; neither of them showing any interest in the stage. But why would they?

All eyes appeared focused on the clock mounted above the stage as the minute hand slowly clicked onto the appointed hour. He moved into position by the curtain as Nils came past and sauntered onto the stage and switched Glen and Steve's amps onto standby. He then went through the motions of testing the microphones as if in anticipation of the band imminent arrival on stage.

The moment the Pistols were meant to come on stage came and went, and as each minute slowly ticked by anxious murmurings began rippling through the hall. The press had scented that something was amiss and were now focusing their cameras on the bemused mayoral party.

Malcolm was retreating back towards the door when he heard the telltale scraping of chairs. He turned and watched the red-faced committee frantically fending off reporters as they headed for the door before slipping out to meet up with Nils backstage.

♪♪♪

While the Leisure Committee were being led a merry dance at the Kings Hall, back at the hotel Mick, Joe, and Paul had called an impromptu behind-closed-doors meeting of their own. Rob Harper, who'd recently taken over the drum stool from the departing Terry Chimes, had yet to give any indication as to whether he wanted the job full time so hadn't been invited.

"What the fuck's goin' on, Bernie?" Joe asked. "Glen told Mick that loads of dates have been cancelled."

"Well, Glen shouldn't go telling tales out of school," Bernard retorted.

"So, it's true?" Joe pressed.

"To some extent it's true," Rhodes nodded.

Mick was perched on the windowsill, a Yellow Pages resting across his knees to serve as a makeshift skinning-up pad. "Glen says tonight's show is off, an' all," he said, while busily crafting a spliff with a bit of cannabis he'd managed to cadge from Goodman before the engineer had departed for the Kings Hall.

"If tonight's show is off then its only because Malcolm has refused to agree to the local council's demand that the Pistols perform the private matinee show," Rhodes shrugged. "I for one don't blame him because it's censorship, pure and simple. And we cannot be seen to be giving in to censorship."

"And who's 'we', exactly?" Joe asked.

"Well, it was Malcolm's decision, obviously," Rhodes replied while casting an anxious eye towards Mick. It had been less than a week since the group's cameo appearance on London Weekend Television's Punk Special with Janet

Street-Porter, during which Mick had castigated the hippy generation for having "smoked too much dope". "But I feel we should back his decision one hundred per cent."

"No one's sayin' that we don't back the decision," Mick fired back. "There's no way we'd play if the Pistols couldn't. All we wanna know is where does it leave us?"

"How do you mean?" Rhodes asked, sensing Mick was in one of his more antagonistic moods.

Mick paused while running his tongue across the cigarette papers to seal the spliff before responding. "We came on this tour to try and build up some sort of reputation outside of London. But how are we gonna do that if we don't get to play anywhere?"

"But think of the exposure you're getting from all this," Rhodes countered, pointing to the newspapers on his bedside table.

"I can think of the exposure that the Pistols are getting," Joe sneered. "There ain't no mention of us in any of those is there?" he said, following Rhodes' gaze.

Rhodes shook his head dismissively "Forget the tabloids, Joe. It's the music papers that count. We're starting to get some major exposure. That feature that appeared in *Melody Maker* the other week was fantastic," he said in reference to Caroline Coon's 'The Clash: Down And Out And Proud' article. "I suggest you two take a leaf out of Paul's book and start dating a music journalist."

Mick popped the spliff into the corner of his mouth while reaching for his lighter. "Ah, but will Paul still be dating a journalist once Caroline finds out about his fuckin' off up to Birmingham with Patti Smith," he smiled over at Paul who was sprawled on one of the beds idly gazing up at the ceiling. "Our name will never darken the *Melody Maker*'s pages again."

"We had a gig coming up at Barbarella's, didn't we?" Paul grinned.

"And that show at Barbarella's was a classic example of what we can achieve," said Rhodes.

"How do you mean?" Mick asked, taking a last toke before passing the spliff to Joe.

"I would have thought that was obvious," Rhodes frowned. "Didn't you sense the energy and excitement coming from the crowd as a result of Joe's altering the lyrics from 'London's Burning', to '*Birmingham's*' Burning'?"

"I only did it to add a little local flavour," Joe shrugged. "It weren't no biggie."

"Oh but it was, Joe!" Rhodes countered, becoming more animated. "It was a huge 'biggie'. You need to do the same in Leeds, Glasgow, Manchester . . . and wherever else we play for that matter."

"Billericay's burning with boredom now," Mick chuckled.

"Is this all part of this two-step plan you keep bangin' on about?" Joe asked, in reference to Rhodes' strategy for The Clash. A strategy that wouldn't only serve to establish The Clash in their own right, but would also see them headlining the kind of events where they had previously played second fiddle to the Sex Pistols.

"Some plan," Mick scowled. "Where are these special gigs you keep promisin' us anyhow?"

Rhodes was momentarily taken aback by Mick and Joe's two-pronged attack. "Well, what about the shows at the University of London Union, and the ICA?" he challenged.

"What was so special about the ULU show?" Mick fired back. "There ain't nothin' fuckin' special about bein' third on the bill to Shakin' Stevens and the Sunsets from what I can see."

"At this stage it's all about getting yourselves known," Rhodes said. "And the fifth November show at the Royal College of Art was a tremendous success!"

"That's as maybe," Mick grudgingly conceded. "But it didn't bring Polydor Records knockin' on the door like you promised."

"Both Chris Parry, and his A&R director Jim Crook, were in the audience that night," Rhodes retorted. "And the reason that they didn't come knocking on my door after the show was because Joe threatened to smash Jim Crook's face in!"

"Only cos I thought it was him that threw the bottle which nearly took my fuckin' head off," Joe said sheepishly.

Paul sat up to accept the spliff from Joe. "We're never gonna get a record deal at this rate," he said ruefully. "Even the fuckin' Vibrators have got a deal!"

"And the Stranglers," Joe added.

"What was the name of that three-piece, Joe?" Paul asked. "The one we saw playin' outside Rock On in Newport Court on the day of the ULU gig?"

"Um, the Jam; wasn't it?" Joe shrugged. "Why do you ask?"

"Caroline says they've been offered a deal by Chiswick."

"What about those demos we did for Polydor?" Mick asked Rhodes, referring to the band's recent visit to Polydor's recording studio where they recorded five songs with Guy Stevens.

The Clash had recorded "Career Opportunities", "White Riot", "London's Burning", "Janie Jones", and "1977". The session had brought mixed emotions for Mick. Stevens had worked with his schoolboy heroes, Mott The Hoople, but the maverick producer had also been instrumental in getting him sacked from a band called Violent Luck a couple of years back. Although Mick hadn't lost any of his admiration for Stevens' mercurial talents, the humiliation had left psychological and emotional scars that had yet to properly heal.

Rhodes was becoming exasperated by their pessimistic attitude. "Look, everything is going according to plan. No one anticipated all this was going to happen, but we just have to make sure we make the most of whatever opportunities come along while we're on this tour. Our show of solidarity with the Pistols will reap its own rewards."

"The Pistols don't give a fuck about us!" Paul said, blowing a smoke ring at Rhodes.

"Why should they?" Mick added.

"Malcolm will remember our show of loyalty," Rhodes pressed.

"I doubt that Malcolm knows the meaning of the fuckin' word, Bernie," Joe sneered.

"Because if he did, then we wouldn't be sitting here having this conversation, would we?"

"What do you mean?"

"If Malcolm was as loyal as you say he is, then you'd be co-managing the Pistols instead of dickin' around with us."

"Then it's lucky for you that I'm not co-managing the Sex Pistols, isn't it? Or you'd still be fronting the 101ers."

"At least I got to play with the 101ers," Joe sulked. "All I've done on this tour so far is sit around on my fuckin' arse! This is the Pistols' time because they're front-page news now, and no one's gonna give a flyin' fuck about what we think."

Rhodes started pacing the room. "You need to start thinking about the bigger picture, Joe. "Thanks to Bill Grundy, the Sex Pistols are now the most famous group in the country. But the tabloid press have got their teeth into them now, and they won't be letting go in any time soon. Mark my words, 1977 is going to be the year of punk. And I'm willing to bet you right now that come Easter there will be hundreds of kids up and down the country in need of a group to rally behind."

"And you think that's going to be us?" Joe asked.

"Why shouldn't it be you?" Rhodes gasped. "The Sex Pistols' flame might be burning bright right now, but it ain't gonna last."

"And how do you know that?" Mick asked.

"Do you honestly think I wasn't expecting Malcolm to fuck me over with the Pistols? I knew he wouldn't be able to help himself, so I got my revenge in early by planting a bomb under his chair – an obnoxious bomb from Finsbury Park. Don't forget, it's only down to me that Malcolm agreed to give Lydon a chance-" "No, it weren't," Mick interjected.
"Oh, but it was, Mick," Rhodes smiled. "Steve certainly didn't want John in the band, and Paul and Glen weren't too sure either – regardless of what they might say now. When we met up with John that night at the Roebuck, the night he did his audition at the shop, I knew Malcolm had finally met his match." He paused while removing his glasses and giving the lenses a cursory wipe. "Trust me," he continued after slipping his glasses on again, "John will fuck Malcolm over. It won't be today, or next week. It might not even be next year, but it will happen. And when it does the kids are going to want another standard bearer. So it's either you or the Damned . . ."
"Fuck them and the hearse they rode in on," Paul chuckled, slumping back down against the pillows as the weed began to take effect."

♪♪♪

The Damned hadn't ridden into Derby in a hearse, but as Malcolm hadn't thought to keep them in the loop as to what was occurring at the Kings Hall they were nevertheless left feeling like spare pallbearers at a funeral. While Rick Rogers was off in search of a phone so that he could find out what was going on, the band were holed up in a roadside café just off the M1 pondering their situation.
"I knew we shouldn't have come on this poxy tour," Rat grumbled, blowing into his mug of tea. "Malcolm and Bernie were treating us like dog shit before the Pistols went on telly, so it's only gonna get worse Come to think of it, Bernie's treated me like shit since the day I met him."
"Do you remember that day at Praed Street when you turned up for your audition," guitarist Brian James grinned.
Brian, like Rat, had encountered Malcolm and Bernard whilst temporarily playing with London SS. At the time of his responding to Mick Jones and Tony James' *Melody Maker* classifieds ad back in July '75, he'd been trying his luck on the continent with his own Stooges-esque outfit, Bastard. Having recognised a couple of kindred spirits in Mick and Tony, he'd returned to Belgium to break the news that he was quitting Bastard, as well as sort out his affairs. He'd been with London SS six months or so by the time Rat came

through the group's Praed Street rehearsal door in response to yet another *Melody Maker* ad.

Despite lacking the prerequisite Johnny Thunders image that Mick, Tony, and Brian were seeking, coupled with his admitting to having contracted the highly-contagious skin disease, Scabies, they were suitably impressed with Rat's aggressive drumming style to offer him the gig. However, within a week, Mick, Tony, and Bernard had decided Rat's face wasn't going to fit after all, and told him he was out. Brian couldn't believe they could be so obtuse, as Rat was by far and away the best drummer they'd auditioned. He didn't give a fuck what people looked like as long as they could play. He'd been steadily tiring of Bernard's oppressive mandate by then anyway, and on hearing they wanted rid of Rat he'd packed away his guitar and headed out of the door. "They've never forgiven us for playing the European punk festival," Brian shrugged.

"As if we were gonna turn down an opportunity to play abroad just because of the Pistols," Rat sneered as Sensible collapsed into the seat next to him.

He and Sensible, whose real name was Ray Burns, had met whilst working together as cleaners at Croydon Fairfield Halls. He was something of a multi-instrumentalist as he could play bass, guitar, as well as keyboards. He'd been playing with the Johnny Moped band when Rat had poached him to play bass in The Subterraneans; the ad hoc group he and Brian were putting together in order to perform a one-off show at a Women's Lib festival in Cardiff.

The Cardiff gig had come about owing to Malcolm having approached Rat shortly after his expulsion from London SS. Malcolm had suggested Rat join forces with Nick Kent, the celebrated *NME* journalist who'd jammed with the fledgling Sex Pistols prior to Rotten's arrival, and his on/off American girlfriend, Chrissie Hynde, whom Malcolm knew from her briefly having worked in SEX. When Kent and Chrissie had given back word owing to their disintegrating relationship, Rat called on Brian and Ray.

With the Subterraneans only intended as a one-off appearance, Rat had brought Brian and Ray along when he was reunited with Chrissie Hynde for another of Malcolm and Bernard's makeshift projects, Masters of the Backside, a.k.a. Mike Hunt's Honourable Discharge.

Perhaps not surprisingly, the project didn't get much beyond the planning stage, and when Chrissie elected to forge an alternate career path, the trio had held auditions for a singer. The two main candidates were John's mate Sid, and Dave Vanian, the singing gravedigger whom Brian and Rat had first encountered at the Nashville Rooms a couple of months earlier. When Sid failed to show up, Dave got the gig by default.

"If you ask me, I don't think Malcolm's forgiven us for what happened at the 100 Club Festival, either," Sensible said, suddenly raising a bum cheek and farting. "And our record's better than theirs . . . Cor, there's nothing quite like the smell of semi-digested sausage, bacon and eggs in the morning," he chuckled as Vanian sat down next to Brian.

"Yeah, I still feel guilty about Sid hitting the pillar instead of me with the beer glass," he deadpanned. He, like the rest of the group, had long-since grown accustomed to being stared at in the street, and was therefore unmindful of the slack-jawed stares from the café's other customers.

"That's because if it had of hit you the Pistols wouldn't have lost their cosy Tuesday night residency," Sensible grinned. "An' we'd still be able to play there."

"I was choked for them," said Vanian. "Do we know what's happening yet?"

"Rick's gone to find out," Brian answered before returning his attention to the smattering of snowflakes that were coming to rest on the outside window.

"While you were in the khazi, I was saying how it was a mistake for us to come on the tour," Rat said for Vanian's benefit. "It's not as if we even needed to, either; cos we've got loads of our own gigs coming up. And a new album to finish . . ."

"Well, we're here now so we might as well make the most of it," Vanian shrugged.

"Oh yeah, hangin about transport cafés being bored shitless is the reason why I started playin' drums in the first place."

"And there was me thinking it was because you didn't want to clean shithouses for the rest of your life," Sensible grinned.

Chapter Nine

The [Sex] Pistols were due to perform at 3.30pm and the place was awash with national newspaper reporters and cameramen as well as a large contingent of police outside in case of any rumoured demonstrations by the National Front or irate parents (neither demonstration happened).

But by 4.30pm the group had not arrived and councillor [Len] Shepley announced that the group had refused to appear at the preview unless the committee would also attend the show that evening. But the committee refused to agree and the show was cancelled. At one point it was suggested that the other groups on the tour – The Damned, The Clash, and The Heart Breakers – might appear without the Pistols but no sooner had the committee agreed than the managers of the other bands said that their groups would not appear without the Sex Pistols. **Sounds, Saturday, 11 December 1976**

Despite Fleet Street having plagued their every turn during the last five days upon arriving at Leeds Polytechnic on the Monday afternoon for the soundcheck the tour party was still taken aback on finding the entrance teeming with the familiar throng of trench-coated reporters - all of whom were seemingly determined to continue, or even exacerbate the ongoing witch-hunt against the Sex Pistols. It had been the same when they'd checked in at the Dragonara Hotel the previous evening when they were once again forced to remain on the coach whilst McLaren and Nils Stevenson took care of the bookings. Indeed, the number of reporters gathered outside the hotel had outnumbered the audience at the Fordham Hotel on their only previous visit to the city back in September.

The reporters had set up camp en masse in the Dragonara's bar and had refused to budge until being given something of note for their respective editors. Thinking that his charges were safely holed away in their rooms, McLaren had held a spur-of-the-moment press conference in the hotel's foyer. After fielding by now run-of-the-mill questions about the tour cancellations, as well as being asked for his thoughts as to whether the Sex Pistols would feature on the agenda at EMI's impending Annual General Meeting set for tomorrow afternoon, he'd gleefully informed the gathering that the Pistols would be unveiling a new song called "No Future". Needless to say, hearing the Sex Pistols had penned a song with an opening couplet likening the British Establishment to Hitler's Nazis was enough to have the reporters fighting for the hotel's phone. Malcolm's quote about how the song would be the high spot of the Polytechnic show had appeared in that day's *Daily Mirror*.

McLaren's quote had only made the final paragraph as the bulk of the *Mirror*'s latest condemnation focused on the "bad" and "ugly" Sex Pistols having supposedly wrecked the Dragonara's lobby by uprooting ornamental plants, hurling pots around, and scattering soil over the carpets. Of course, what the article neglected to mention was that it was the same *Mirror* reporter who'd cajoled Steve and Paul into throwing a few ornamental plants around the foyer, or that the enterprising hack had first slipped the Dragonara's manager £25 to cover the cost of replacing the ornamental plants and having the carpet cleaned. Despite Nils' best efforts, Steve and Paul had managed to sneak downstairs and were heading for the hotel bar when the *Mirror*'s eagle-eyed reporter – having no doubt recognised Steve as being the one who'd called Bill Grundy's bluff on TV – got to work.

On hearing about the plant-throwing escapade McLaren had tore into Steve and Paul, if only because of what further damaging headlines might do to their already strained relationship with EMI. Thankfully, Frank Brunger had called his bosses to assure them that the plant-throwing antics had been wilfully set up by the unscrupulous *Mirror* reporter.

♪♪♪

The show was being staged in the Polytechnic's sports hall. The Pistols were onstage running through "No Lip" when John suddenly bolted from the stage. Glen was surprised John had lasted as long as he had. Steve and Paul were also looking decidedly worse for wear despite their attempts at a "hair-of-the-dog-that-bit-you" cure all. He was momentarily tempted to go outside and drag one of the reporters into the toilets to prove the Sex Pistols didn't throw up on stage as some of them were claiming.

Before leaving Derby, Frank Brunger's fellow EMI staffer, Mike Thorne, who was tagging along in an unofficial capacity, had called Manchester Square to give an unbiased report on the Leisure Committee situation. He'd also suggested that it might be good for morale if EMI picked up the tab for a communal meal in the Dragonara's restaurant as this was standard practice when one of their artists was out on tour. Despite Thorne and Malcolm's repeated pleadings the meal had proved a boisterous affair, which was hardly surprising seeing as everyone was ordering rounds of triple vodkas on the rocks.

Following on from the meal, the party had relocated to the city centre; the idea being they'd find some accommodating Yorkshire lasses to bring back to the hotel. However, with it being a Sunday night - and a cold, miserable one at that - the only accommodating females to be found were the ones demanding recompense for their favours. Indeed, the only one to get lucky on the night was their security guy, "Fat Freddie", whose eighteen stone frame made him a formidable proposition for anyone thinking of taking a swing at one of his charges.

Drawing on his years of experience out on the road with various bands, Freddie knew when best to stick or twist. Having feigned total disinterest in accompanying the others into the centre, he'd set to work on the hotel's receptionist. Having cajoled her into accompanying him up to his room he'd called down for room service and with the aid of some decent claret had proceeded to charm her into joining him in the bath. This, however, was where Freddie's amorous intentions hit the skids as owing to Freddie's bulk the two lovebirds somehow managed to get themselves wedged in the tub and had to call for assistance.

Rather than break communal bread at the Dragonara, or accompany the others on a boozy pub crawl, Glen and Mick had opted to venture out into the night to see what gastronomic delights Leeds city centre had to offer two discerning Londoners. Aside from it being a Sunday evening, their gourmet options were further restricted, however, owing to Mick having given up meat. After what appeared to be a fruitless trawl, they eventually happened upon an Italian restaurant. However, owing to the lateness of the hour the only none meat option available on the menu was grilled trout. And when the food arrived, Mick was horrified to find the trout was still in possession of its head; its glazed eye staring accusingly up at him from the plate. The waiter had been so surprised at Mick's insistence that he take the dish away and remove the head that he'd momentarily dropped his fauxItalian accent. Although he'd readily acquiesced to Mick's demands, he'd return a minute or so later with a shrivelled lettuce leaf separating the freshly-severed head from its body. Needless to say, Mick and Glen beat a hasty retreat to the Dragonara in the hope they might be able to order room service.

With Steve and Paul having downed tools the moment John fled the scene in search of a toilet, Glen found himself cutting a forlorn figure up on the stage. He was thinking about taking a breather himself when Malcolm came bursting through the door at the opposite end of the hall. He could see Malcolm was clutching a folded newspaper. From the look on his face as he strode towards the stage, Glen instinctively knew it was a copy of that day's *Daily Mirror*.

"Where are the others?" Malcolm demanded, gazing about the hall.

Glen placed his bass on its stand. "John's probably still talking to God on the porcelain telephone. I've no idea where Steve and Paul are."

Malcolm remained silent whilst casting an eye over the motley assembly of musicians and their entourages who'd taken up position against the far wall; all waiting patiently for their respective soundcheck. "Have you seen this?" he said at last, thrusting the paper under Glen's nose.

Glen's initial assessment had proved incorrect, as the newspaper was actually a copy of The *Sun*. As Malcolm had already folded the paper to the relevant page, Glen was expecting to find another lurid account of Steve and Paul's flower rearranging at the Dragonara. Instead he found it was an article relating to a female Liverpool councillor called Doreen Jones, who'd apparently succeeded in her quest to cajole her council colleagues into placing a special banning order on all punk rock groups that coming weekend. "We already knew Liverpool was off," he shrugged.

"I'm not talking about that!" Malcolm snapped, taking a step closer to Glen and stabbing a finger at the article's final paragraph. Glen ran his eyes over the paragraph in question which had Rick Rogers saying how The Damned were happy to play the Kings Hall. "Can you believe such treachery?" Malcolm seethed, glancing over his shoulder to where Brian James and the rest of The Damned were sat huddled together looking suitably bored.

Glen already knew from speaking with Rat that Rogers' comments had come before he'd learned about Malcolm's turning the tables on the Leisure Committee. "But they didn't know what was going on, did they?" he said, following Malcolm's gaze. "You kept us in the dark until the last minute."

"What was that contraption that Alexander Graham Bell invented a hundred years ago? Oh yes, the *fucking telephone*!"

"Well it doesn't matter now, does it?"

Malcolm stared at Glen as though he were an imbecile. "Doesn't matter? Of course, it fucking matters! "By saying they were happy to play, they've undermined my authority." "Why don't you invite them onto the coach?" Glen suggested. "It's not like we haven't got the room, is it? We could drop them off at wherever they're staying after the shows."

"Invite them onto the coach? I'm seriously considering throwing them off the tour."

"Throwing who off the tour?" Glen and Malcolm both spun round to find John standing with his arms resting on the lip of the stage eyeing them suspiciously.

"Keep your voice down, John," Malcolm hissed.

"He's struggling to keep anything down at the minute, aren't you mate?" Glen smiled.

"Who are you callin' 'mate'?" John snarled. "So, who are you throwing off the tour?" he asked turning towards Malcolm. "If you want my opinion, we could dispense with the fuckin' lot of 'em."

"Why don't we just let things be," said Glen. "We're finally getting the chance to play, aren't we?"

"Trust you to drop a fuckin' Beatles song into the conversation," John sneered.

"Here we go again,' Glen groaned. "How many times do I have to tell you, John; I don't like the Beatles per se, I just appreciate elements of what they do. And anyway, it's 'Let It Be'."

"I know what it's fuckin' called!" John snapped as he set off towards the fire exit. "And watch who you're callin' 'Percy'."

"'Percy'?" I said '*per se*'. It means–"

"I know what it fuckin' means!" John shouted over his shoulder. "See you next Tuesday!"

"Why's he keep sayin' that?" Glen frowned. "He's said that to me a lot of late."
"Come on, Glen," Malcolm grinned. "It's an acronym. Well, sort of. You went to grammar school, I'm sure you'll work it out."
Glen stood gazing about the hall. *An acronym, eh? See you next Tuesday? See you . . . C . . . U . . . N . . .* "Oh, very droll," he shouted over to the fire exit.

♪♪♪

Malcolm was relaxing in the bath when there was a knocking at the door. He ignored it; thinking whoever it was would go away. When the knocking continued he lifted himself out of the bath, grabbed a towel from the rail, and started towards the door, leaving a trail of soggy footprints in his wake. He stopped suddenly upon realising it could well be a reporter. "Who is it?" he asked tentatively.
"It's me, Ray," Ray Stevenson said from the other side of the door.
Malcolm opened the door to the photographer. "What've they done now?" he asked resignedly.
Stevenson stepped past Malcolm into the room. "There's a film crew from Yorkshire Television downstairs. They'd like to interview the Pistols, or someone connected to the group."
"Would they now," Malcolm sighed. "And many times must I remind people that it's '*Sex* Pistols'."
What do you want me to tell them?"
"Tell them no."
"Are you sure?" Stevenson asked. "It'll give us some free publicity for tonight's show."
"Free publicity," Malcolm chuckled to himself. "I'd say that's the least of our concerns right now, wouldn't you?" He walked across to the dressing table. "On second thoughts, it would allow a chance to set the record straight."
"Do you want me to round up the boys?"
"By all means," Malcolm nodded to Stevenson in the mirror's reflection. "But tell them they aren't to speak with the television crew or anyone from the press. We can't risk a repeat of what happened at the hotel yesterday so close to EMI's AGM - regardless of who was to blame. Now, if you'll excuse me," he added walking towards the wardrobe, "I need to get dressed."

The four Sex Pistols shuffled into the hotel's dining room where the interview was to be conducted. They took up positions by the windows in direct line of the camera yet far enough away to prevent a stray comment being picked up by the boom. As they'd be setting off for the Polytechnic immediately after the interview they were all dressed in their stage gear. As per Malcolm's instructions, they are all wearing clothing from SEX. John is sporting a vermillion-red waistcoat over a white shirt, and a pair of bondage trousers; Glen a red parachute shirt; Paul a mohair sweater. Steve is bedecked in black biker jacket and leather trousers, but a Hangman's Noose string jumper shows beneath his jacket.

After taking his seat opposite Yorkshire Television's anchorman, Ken Rees, Malcolm casually removed his mohair sweater to reveal an Anarchy shirt beneath.

"Good evening, Mr. McLaren," Rees said extending his hand. "Thank you for agreeing to speak with us. We should be good to go in a couple of minutes."

Malcolm placed the sweater loosely about his neck. "It's my pleasure," he smiled, giving Rees' hand a quick shake.

Rees leaned closer to Malcolm. "I have to say that's a rather interesting shirt you're wearing."

"Do you remember the Wemblex brand from the sixties?" Malcolm asked Rees.

The pinstripe shirts were part of a bankrupt stock he and Westwood had bought on a whim a few years earlier. Turning the shirts inside out, they'd hand-painted stripes of varying hues over the body and sleeves while attaching hand-made patches bearing situationist slogans such as "Prenez Vos Desirs Por la Realite", and "A Bas le Coca Cola". Using a child's stencil kit they then adorned the shirts with slogans such as "Only Anarchists Are Pretty" or "Dangerously Close To Love". The finishing touches included Mao-style red armbands declaiming "Chaos", Nazi eagle patches sewn upside-down on the collars, and silk patches of Karl Marx that Malcolm had happened upon in a shop in London's Chinatown that specialised in Maoist literature.

"We've been selling them in the shop for about six months now. I've got a spare one if you're interested?"

"Not really my style," Rees smiled. "How much do they go for?"

"Twenty-five pounds."

Rees was flabbergasted. "I could get five shirts from Marks and Spencer's for that,"

"Quite," Malcolm smirked

"We interviewed Dr. Nashenter earlier this afternoon."

"Dr. Who?"

"No, Dr. Nashenter," Rees chuckled at his own joke. "He's the Dean at Leeds Polytechnic."

"Oh, I see," Malcolm nodded. "What did he have to say?"

Rees glanced down at his notes. "He said that while he thought the Sex Pistols 'puerile' and 'disgusting'" – he paused again to glance over at the band – "in accordance with the constitution and articles of the government of the Polytechnic he was powerless to prevent the concert from going ahead as the decision rested with the student union."

"Pity the Dean at East Anglia University didn't think to abide by the constitution and articles of the government at his own school," Malcolm responded.

"Dr. Nashenter also told us that the Polytechnic is staging a production of Handel's Messiah this evening within the faculty's main hall," Rees continued. "He found it highly amusing that such widely-contrasting streams of prayer would be simultaneously emanating from the two halls." When Malcolm didn't offer a response he forged on. "I was wondering if there's any chance that we can bring Johnny over during the interview to ask his opinions on the recent assassination attempt on Bob Marley. I mean, with all the hullabaloo surrounding the Sex Pistols at the moment it must have crossed Johnny's mind that someone might try to get at him. And Marley's manager was also–" he fell silent on seeing the line producer signalling to him. "We're ready to begin.'

Malcolm shifted in his seat and glanced over his shoulder as if to satisfy himself the band were behaving before turning back to face Rees.

Rees consulted his notes again. 'I'd like to start by asking if it's true what happened in Derby."

"What do you mean?" Malcolm asked, absently toying with his address book, which lay on the table in front of him.

"That your group refused to perform in front of the town's Leisure Council," Rees asked.

"Why should we have to perform to some old fuddy-duddies who have no concept of what the Sex Pistols are about?" Malcolm said matter-of-factly. "It's the kids we want to play to."

"But the council wanted to vet your group's act because they were worried," Rees pressed.

"Worried about what?"

"About the group's performances on stage."

"What about them?"

"It's said that you're sick on stage. You spit at the audience and so on." Rees paused momentarily for effect. "I mean, how can this be a good example to children?"

"People are sick everywhere," Malcolm replied blithely. "People are sick and fed up of this country telling them what to do," he added, skilfully deflecting the question away from the Sex Pistols and onto his own view that the British public should wake up and refuse to tolerate government censorship.

"But not getting paid for it," Rees countered.

"Pardon?"

"But not getting paid for putting on that sort of show."

"Well nor are we. We ain't even being allowed to play."

"In fact,' Rees continued, "you're acting as spokesman for the group today."

"Yes, indeed."

"Have you stopped them from talking to us?" Rees asked, glancing over at the group as John suddenly leaned forward and placed his hand up against his face to mask what he was saying to the others.

"Not at all," Malcolm shrugged. "They're just so disgusted by our having to answer so many questions about something so simple."

"Do you feel the publicity following the Thames Television interview has been damaging . . . or do think it has helped you?" Rees asked.

"I don't think it's been damaging. Far from it. Whether it's helping us is another matter. The point is people are getting very disappointed by the fact that kids who have bought and purchased tickets of these venues that are now being cancelled are having to travel further a field to see the band of their choice."

"What sort of future do you see a band like the Sex Pistols having . . . a long future?"

"I do indeed," Malcolm nodded. "I think, I think at least they're standing up and . . . ah, not tolerating any form of censorship in their act. And in that sense it's exhilarating a lot of young kids around the country, and giving them confidence to stand up and say what they want."

"Would you not agree in any way that the packed halls which you're playing to - wherever you get a concert launched - are entirely due to the bad publicity that you've had?"

"Not at all. Many dates were sold out long before."

"How do you react to the reputation that you're group is the most revolting in the country?"

"Look," Malcolm sighed, becoming increasingly irritated by Rees' mundane line of questioning. "Our group is creating a generation gap for the first time in five years in this country and a lot of people are feeling genuinely threatened by it. If the kids wanna buy the record it's called 'Anarchy in the UK', it's out in the shops and they can make their own decisions. And their mothers," - he added before Rees could interrupt him - "they can ask them to equally make their decision about it. And if the mothers care anything about their young kids they should be up in arms about having councillors, of which they are paying taxes to, to tell, to, to, to be angry with them about not allowing their kids to go in to the concerts and making their own choice."

"But let's be absolutely frank about it,' Rees said, while acknowledging his line producer's signal that he needed to wrap things up. "Do they enjoy being known as a revolting group?"

"Every young kid is, is ah . . . is ah . . ." Malcolm paused while he sought to find the right words, "finds enjoyment in being known as revolting."

"Thanks for that, Malcolm," Rees said. "I'm more of a classical man myself, but I wish you and the Sex Pistols every success. He looked past Malcolm on seeing the band sidling towards them. Benjamin Britten had died from congestive heart failure two days earlier, and thought he might have a little fun by testing their perceived ignorance. "Could I ask you boys for your reaction to the death of the nation's first musical peer?" he asked, getting to his feet.

"Which pier's that then?" Steve shrugged. "Brighton?"

"Yeah, that's right, you oaf," John cackled. "Benjamin Brighton."

Chapter Ten

THE BAD AND THE UGLY
The Sex Pistols were busy making a nuisance of themselves again yesterday.
The four-man Punk Rock group wrecked the lobby of a luxury hotel, uprooting ornamental plants, hurling pots around the room and scattering soil over the carpets.
The vandalism at the four-star Dragonara in Leeds was the prelude to a Punks' concert in the city tonight. Ten shows scheduled for other towns have been cancelled by worried managements since the foul-mouthed group angered millions of TV viewers last week.
A Mirror man who watched the group go wild at the Leeds hotel said: As they walked away they shouted, "Don't blame us. That's what you wanted. Send the bill to EMI" – their record company.
Tonight's show will be staged at Leeds Polytechnic. The group's manager, Malcolm McLaren, said that the high spot would be a song that opens with the words, 'God Bless the Queen and her fascist regime."
Daily Mirror, Monday, 6 December 1976.

Despite the brouhaha surrounding the new 'punk cult' in the wake of the Sex Pistols' appearance on *Today*, the Polytechnic's sport's hall was only half-full when The Clash finally got the Anarchy Tour underway. Strummer, Jones, and Simonon took to the stage sporting customised paint-splattered shirts bearing stencilled political slogans, replete with matching armbands. Strummer's green shirt bears the stencilled slogan: Social Security £9.70. He sees this as a means of communicating with the audience. To show them that while £9.70 per week may not seem much to live on, it was enough to get a band started. Enough to spark a musical revolution . . .

Given the media's fixation with the Pistols over the past five days, Strummer attempted to incite a reaction from the crowd with an Orwellian gambit in declaring he'd spent the previous forty-eight hours thinking "Big Brother was really upon them" before hitting the opening chord of the A/D/A/D/A/D/D/A intro to "White Riot". The response when the song comes to an end, however, is lukewarm at best. As though it was only the Pistols being catapulted onto the front pages that had forced them away from a night in front of the telly. The Clash were nonetheless determined to enjoy themselves; their pentup frustrations at having spent the last few days living a goldfish-bowl existence giving vent to a blistering performance.
Without pausing for breath they plough into "I'm So Bored With The USA", the first song that Jones and Strummer had collaborated on. Mick's original title for the song was "I'm So Bored With You", with a lyric centring around a waning romance.

Sentimentality didn't feature in the Strummer lexicon, however, and there was no arguing it had been his insistence at adding the "S" and the "A" that had given the song a whole new dynamic. Their thirty-minute set is bristling with other high-octane numbers such as recently penned "Hate & War", "Cheat", and "48 Hours". They bring the performance to a frenetic close with the apocryphal, "1977". The sound is woefully muddy owing to Dave Goodman having spent the afternoon holed up in the student union bar with Roadent and Keeth Paul. Despite the Clash having brought Mickey Foote along to work their sound, Goodman was refusing all entreaties to return to the bar.

By the time The Heartbreakers came out on stage the audience had swelled considerably in both number and volume, as those preferring to remain ensconced within the adjoining Student Union bar rather than sample what The Clash had to offer weren't going to pass up the chance to see punk rock New York style. And the Heartbreakers were not about to disappoint. Thunders is the epitome of guttersnipe cool, and his only half-joked query as to whether there were "any junkies in the house" serves as the perfect prefix for their opening number, "Born to Lose". His and Nolan's reputations may have preceded them, but those in the crowd hoping to hear The Heartbreakers play any Dolls numbers were the ones going to be left heartbroken. They are hampered by Keeth Paul's haphazard fumblings at the mixing consol, but Thunders is sufficiently long of tooth to know how to compensate and he and his fellow 'Breakers effortlessly build up the momentum with angst-ridden three-minute melodramas such as "Get Off The Phone", "It's Not Enough", "Baby Talk", "Take A Chance With Me", that – while imbued with nihilist twist - weren't all that far removed from the vignettes by The Shangri-Las, The Angels, The Shirelles, and other all-girl groups that Thunders had grown up listening to. Their set also includes a mean cover of The Contours' 1962 hit, "Do You Love Me", and they bring their UK debut to a climactic finale with the heavily drug-referenced, "Chinese Rocks". Thunders' leather motorcycle jacket, drainpipe jeans, and winkle-picker boots ensemble would be considered a little clichéd on New York's Lower East Side, but there was no arguing that it brought a little piece of rock'n'roll celebrity to warm the cockles on a cold December Monday evening in West Riding.

Next up are The Damned who are greeted with a raucous cheer intermingled with a few mock wolf whistles owing to Captain Sensible's sporting a nurse's uniform. The beshaded bassist has garnered something of a reputation for camping it up on stage, and had also brought along a ballerina's tutu. Brian and Rat are in jeans and T-shirts, but Vanian has developed his own onstage alter-ego. He is dressed head-to-toe in Bela Lugosi black, with his face smeared in theatrical greasepaint, and his brilliantined hair swept back off his forehead. When reviewing a Damned show from the previous month, the *NME* described him as being a "runaway from The Addams Family."

Since making their debut supporting the Pistols at the 100 Club back in July they have gigged extensively up and down the country - playing seventeen shows in November alone. Unsurprisingly, they open with "New Rose", which much to McLaren's chagrin, has inadvertently earned them a lasting place in musical folklore for being the first official punk rock single released in the UK.

During the opening number, Sensible engages with those kids huddled together at the front of the stage who are clearly here for the music rather than the potential mayhem. At the song's end he gulps down the remainder of his lager and sprays them with lager causing several fans to retaliate in kind. Although it was meant as a harmless bit of fun to liven up the proceedings, the Captain was inadvertently playing into the hands of the journalists standing at the rear of the hall.

The Damned are already working on their debut album at Pathway Studios in Islington, with their Stiff Records label mate Nick Lowe serving as producer. While they too suffer from Goodman's afternoon binging, songs such as "Feel The Pain", "See Her Tonite", as well as the rumoured follow-up single, "Neat, Neat, Neat", are evidence enough that The Damned are on a self-propelled upward trajectory. They bring their set to a frenetic close with a searing version of the Stooges' 1970 hit "I Feel Alright", which elicits a favourable response from the majority of the audience.

Little could they have known as they departed the beer-sodden stage, however, that Malcolm had decided to throw them off the tour for their perceived treachery? Whilst they'd been out front entertaining the crowd, Rick Rogers was backstage frantically pleading the group's case that their supposed duplicity had come during the time-frame when it had seemed that Malcolm was acquiescing to the Leisure Committee's demands. And that seeing as it was Malcolm's insistence that Stiff foot the bill for The Damned during the tour that had resulted in Jake Riviera have them travel separately, he could hardly then blame them for failing to second guess his intentions. His pleas, however, had fallen on deaf ears.

♪♪♪

The Damned's camp theatrics have helped liven up proceedings somewhat, but the Sex Pistols nevertheless emerge to stilted applause. While Steve and Glen check their instruments are still in tune John surveys the audience casually running his fingers through his ginger spiked coif whilst taking occasional sips from a can of lager. There had been times whilst they'd been traversing the length and breadth of the country playing every shithole imaginable trying to create a buzz about the group when he'd wondered whether he was wasting his time. True, their hard work had secured them a recording contract with EMI, but outside of London, and certain other cities such as Manchester and Birmingham, they'd largely struggled to make much of an impression anywhere else. Indeed, there'd been occasions when they'd outnumbered the audience. Now, however, thanks to an unscheduled appearance on an insignificant regional TV show, the Sex Pistols were the most famous group in the country. And of course, his being the singer meant he was the group's public face – whether certain other members liked it or not - and he was going to enjoy every minute of his new-found celebrity.

John continued to stare into the void, only coming to life as the G/F/Em/D/C intro to "Anarchy in the UK" fills the smoke-filled air. He is the antichrist, and an anarchist. He doesn't know what he wants, but he knows how to get it . . . he wants to destroy the passerby. At the song's finale he grabs another lager and raises the can aloft in acknowledgement of those who are in ecstasy at seeing their heroes in the flesh, and would have braved the weather regardless of the group's new-found infamy in the wake of the *Today* debacle. Unfortunately, their efforts are easily drowned out by the derogatory heckling from the otherwise silent majority, but John is in defiant mood and has been relishing the opportunity to engage his supposedly-intellectual crowd in a bout of verbal sparring. "You're not wrecking the place," he spits derisively. "The News of the World will be really disappointed!" The badinage is cut short, however, when Steve, having now discarded his leather jacket, powers into "I Wanna Be Me".

When their version of "Steppin' Stone", which was originally recorded by Paul Revere & the Raiders in May 1966, before receiving mainstream success thanks to The Monkees six months later, normally served as a reference point for the uninitiated fails to ignite the crowd John vents his spleen by informing them that if they didn't like what's on offer then they knew where the exit door was. The next song, the much-vaunted "No Future", does at least elicit a reaction, but as soon as the song comes to an end the audience slips back into its semi-lethargic state.

John then attempts to stir things up by berating the crowd for what he sees as their collective conservative attitude. This, however, only brings another wave of catcalling, with one wag cheekily demanding his money back. John retaliates in kind by pointing out that anyone incapable of appreciating what the Sex Pistols were about should head for the exit and do something more meaningful with their time.

The Sex Pistols have been covering The Who's 1966 hit, "Substitute", since their earliest shows. The song had recently made a surprise return to the UK singles chart following a resurgence of interest in Messrs Daltry, Townsend, Entwistle, and Moon on the back of the *Tommy* film. As with "Steppin' Stone" it usually serves as a conduit capable of traversing the musical boundaries, but when it fails to draw much of a response John again derides the crowd's continued show of apathy as being the result of the local council having perhaps imposed a ban on handclapping.

With John having given up the ghost of trying to draw blood from the stone, the group soldier on through the remainder of the set before bringing the evening to a close with their version of the Stooges' classic, "No Fun".

♪♪♪

The Anarchy Tour was finally underway, but with Rank Leisure steadfastly refusing to reconsider its "anxieties over security aspects" for the show at Bournemouth's Village Bowl, McLaren ordered the bus to head back down the M1 to Sheffield in the hope that the tentatively booked alternative show at the city's university might still be on the cards. To everyone's dismay, Goodman had somehow managed to get himself – and the PA – stranded in Berkshire after taking a wrong turn-off from the motorway. This, however, was rendered little more than an irritation when the university's faculty decided against opening its doors to the Pistols.

Grateful for a temporary sanctuary from the prying eyes of the press, the tour party entrenched themselves in the university's student union bar where they'd whiled away the afternoon holding an in-house debate on Malcolm's decision to throw The Damned off the tour. The decision had brooked no argument from either Rhodes or Childers. Rhodes' had long-objected to his charges having to go on before The Damned, while their removal meant a larger percentage of the door receipts for the Heartbreakers.

The Damned had no sooner returned to London when Stiff Records issued the following statement to the music press:

> "Following reports that the Sex Pistols have fired the Damned due to various oblique reasons, confirmation is given that the Damned will not be appearing at any more of the Pistols' dates. No further dates are planned at the present for the group. They will instead return to the studio to complete their first album with producer Nick Lowe, which Stiff plan to release early in the New Year."

Satisfied that Goodman had found his bearings, McLaren spent a futile hour on the phone trying to cajole Dr. Nashenter into allowing a second date at Leeds Polytechnic for the Wednesday evening. Even if Nashenter had given his blessing, playing two shows within three days in the same city was surely tempting fate. And the Leeds show had been far from a sell-out. Another factor to consider was that with The Damned having now been expunged, there was no guarantee the Polytechnic's cash-conscious students would be willing to hand over the same admission price for a truncated bill.

Chapter Eleven

PISTOLS FIRE BIG BLANK

SEX PISTOLS Leeds: THE SEX Pistols were met with jeers on the first night of their troubled-hit tour, at Leeds Polytechnic.

Scores of fans walked out and lead singer, Johnny Rotten yelled at those that remained: 'You're just a load of dummies – you're dead!' But in fact it was punk rock that was in danger of dying. The group was met with hoots of laughter as they tried in vain to whip up excitement.

They kicked off with a swipe at Bill Grundy and the Queen, and then they broke their manager's orders by using a string of obscenities. Their music was predictably loud and crude but alas it was also dismally disappointing – relentless and unimaginative.

When the group waited among cat-calls to do an encore, Rotten turned upon his fans and snarled: 'Has the council banned you from clapping? If you don't like us, you know where the exit is.' Record Mirror, Saturday, 11 December 1976.

Glen was looking forward to playing Manchester again. This was their first visit to the Electric Circus, but if the response was anything like those the Pistols had received at the two shows they'd played at the Lesser Free Trade Hall during the summer then it promised to be a good night. The first Lesser Free Trade date at the beginning of June came about thanks to Buzzcocks' frontman and guitarist, Howard Devoto and Pete Shelley, having felt compelled to check the Pistols out after reading the *NME*'s "Don't look over your shoulder, but the Sex Pistols are coming" review of their appearance at the Marquee Club supporting Eddie and the Hot Rods in February; the band's first substantial exposure. He could remember the rush of excitement on turning the page and seeing John's face staring out at him. Support acts seldom got a mention in a live review, but Neil Spencer had devoted his entire review to the Pistols with no mention of the Hot Rods whatsoever.

It was their reading about how the Pistols had covered the Stooges' "No Fun". The review hadn't the song itself, but just the mere mention of the Stooges had proved sufficient for them to borrow a friend's car and head for the bright lights of London. At the time of course, Buzzcocks hadn't existed anywhere outside of Devoto and Shelley's minds. Indeed, they were still known to one and all as Howard Trafford and Pete McNeish. Having stopped off en route to pick up their pal Richard Boone, who was now managing Buzzcocks, they'd arrived in London hoping the Pistols would be playing in the capital that weekend. They'd bought a copy of that week's *Time Out*, and on finding no mention of the Pistols within its pages, the trio had called the *NME*'s offices in Carnaby Street. As luck would have it, Neil Spencer took the call. Though Spencer didn't know much more about the Pistols than what he'd written up, he was able to point them to SEX. *Time Out* would at least prove useful in providing Buzzcocks with their name thanks to the tagline in a review of that week's episode of *Rock Follies*, ITV's new musical drama following the fortunes of a fictional all-girl trio called the "Little Ladies".

The Pistols were in fact playing two shows that weekend: the first being support to Screaming Lord Sutch at the Bucks College of Higher Education's Valentine's Ball in High Wycombe, the second in support of Mr. Big in Welwyn Garden City. It was after the Welwyn Garden City date that Devoto and Shelley approached Malcolm with an offer for the Pistols to appear at the Bolton Institute of Technology where they were both enrolled. When the college's Student Union refused to give up a Friday night to a London-based act they'd never heard of, Devoto and Shelley booked the Lesser Free Trade Hall.

It had proved a pivotal evening as by the time the Pistols returned to the Lesser Free Trade Hall just six weeks later, the majority of those in attendance at the first show had since formed their own bands. Devoto and Shelley had also managed to get Buzzcocks in time for the second date. It was at the second Lesser Free Trade Hall show that the Pistols had debuted "Anarchy In The UK".

The Lesser Free Trade Hall shows had also brought the Pistols to the attention of Tony Wilson. Aside from his co-presenting *Granada Reports*, the north-west's equivalent to *Today*, Wilson also fronted Granada's late-evening culture, music and events show *So It Goes* that went out Sunday night at 10.30. With the Pistols being as yet unsigned, Wilson had gone out on a limb in badgering his bosses to have the Pistols on *So It Goes*. As Granada had close links with London Weekend Television, the show was also broadcast throughout the London area.

Jordan's stubborn refusal to remove the swastika armband she was sporting had caused a bit of consternation amongst the production crew; the studio bosses giving her an ultimatum: that she either agree to covering up the offending insignia with gaffer tape, or be ejected from the studio.

They'd met the comedian Peter Cook, who'd been invited on to talk about the new *Derek and Clive* album. *So It Goes* had its own resident comedian, a balding Aussie called Clive James. Aside from delivering a topical monologue each week, it was James' job to warm up the predominantly student-based studio audience before the show and during the commercial break. James had thought to impress Cook by poking fun at John's attire, but John had made mincemeat of him.

Each act was allotted a three and a half minute timeslot. He could remember Wilson impressing upon them the importance of their adhering to the show's strict timetable. They were the last act on, but instead of bringing "Anarchy" to an end on cue they'd continued playing; the wailing feedback from Steve's Les Paul all but drowning out Wilson's attempts to bring the show to a close. Glen was still picturing the jaw-dropping reaction from the *So It Goes* audience when the bus drew to a halt outside the Midland Hotel. He wasn't surprised to see the entrance to the hotel teeming with reporters; even recognising a few faces. There was something different about them today though. They seemed more animated than usual. Malcolm had barely time to step onto the pavement before they surrounded him.

EMI had announced they were withdrawing finance for the tour.

"Can you hear what they're shoutin after Malcolm?" Mick gasped, turning to Glen.

"That EMI have announced they've withdrawn finance for the tour," Glen nodded, watching Malcolm fending off reporters as he made his way inside the hotel.

"Can't be true, can it?" Mick asked while flashing a v-sign at a reporter that had come up to the window.

"Leslie Hill didn't mention anything about it to Malcolm when they spoke on the phone yesterday," Glen sighed. "But a lot can happen in twenty-four hours, and this lot obviously got their info some somewhere."

The band hadn't met Hill before the press conference at Manchester Square the previous week. Hill was unquestionably an EMI company man, but Glen had sensed they could trust him not to feed them any bullshit. After all, he'd proved true to his word in resolving the dispute with the packers at the pressing plant, and had appeared genuinely concerned about the disruption the halt had caused. With the leading high street chains such as Woolworths, W.H. Smiths, and Boots refusing to stock "Anarchy", their only hope in reaching the charts was in getting the record out to as many independent outlets as possible.

Another on-going problem that was hindering the record's chances of course was that apart from John Peel, every other DJ at Radio One was refusing to play the single. This deliberate blackballing had extended to commercial stations including Capital Radio. Aiden Day had supposedly announced on air that he would rather quit the station than play "Anarchy". He'd been baffled to hear Radio Luxembourg was also refusing to give the record any airplay – especially seeing as they'd enjoyed cocking a snook at the authorities by not paying for a license. They even went as far as giving Tony Prince a one-night suspension for sending an on-air invitation to the Sex Pistols to perform live on his show.

At that moment Rhodes got to his feet. "Do you reckon it's true, Bernie?" Mick shouted over.

Rhodes advanced to Mick and Glen. "Do I reckon what's 'true'?"

"That EMI have pulled the tour support," Glen asked

"Why would EMI settle an outstanding hotel bill one day, and then withdraw its support for the tour the next?"

"They had their AGM the yesterday, though," said Glen. "But I guess we're about to find out if it's true or not," he added on seeing Malcolm emerge from the hotel, brushing off renewed petitions from reporters as he came bounding down the steps and back onto the bus.

"Is it true, Malcolm?" John shouted up. "Are we goin' home?" "Yes and no," Malcolm replied, advancing along the aisle.

"What the fuck does that mean?"

"Yes, it's true that EMI have pulled our tour support. But we won't be returning to London . . . at least just yet."

"What we doin' then?" John sneered. "Havin' a fuckin' whip round?"

"As luck would have it," Malcolm continued ignoring John's comment, "Sophie says a cheque from EMI Publishing has arrived at the office. I must admit to finding the irony amusing. That one arm of EMI is doing all it could to rein us in, while the other has provided us with the means to carry on."

"How much is it for?" Steve shouted.

"The only numbers you need concern yourself with Steve are the ones you're going to be playing tomorrow night," Malcolm smiled.

"Why shouldn't we fuckin' concern ourselves with the numbers?" John challenged. "It's a cheque from EMI Publishing ain't it? We write the songs . . . not you."

"You're quite right, John," Malcolm nodded. "You write and perform the songs, while I'm the manager. And as manager, I take care of the business side of things."

"Who told you EMI had pulled the support?" Glen asked Malcolm, while flashing a look at Rhodes.

"It was Leslie Hill," Malcolm replied, glancing out of the window at the reporters. "He apologised, saying the decision was taken higher up the chain. I've spoken with Stephen, and he's looking into where we are from a legal standpoint."

"Who's Stephen?" Mick asked, giving Glen a gentle dig in the ribs

"Stephen Fisher. He's Malcolm's partner in Glitterbest, the company they set up to look after our interests. They each have a fifty per cent stake."

"How much does Malcolm take? His cut, I mean."

"Twenty-five per cent."

"An' how much does this Fisher bloke take?

"Dunno, I think Malcolm pays him out of . . ." he suddenly fell silent on seeing Malcolm glaring at him.

"If you and Michael are quite finished, Glen . . .?"

"Sorry Malcolm," Glen mumbled, shifting in his seat.

"As I was saying," Malcolm continued, "Leslie Hill suggested we cut our losses and return to London. Until speaking with Sophie, I have to say I had to agree with him that it was the only viable course of action. Thanks to Terry at EMI Publishing, however, we can stick two fingers up at Sir John Read and the other stuffed shirts at Manchester Square. The longer we can stay on the road, the longer we'll continue to generate publicity. And drumming up publicity of course is the whole point of this tour. Now, with this rabble showing no sign of dispersing," he said, glancing out the window, "we'll follow the same procedure as we did in Derby. Nils and I will go inside and take care of the checking in. You're all to go straight up to your rooms, and under no circumstances are any of you to speak with the press. Are you listening Steve and Paul?"

♪♪♪

Malcolm was naturally anxious to avoid any incidents which might further damage the Sex Pistols' standing within EMI. With the reporters gathered in and around the Midland Hotel's foyer sensing another banner headline, and showing no sign of dispersing until they got their story, he was once again forced to order everyone to their rooms. Following another lengthy conference with Stephen Fisher, he'd put in a second call to Leslie Hill to inform the latter of his decision to carry on regardless with the tour. The irony that EMI moneys were allowing Malcolm to keep the Sex Pistols on the road wasn't lost on Hill either, but with his having already expressed his personal support for the group there was nothing he could do but make contingency plans. The first of these was to inform Malcolm that Frank Brunger, would from this juncture on, be acting as an on-the-road liaison for the remainder of the tour.

Malcolm's first thought upon hearing this was to suggest that Brunger accompany them on the coach. He immediately checked himself, however, after remembering that it had been Brunger who'd - albeit inadvertently – earned Dave Goodman's enmity over the production credit mix-up on the single. He was rooming with Goodman and didn't want any unnecessary aggravation.

Once Hill was satisfied that his envoy would receive a cordial welcome in Manchester he then proceeded to give Malcolm a summary of the previous day's events at the company's AGM.

Firstly, he gave an outline of the brief that he'd prepared for the meeting, which outlined his plans for the Sex Pistols to go into the recording studio later that month with Mike Thorne, to record a second single scheduled for release in early February 1977. This would be followed by an album, with a scheduled release date for the following March or April. The brief also included a mention of Brunger's appointment as the company's onthe-spot representative, and that the Harvest man's sole duty would be to provide EMI with a true account of what was happening on the tour. He'd also attempted to assuage his superiors further by bringing attention to the fact that – regardless of what was being reported in the tabloids – the Sex Pistols had visited Manchester Square on at least ten separate occasions within the previous three weeks and nothing untoward had ever occurred. Hill had also enlisted the help of Nick Mobbs, who was head of EMI's A&R Department, and the man responsible for signing the Sex Pistols to the label.

Hearing Mobb's name reminded Malcolm of his visits to Manchester Square, and his battle to convince the 30-year-old, denim-clad A&R chief of the Sex Pistols' worth. Despite his having been dragged to the Midnite Special showcase at the Screen On The Green at the end of August by an enthusiastic Mike Thorne, as well as his cutting short a trip to Venice under his own volition to see Wings in order to see the Sex Pistols playing in Doncaster the following month, Mobbs had remained sceptical about whether the Pistols' rough-and-ready stage act would translate to vinyl. However, having been won over by Malcolm's spiel, Mobbs finally capitulated and went upstairs to present the group's case to Bob Mercer, the head of EMI's Group Repertoire Division.

According to Hill, Mobbs had gone on record to say that he felt that the violence aspect surrounding the Sex Pistols had been blown-up out of all proportion, and that it was certain sections of the group's audience that were in fact responsible for the purported flare-ups at their concerts - although he had been willing to concede that such instances could rub off on the performers themselves. He'd also attempted to play down the tour's cancellations and highlighted the one at Derby which, according to the information gleaned so far, had been cancelled due to the fact that fifty members of a motor-cycle club had made a blockbooking and were expected to cause trouble inside the venue. In addition to this, it was also understood that the fascist National Front were planning to stage a protest outside the venue and, it had been at the label's behest the show be cancelled rather than as a result of the Sex Pistols' refusal to perform before the town's Leisure Committee as reported in the press.

Between them, Hill and Mobbs had managed to play down the plant throwing incident at the Dragonara by proving the whole episode had been wilfully engineered by a reporter from the *Daily Mirror*. And that the hotel manager's chief concern had not been about the Sex Pistols' supposed reputation, but rather the behaviour amongst the large contingent of reporters who were constantly hanging around the hotel lobby causing a nuisance to his other guests. Hill had concluded his brief by exonerating Eric Hall, whose decision it had been to book the group onto the *Today* show, whilst attaching sales figures to date for "Anarchy In The UK" in the hope that they might help sway any corporate decision on the label's future relationship with the group.

On Malcolm's insistence, Hill had then proceeded to read out verbatim a statement from EMI's chairman, Sir John Read, which had subsequently been sent out to the company's shareholders in the form of an official EMI newsletter. The statement was entitled: Comment on Content of Records by Sir John Read, Chairman.

During the course of today's Annual General Meeting, Sir John Read, Chairman of EMI Group said:
The EMI Group of companies operates internationally and has been engaged in the recorded music business for over 75 years."

During recent years in particular, the question of acceptable content of records has been increasingly difficult to resolve – largely due to the increasing degree of permissiveness accepted by society as a whole, both in the UK and overseas. Throughout its history as a recording company, EMI has always sought to behave within contemporary limits of decency and good taste – taking into account not only the traditional rigid conventions of one section of society, but also the increasingly liberal attitudes of other, perhaps larger, sections of society at any given time. Today, there is in EMI's experience, not only an overwhelming sense of permissiveness – as demonstrated by the content of books, newspapers, and magazines, as well as records and films – but also a good deal of questioning by various sections of society, both young and old, e.g. what is decent or in good taste compared to the attitude of, say, 20 or even 10 years ago?

It is against the present-day social background that EMI has to make value judgements about the content of records in particular. EMI has on a number of occasions, taken steps totally to ban individual records, and similarly to ban record sleeves, or posters, or other promotional material which it believed would be offensive.

The Sex Pistols incident, which started with a disgraceful interview given by this young pop group on Thames TV, last week, has been followed by a vast amount of newspaper coverage in the last few days. Sex Pistols is a pop group devoted to a new form of music known as 'punk rock'. It was contracted for recording purposes by EMI Records Ltd in October, 1976, - an unknown group offering some promise, in the view of our recording executive, like many other pop groups of different kinds that we have signed. In this context, it must be remembered that the recording industry has signed many pop groups, initially controversial, who have in the fullness of time become wholly acceptable and contributed greatly to the development of modern music.

Sex Pistols have acquired a reputation for aggressive behaviour which they have certainly demonstrated in public. There is no excuse for this. Our recording company's experience of working with the group, however, is satisfactory. Sex Pistols is the only 'punk rock' group that EMI Records currently has under direct recording contract and whether EMI does in fact release any more of their records will have to be very carefully considered. I need hardly add that we shall do everything we can to restrain their public behaviour, although this is a matter over which we have no real control.

Similarly, EMI will review its general guidelines regarding the content of pop records. Who is to decide what is objectionable or unobjectionable to the public at large today? When anyone sits down to consider seriously this problem, it will be found that there are widely differing attitudes between people of all ages and all walks of life as to what can be shown, or spoken, or sung.

Our view within EMI is that we should seek to discourage records that are likely to give offence to the majority of people. In this context, changing public attitudes have to be taken into account.

EMI should not set itself up as a public censor, but it does seek to encourage restraint.

The board of EMI certainly takes seriously the need to do everything Possible to encourage the raising of standards in music and entertainment.

By the time Hill had finished reading out Read's non-too-festive missive - which was almost puritanical in its moral-mongering - Malcolm was suffering from a severe case of cramp in his left hand from holding the receiver tight against his ear. However, he instantly forgot about his discomfort upon hearing Hill mention that EMI would be reviewing whether to release any more Sex Pistols records. The tingling pain in his fingers shot straight to his head as his already troubled mind began swimming with a plethora of scenarios – none of which were particularly palatable from where he was standing. The possibility of EMI dumping the Sex Pistols was mortifying enough, but if the label instead chose to sit on the group - as they were perfectly entitled to do under the terms and conditions tucked away in the contractual small print - whilst simultaneously refusing to release any more records, it would effectively reduce them to a live act. The mere thought of the Sex Pistols being shackled at a time when The Damned were recording their debut album was simply more than he could stand.

Hill must have sensed Malcolm's frustrations, and tried to sugar-coat the potential cyanide pill by reconfirming his continued personal support for the Sex Pistols. He also assured Malcolm that he would do everything within his power to ensure that the group went into the recording studio with Mike Thorne at the earliest given opportunity.

♪♪♪

Goodman was trawling the Midland's corridors in search for Glen and Mick's room. There was no show that evening, and he was hoping to instigate a get-together similar to the aftershow they'd enjoyed at the Dragonara two nights ago. The party had carried on well into the early hours and would live long in the memory; the only downside was that his hash stash was now the size of a malteaser. At this rate, he'd be dry before the week was out. He'd contemplated ringing Kim, his PA-hire business partner. It was Kim that had supplied him the hash, but he wasn't sure if his call would be welcomed right now. With the Pistols hiring the PA, Kim had taken it as a given that he'd be coming along on the tour. Malcolm, however, had had other ideas. The Clash and The Heartbreakers were bringing along their own people, and Malcolm had been anxious about their being too many cooks in the kitchen. Reading between the lines, he knew that was Malcolm's polite way of saying he wasn't prepared to put any money in the pot for Kim's wages. Kim had not been best pleased when he'd called round his place on the eve of the tour to collect the hash – even more so on espying Malcolm sitting in the van. Goodman's on-the-road tour specials had become the talk of the Speakeasy. He never minded sharing them, either. What he did mind, however, was certain people Bogarting them. Since the first night at the Crest Hotel, Rotten had made a point of being next in line after himself and Caruzo. And once Rotten got his paws on a spliff, that was it. Goodnight Vienna! At last night's gathering he'd taken a near-full spliff into the bathroom with him and locked the door. Corkie and the rest of the Brummie road crew weren't putting up that, though. They'd busted in the door and threatened to drown Rotten in the bath unless he relinquished the spliff.

When Rotten emerged from the bathroom he'd sulkily grabbed up a half-eaten sandwich from the dresser and pitched it at Corkie. Corkie had ducked, and the sandwich had caught Mick Jones on the side of the head. Mick had thrown a hissy-fit about the mayonnaise getting in his hair and hurled his beer at Rotten. That had been the signal for an all-out beer and foot fight. The carpet and quilts had got a soaking, but other than a couple of pillows getting ripped up no one would have been any the wiser. That was until Jerry Nolan got involved. He'd taken umbrage at being wrenched from his drug-induced oblivion in the next room, and put his boot through the door.

He was chuckling at the memory of Nolan's threatening to tear someone a new arsehole when the man himself stepped out of the lift further along the corridor. Goodman was amused to see the bag the drummer had clutched under one arm was brimming with apples.

"Hey, Dave, my 'good man'," Nolan nodded. "Who you lookin' for?"

Goodman was relieved to see Nolan's mood from the night before had lifted. "Hi Jerry, do you know the number of Glen and Mick's room?

"No, but I just seen Glen down in reception. He looked kinda troubled. Could have been his hangover, I suppose."

"How's your head today?" Goodman asked with a knowing smile.

Nolan looked genuinely perplexed. "Me? I didn't have no hangover . . . Oh, I see what you're getting' at. Let's just say you guys have your poison, and we have ours. You still holdin'? Johnny could use a little somethin' to take the edge off. I know I could."

"'Doctor Feel-Goodman' at your service," Goodman grinned, pulling a ready-rolled spliff from his pocket. Goodman found Thunders sitting cross-legged on his bed tinkering away on his guitar when he followed Nolan into the room. "Look who I found wanderin' the halls," Nolan said, grabbing an apple from the bag and taking a bite. Goodman walked across and sat in the chair by the window. "Sounded good what you were playing, Johnny," he said, popping the spliff into the corner of his mouth and plucking a lighter from the pocket of his dungarees.

"It's somethin' I've been messin' about with," Thunders nodded absently before scrambling off the bed and replacing the guitar in its case. Goodman was immediately struck at how small in height Thunders actually was. He couldn't have been much over five foot five. He'd certainly looked a hell of a lot taller in the Dolls, but that had obviously been the bouffant hair and stack heels. "Johnny's savin' that riff for the album," said Nolan, collapsing on his bed. Goodman satisfied himself that the spliff was lit before responding. "What album? You boys close to securing a deal?"

"We're thinkin' about stayin' here once the tour's over," said Nolan. "London, that is."

"Yeah, Leee thinks we'll have more chance of gettin' a deal over here," Thunders nodded. "None of the labels back home will touch us. They don't think we'll live long enough for them to recoup their investment." Goodman handed the spliff to Thunders. "Well, if you need a producer . . .?" "Sure, you can throw your hat into the ring," Thunders nodded.

"And me and Caruzo are looking to set up our own label."

"No offence, Dave," Nolan smiled, "but we're hopin' Leee can secure us a deal with one of the majors."

"It might take some time," Thunders nodded, holding the spliff out for Nolan, "but we got plenty of that."

"Yeah, all you'll need is to get an extension on your work permits," Goodman nodded.

"That should be easy enough."

"Work permits?" Nolan frowned. "I don't know nothin' about any work permits."

"You need them to work over here," said Goodman. "Malcolm must have sorted out the permits for you."

"And what if Malcolm didn't bother with these permits?" Thunders asked. "What would happen if the authorities found out we don't got no permits?"

"I should imagine you'll be put on the next plane to New York."

"Oh, I . . . Where you goin', Jerry?" Thunders asked on seeing Nolan leap from his bed heading for the door.

"I'm goin' to go talk with Leee about these permits," Nolan said from the doorway. "And if Leee don't know nothin' about them, I'm gonna go look for Malcolm. And if he don't give me the right answers to my questions, I'm gonna kick his skinny, Limey ass all the way back down to London if necessary!"

♪♪♪

Glen was sat tucked away in a secluded corner of the Midland's reception area gathering his thoughts. He spotted Pete Shelley and Buzzcocks' bassist Steve Diggle come through the door and make their way over to the reception desk, but made no effort to make them aware of his presence. This wasn't out of any deliberate show of rudeness as he had got on well enough with them during the Pistols' previous forays to Manchester. It was simply because the last thing he wanted to do at that particular moment was talk shop. He was amused to see Diggle up to his usual tricks eying up the maids making their way down the stairwell while Shelley was speaking with the receptionist. Diggle continued watching the girls as they made their way across the foyer, and for a heartbeat Glen was sure he'd been spotted. He relaxed again on seeing the two Buzzcocks making for the lift, while offering a silent prayer to whichever god it was that protected disgruntled bass players from unsolicited interruption. He was also tempted to have a quiet word with St. Jude, as he now convinced more than ever that his being a Sex Pistol was a lost cause. It just wasn't worth the effort. No, that wasn't strictly true. It was being in the same band as John that was proving unbearable. It didn't matter what he said nor did, John would always find fault: be it over his musical tastes, his opinions, his choice of friends - especially his friendship with Mick. Even his toiletry habits had been called into question! Or was that Steve? No matter, John would have stuck his oar in. And now, from what Mick had overheard, John was questioning his "suitability" for wearing clothing from the shop. It was like being back at school. Dealing with John had been difficult enough before they'd gone on the *Today* show, but now that he was intent on living up to his press persona he was unbearable to be around. He'd known John was going to be trouble the moment he'd walked through the door at The Roebuck that balmy August evening. His surly attitude and sarcastic putdowns had driven Malcolm to despair, while Steve had threatened to black him one before they'd even got as far going over to the shop for the audition. That had been farcical experience in itself. Malcolm had thrust a plastic showerhead that he'd found under the counter into John's hand, and told him to sing along to Alice Cooper's "I'm Eighteen" on the shop's jukebox. John must have felt pretty stupid singing into a plastic showerhead. He hadn't known the lyrics either, and had warbled the chorus over and over while lurching about like Quasimodo on acid. There's been something about him though. Despite Steve's protests, everyone agreed it was worth giving John a tryout at their rehearsal place over in Rotherhithe. It was above a pub called The Crunchie Frog, if he remembered rightly. Of course, in the interim Steve had convinced Paul that John was a timewaster and wouldn't show for the rehearsal. Well, if Steve and Paul weren't bothering, he certainly wasn't going to schlep all the way to Rotherhithe on the off-chance. The trouble was, John did show up at the pub, and he hadn't been best pleased. In fact, it was his managing to calm John down when he'd called the following day, and his cajoling Steve and Paul into giving John a chance, then he was even be in the band. What thanks had he ever got for that?

The funny thing was he and John had actually worked well together in the beginning. They'd playfully come up with the underwater themed lyric to "Submission" in answer to Malcolm's suggestion they pen a song about sexual bondage. And it was down to his musical savvy that they'd come up with a tune to fit John's poem-esque lyric to "No Future". They'd been at Wessex Studios trying to record "Anarchy" with Dave Goodman. During a break he'd started tinkering about with an A-Flat/ A-Major/ C-Sharp/D-Major melody on the studio's Bösendorfer Grand piano. He was no Liberace, but the lessons he'd begrudgingly taken whilst at grammar school meant he could chop out a melody whenever the occasion arose. John had been sat huddled in a corner scribbling away when he'd suddenly sprang to life yelling at him to keep playing. When they'd started working on the tune for real Steve had refused to play "wanky Beatles chords" as he called them. And while Steve's barre chords had changed the tune to "No Future" beyond all recognition, they'd chalked up another song.

He was chuckled to himself wondering what Steve or John would say if they knew he'd lifted the original melody to "No Future" from a Don Partridge song when he heard his name being called. He looked up to find Malcolm striding towards him, flanked on either side by a Buzzcock. "C'mon boy," Malcolm said, motioning Glen to his feet. "Why, where're we going?" Glen asked, reluctantly getting to his feet and slowly making his way towards them.

"Pete and Steve have suggested we mark their filling in for the Damned tomorrow evening with a celebratory drink at Tommy Duck's," Malcolm beamed. Tommy Duck's, or "Tommy Duckworth's" to give the pub its proper name, was legendary throughout the north-west of England. Its walls were decorated with a priceless collection of Victorian theatre and music hall posters, while another unique feature was its having a skeleton encased within a glass-topped coffin serving as a table. The pub's main selling point was its ceiling being festooned with scores of pairs of knickers, ranging from the skimpiest bits of lace to capacious bloomers.

Chapter Twelve
CALL FOR BOYCOTT ON SEX PISTOLS

An outraged Liverpool Councillor to-day called for a boycott on punk rock group Sex Pistols – who vow to sidestep a ban on their city concert.

Councillor Doreen Jones plans to demonstrate outside the club where they are to play in a bid to dissuade youngsters from seeing the group.

"Let's show the rest of the country Liverpool is too good for this sort of rubbish. We don't want them here," she said.

Liverpool Echo, Tuesday, 7 December 1976.

Throwing The Damned off of the tour gave McLaren immense personal satisfaction. He just wished he could have seen Jake Riviera's face when Rick Rogers had called Stiff's offices with the news. There was no point in trying to guess what the reaction was going to be amongst those that had already purchased tickets for the following evening's show at the Electric Circus, but hopefully the inclusion of Buzzcocks would suffice. And inviting Buzzcocks onto the bill would elevate them above Slaughter and the Dogs in the local pecking order. Howard and Pete had generously invited their Wythenshawe-based neighbours onto the bill at the second of the Lesser Free Trade Hall shows. There was denying the more established Dogs had proved as good as their word in bringing a sizeable number of punters through the door that night, but McLaren couldn't bring himself to forgive their designing a poster for the show and placing themselves as headliners.

Richard Boone had made a brief appearance at Tommy Duck's the previous evening, and before leaving McLaren made arrangements with Boone to meet at the hotel to discuss over breakfast the possibility of Buzzcocks replacing The Damned for the remainder of the tour. He'd set off for the restaurant a half-hour early hoping to enjoy some solitude before Boone's arrival. En route he decided to check at reception to see whether there were any messages for him. No sooner had he approached desk, however, when the manager emerged from a side office to inform him he would like a word. Fearing the worst, he'd followed the manager back inside the office. He'd felt the knot tightening in the pit of his stomach as the manager explained how he'd spent the morning dealing with the complaints filed against his charges' unruly behaviour during the night. He'd then served notice on the tour party, giving them one hour to vacate the hotel before he called the police. This was the last thing Malcolm needed, and he tried placating the manager by offering him the cash to cover the cost of whatever reparations might be required. The manager, however, was not to be dissuaded.

Knowing that Nick Mobbs had made the journey up to Manchester to catch the Electric Circus show, Malcolm went in search of Mobbs' room in the hope that the A&R chief might be in possession of a company chequebook. Though sympathetic to Malcolm's plight, Mobbs could only repeat Leslie Hill's warning that if Malcolm wanted to continue with the tour then he was on his own. Mobbs had also let it be known that while EMI had covered the cost of the rooms at the Crest and the Dragonara, the label wouldn't be covering the exorbitant room service bills that had been run up during their stays. These costs would be deducted from the royalties thus far accrued from the sales of "Anarchy In The UK".

Malcolm managed to solve the hotel situation in procuring rooms at the Belgrade Hotel in nearby Stockport. However, they arrived at the Belgrade an hour or so later to discover the manager had since undergone a change of heart. Rather than listen to Malcolm's overtures, he'd took up a stance in the doorway posing with his arms outstretched for the smattering of reporters that had followed in the coach's wake, and was clearly relishing his every moment in the media glare. Malcolm had entrenched himself in a nearby public phone box, painstakingly going through the hotel listings in the Yellow Pages in search of an alternative sanctuary. There were several decent hotels within a ten-mile radius of the Belgrade. Each also had rooms available for that night, but none proved willing to take the Sex Pistols' shilling. He'd about given up hope when he'd struck gold in securing a block-booking at the Arosa Hotel in Withington. The Arosa's amenities were a far cry from those to be had at the Midland, but it was infinitely preferable to spending the night on the bus. Later that same day, John and Nils were in their room ruminating over Sir John Read's comment at EMI's AGM about the label considering whether to release further Sex Pistols product. "I reckon it's a bluff," John sneered, tugging a can of Harp lager free from the four-pack he was cradling between his legs. The Arosa might not have been able to offer room service, but there was at least an off-license within walking distance. "They ain't gonna sit on us. If they did, it would be as good as writing off the £40,000 because they'd have to pay us the other £20,000 next October." Nils sat idly toying with the hem of his mohair jumper. "True, but £40,000 is peanuts to a company the size of EMI. And they'll most likely recoup most of that with worldwide sales of 'Anarchy'."

"Then we'll turn the tables."

"How?"

"By not doing any more recordings for 'em," John said, punctuating the air with the tip of his cigarette.

"But Malcolm's desperate to have 'No Future' out in time for the Jubilee, isn't he?" Nils countered

John blew a smoke-ring up at the ceiling, watching the ring slowly expand and lose its shape as it dissipated. "I didn't fuckin' write it for the Jubilee," he said, twisting on his elbow so that he was facing Nils. "To be honest with you, I didn't even know there was a Jubilee comin' up! Have you heard Malcolm wants us to change the title to 'God Save The Queen'? Fuckin' cheek! He don't even fuckin' understand the lyric!" he spat, jabbing the air again with his cigarette for emphasis. "That quote he gave in the papers the other day. Where he says it starts with 'god bless the queen and her fascist regime' . . .?

"Well, you know what Malcolm's like when he has an audience," Nils grinned. "And changing the title would dilute the meaning," John continued his harangue. "I called it 'No Future' 'cos if your man in the street don't wake up and see he's bein' taken for a fuckin' ride by the establishment then he ain't gonna have a future. Nor will his kids, and their kids, ad infinfuckinitum."

"I hear Glen wants 'Vacant' to be the follow-up single," said Nils.

"Don't get me started on that fuckin' cunt!" John groaned. "It was bad enough being in a band with him before the Grundy thing. Glen just wants everything to be 'nice', wants us to be like the Bay City fuckin' Rollers or somethin'! Like that was ever gonna fuckin' happen!"

"Yeah, but–"

"If you ask me, Glen still wishes Malcolm had convinced that Jock fucker from Slik to join the band. "You know the one I'm on about? Midge somethin' or fuckin' other . . . It was while Malcolm and Bernie were in Glasgow trying to shift some of Steve's hooky gear. That record they had out last year was fuckin' awful!" "Got to number one on the charts, though didn't it?"

"What's that got to do with anythin'? Clive fuckin' Dunn got to number one!"

Nils decided to have a little fun playing devil's advocate. "Alright then, if you could have any bass player in the Pistols who would it be?"
"Dunno."
"Come on, play the game. You can have any bass player you want."
"Holger Czukay from Can."
"How's he gonna fit in with what the Pistols do?"
John playfully hurled his empty can at Nils. "You said I could have 'anyone'."
"What about from among the bands on the scene?"
"What fuckin' scene?" John asked with a mock-frown. "There's somethin' you're not tellin' me here, isn't there?"
"You didn't hear this from me; right, but Malcolm and Bernie supposedly considered swapping Glen for Simmo."
"Bollocks!"
"Only saying what I heard . . ."
"Does Glen know?"
"Doubt it. Paul and Steve don't know about it "
John narrowed his eyes. "When was this, then?"
"Not that long ago actually," Nils shrugged.
"Who told you?" John pressed.
"Suzi."
"Yeah, like she'd fuckin' what was goin' on," John cackled, tugging another can free and popping the ring-pull. "Do me a favour."
"Straight up!" Nils countered. "She got it off of Viv. Have I told you Suzi's thinking of changing the spelling to "Siouxsie" You know, as in the Indians; Sitting Bull, Custer's Last Stand, an' all that?"
"Only about a dozen times," John said, rolling his eyes. "I didn't think Suzi was stupid enough to believe anything fuckin' Vivienne comes out with?"
"I'm only telling you what she heard," Nils shrugged. "And you'd be surprised at what Malcolm tells Viv. He doesn't keep anything from her . . . He daren't. And you still haven't answered my question. Would you have gone along with it? I mean, Simmo is still learning " John took a drink from his can, swishing the lager about his mouth while contemplating his response. "Too fuckin' right, I would!"

♪♪♪

The Electric Circus in Collyhurst was a former cinema and variety club whose halcyon days were but a sepia-toned memory; a stark sentinel overlooked on all sides by towering monolithic tower blocks. The original Electric Circus had been run from Mr. Smith's nightclub on Brazil Street in the heart of the city's Gay Village; its Collyhurst usurper stealing the name, while taking none of the fame. Collyhurst itself, however, had little need to purloin an identity as it had played a significant role in Manchester's history as the sandstone hewn from its quarries had provided the city with its renowned red-bricked facade. Like the Electric Circus itself, Collyhurst and its environs had seen better days. Its proud residents – many of whom were consigned to a life on government handouts – would have no doubt agreed with the Sex Pistols' nihilistic "No Future" mantra. To the gangs that roamed the streets at night, however, they were a bunch of jumped-up cockneys invading their turf.

When the tour bus parked up on the triangular patch of wasteland directly opposite Electric Circus during the early afternoon there'd been nary a soul to be seen, but as the shadows lengthened in the fading winter light the surrounding neon-lit concrete jungle slowly came to life. For those making their way to the Electric Circus from the city centre, the Rochdale Road was the only viable approach. The gangs knew this, of course, and had posted sentinels to await the arrival of the "vile punk rockers" they'd heard so much about of late. John climbed up onto a chair and peered through a gap in the dressing room's wire meshed windows in time to see a line of mounted police make yet another attempt to disperse the baying mob. "By gum, lads; it's gettin' a bit bloody rowdy out there," he said, adopting a faux northern accent. "Why aren't they sat at home feedin' their whippets and watching fuckin' *Coronation Street* like normal folk?"

"Because it's Thursday, John," Steve Diggle offered, coming over to join John at the window. "And Corrie's only broadcast on Mondays and Wednesdays."

"Most inconsiderate of ITV," John chuckled, draining the last of his Tartan Ale and tossing the empty can into the corner.

"It doesn't sound as though the police are making much headway with the rabble," Malcolm grimaced, as angry shouts of "kill the punks" echoed on the night air. "There's a fuckin' army of Man City fans out there," John said, taking another peek through the window. "They don't have no game tonight cos they were away at Middlesbrough the other night. They drew nil-nil. It was nil-nil when they came to our place back in September an' all; the boring fuckers. You'd expect more from 'em with the likes of Peter Barnes, Joe Royal, and Brian Kidd in the side. They should never have sold Rodney Marsh." "They're probably here because of the football programmes," Malcolm smiled wistfully. "When Sophie and I were putting the tour together, Jamie hit upon the idea of advertising the tour in the match-day programmes of the football teams associated with the towns and cities where we'd be playing. Manchester had a home match coming up against Derby on the day of the . . . on the day of the proposed Derby show" - he hastily corrected himself – "we thought we'd be killing two birds with one stone. Of course, this was before all the hoo-hah."

"It sounds to me like there's more than fuckin' birds getting killed out there," John retorted as a bottle smashed against the mesh. "I don't understand why the police don't just let those fans with tickets inside where they'll be safe?" Malcolm sighed, glancing at his watch. "You boys are set to go on in an hour's time," he said, glancing across to Shelley and Diggle. But unless the police manage to restore some order out there you'll be performing to an empty hall. "We'll treat it like a rehearsal," Shelley shrugged "We should have gone back to the other fuckin' place," Steve said gloomily. "The Lesser somethin' or other "Yeah, why didn't we, Malcolm?' Paul asked.

"Because the Lesser Free Trade Hall is far too small a venue for you now,' Malcolm said, visibly flinching as another barrage of bricks and bottles crashed against the outside wall. "It undoubtedly served its purpose in the past, but you have a major record label behind you . . . and a record climbing the charts."

"You could have booked the Free Trade Hall itself," Glen offered. "It's around the same capacity as the Glasgow Apollo "In hindsight I suppose I should have looked at the possibility," Malcolm conceded. "So we get stuck with playing this fuckin' shit-hole instead," John sneered. He was about to say something else when Dave Goodman came bursting through the door.

"Jesus, it's like a bad night on the Bogside out there!" the engineer gasped. "So it would appear," Malcolm nodded. "But the police are dealing with it, aren't they?" "Well, they're doing the best," said Goodman. "But some of the loonies actually managed to barge their way past the bouncers." "What was that?" Malcolm gasped, glancing anxiously towards the dressing room door.

"Don't worry," Goodman said on seeing the look of panic in Malcolm's eyes. "The Heartbreakers were out onstage. Jerry and Waldo leapt down and steamed. From what I hear the loonies were beggin' the bouncers to save them."

♪♪♪

Howard Devoto stands motionless in front of the microphone surveying the audience as though searching for familiar faces amongst the throng. Since supporting the Sex Pistols at the Lesser Free Trade Hall Buzzcocks have built up a loyal following, and are beginning to make waves on the Manchester music scene. However, the initial excitement that he'd felt from reading about the Sex Pistols in the *NME*, and then seeing the group performing in High Wycombe and Welwyn Garden City is beginning to wane. He's already disillusioned with the scene. He knows in his heart that the frenzied tabloid exposés in the wake of the Sex Pistols' appearance on *Today* will open the floodgates and allow a plethora of inferior groups to jump aboard the bandwagon and proclaim themselves to be punks and surely negate what the Sex Pistols had set out to achieve. Indeed, his disenchantment has reached the point where he's made up his mind to quit Buzzcocks and form a new group more in tune with what he'd originally envisioned for Buzzcocks. Even the prospect of being able to bring forward recording their four-track EP with the money Malcolm is giving them for tonight's show fails to lift his despondency. He knows he has some serious soulsearching to do in the days ahead. When all is ready, Shelley brings his hand down against the strings of his cheap Woolworths guitar, and Buzzcocks launch into their opening number "Breakdown"; its simplistic single chord intro catchy enough to have those gathered at the front of the stage leaping about in time to the music. Their frontman may be suffering from a bout of musical melancholy, but Shelley and Diggle – adeptly accompanied by the fresh-faced John Mayer on drums - are determined to make the most of this unexpected opportunity to participate in a tour that is drawing national press coverage at every turn, and can only enhance their own reputation. Since their official unveiling at the lesser Free Trade Hall they have played a sizeable number of shows in and around their home city, and songs such as "Friends Of Mine", "Time's Up", "Orgasm Addict", "You Tear Me Up", and "Love Battery" are already regarded as crowd-pleasers. Buzzcocks might be considered newcomers on the nascent scene, but they're savvy enough to know that an opening act should never outstay its welcome. They bring their thirty-minute set to a close with a new song called, "I Love You, You Big Dummy".

Before embarking on the Anarchy Tour, The Clash hadn't headlined a show north of Birmingham and yet such is their burgeoning reputation that they are given a thunderous welcome as they emerge from the dressing room and make their way towards the stage. Joe, Mick, and Paul are once again dressed in their customised paint-splattered stage gear, and a brief pause while Joe yells at the hapless Keeth Paul to tone down his over-the-top psychedelic lighting they charge pell-mell into the opening number, "White Riot". Whether it's the enthusiastic reception, or their being spared the discomfiture of having to open - albeit for one night only — but the trio have a collective spring in their step as they throw shapes about the compact stage. They've also obviously learnt from watching The Heartbreakers in Leeds, for they no longer charge through the songs like amphetamine fuelled lunatics. The massed ranks jostling each other for a better position under the lighting at the front of the stage are clearly into The Clash, but some of the more-partisan locals are intent on making life difficult for the London groups and during a break between songs they begin their petty barracking. Under normal circumstances Joe would have tackled the hecklers head on and attempt to either win them over, or at least educate them on the error of their ways. Tonight, however, he is under strict instructions from Bernard to refrain from doing anything that might antagonise the crowd – if only because they will have to pass through the audience while returning to the dressing room. Nonetheless, The Clash's energycharged performance is akin to a souped-up Ford Cosworth V8 engine with Joe's left leg acting as the rev-counter as the group skilfully build up the momentum with each song so that by the time they bring their ten-song set to a climax with "1977", the majority of the audience is demanding more and they are obliged to remain on stage for two encores, which surely stands them in good stead for when they return to the provinces under their own banner.

New York's music cognoscenti readily accepted that The Heartbreakers were never going to be a punk group in the true sense - and not only because of the leather-clad quartet's preference for needles over safety-pins. The more musically astute members of the Electric Circus audience – though probably never having previously heard Thunders and Nolan's latest vehicle – knew that with two former New York Dolls in the line-up, The Heartbreakers were going to play straight-forward, 4/4 time rock'n'roll. With the Dolls having been forced to cancel their proposed show at the Manchester Hardrock back in November 1972 following Billy Murcia's tragic demise, one might have expected Thunders and Nolan to be keen to make up for lost time. However, as Malcolm could all too readily testify, the duo's penchant for putting drugs before duty had been the ruin of many a Dolls show. With Walter and Billy more than willing to help their friends chase the dragon, The Heartbreakers were going to be no different in that respect. Unlike their polished performance of three nights earlier, they appear disjointed and lacklustre and fail to get into their stride until two thirds of the way into their set. This in turn elicits little more than stilted applause from the audience. Unlike The Clash, there are no appeals for an encore.

♪♪♪

With Manchester having now become something of a home from home for the Sex Pistols, the air within the Electric Circus is charged with electric expectation as the group emerge from the dressing room. John, looking resplendent in full bondage suit, leaps up onto the stage and sweeps the microphone stand up into the air as Steve, Glen, and Paul blast into "Anarchy in the UK". He instinctively knows something is wrong with the monitors as he has to screech simply to make himself heard above the backline. The fans, however, care little about the malfunctioning monitors, and leap about en masse punching the air in time to the song's anthemic chorus. At the end of the song John begins berating Goodman over the faulty monitors, but his attempted protest is drowned out as Steve ploughs regardless into "I Wanna Be Me". The monitors are still causing John problems but when the song comes to a close instead of targeting Goodman he instead launches his invective against a small minority that were spitting at him; no doubt having read in one of the tabloids that "gobbing" is how punk rockers were supposed to salute their heroes. While Steve is occupied readjusting the tuning on his Les Paul, John tells those responsible in no uncertain terms that if the spitting doesn't stop immediately then the show will.

Some of those massed over by the bar area take advantage of the lull, and begin hurling abuse at the stage. Those amongst the audience who were in attendance at either of the Lesser Free Trade Hall shows were no doubt expecting John to pick up the gauntlet, but as with Joe Strummer, he appears reticent to take on the hecklers. Instead, he turns his back on the audience and spends the enforced interlude chatting to Paul. The next number is "Seventeen", but while the monitors appear to be working again, it's the Sex Pistols who appear out of sync. It's as though they are suddenly ill at ease with their surroundings, and their performance is suffering as a result. Steve is clearly not happy with his guitar sound, and midway through "Substitute" he brings the proceedings to a temporary halt and sets about giving his Gibson another retuning. This latest interruption triggers another barrage of abuse from those gathered at the rear of the hall; even the kids at the front are beginning to grow restless. Although The Who's classic is completed at the second time of asking, the monitors appear to be playing up again. John is beside himself at having to screech at the top of his lungs and again subjects Goodman to another vitriolic outburst. During "No Feelings" the defective monitors are suddenly rendered the least of the Sex Pistols' problems, because the hecklers are no longer content with hurling insults and set about pelting the stage with anything that comes to hand. John is the obvious target, but Glen is the first to fall victim when a Newcastle Brown Ale bottle smacks him squarely on the forehead almost knocking him clean off his feet. Frank Brunger's fiancée Diane Wagg, who also worked for EMI, had accompanied Nick Mobbs up to Manchester. Along with Mike Thorne, they'd taken up a position by the bar to watch the show. Fearing they might be deemed guilty by association, the four EMI staffers hurriedly retreated to the sanctuary of the dressing room.   Steve, already frustrated by the group's sloppy performance, finally loses his rag after being soaked in beer and challenges the perpetrator to come up on to the stage and face him like a man. The mood within the hall is darkening with each passing second, and the bouncers - fearing what might occur should someone in the crowd decide to accept Steve's challenge - rush toward the front of the stage and form a human barrier. With order appearing to have been restored the group launch into "Liar", but John inadvertently reignites the crowd's alcohol-fuelled antipathy on removing his bondage jacket to reveal a top adorned with Nazi ephemera. When Steve is forced to signal yet another delay so that he can try to sort out his guitar sound, he is instantly targeted by the same mindless idiots that were spitting at John earlier. He threatens to pull the show unless the spitting stops, but realising he's fighting a losing battle he tears into "No Future". This, however, serves as another flashpoint owing to the hot-heads at the bar having read all about the Sex Pistols' ditty which supposedly besmirched their beloved sovereign.

The Sex Pistols bring their set – and the evening - to an end with "Problems", and though the kids at the front plead for "No Fun", there will be no encore. On seeing the group filing from the stage, the troublemakers suddenly surge forward, but the bouncers are quick to respond and escort them back to the sanctuary of their dressing room.

♫♫♫

The hate mob gathered outside the venue was showing little sign of dispersing, and the police appeared to have left the bands to their fate. Malcolm had instructed Andy to take the bus back to the Arosa for safe-keeping with the intention of calling the hotel after the shows. If Andy returned now there was no telling what the mob might do to so tempting a target. He'd got the venue's manager to order several taxis, but the controller had warned that his drivers didn't like venturing out to Collyhurst at this hour. Malcolm couldn't blame them. The taxis had arrived, but Malcolm feared that anyone remotely resembling a Sex Pistol would be strung up from the nearest lamppost as soon as they stepped out the front door. Thankfully, Dave Goodman's flared dungarees and Afghan coat ensemble enabled him to venture outside unimpeded. With the assistance of the bouncers, Goodman had overseen the evacuations. Goodman was in the last of the taxis along with Rotten, Joe Strummer, Mick Jones, and The Clash's soundman Mickey Foot. As with the other taxis, the car was pelted with stones as it sped along Collyhurst Road. But some of the agitators recognised Rotten, and jumped in their own cars to give chase. Indeed, it was only after a *Sweeney*-esque, highspeed chase through Manchester's dimly-lit backstreets that the driver was able to shake off their pursuers. Rather than head for Withington, however, they had the driver take them into the city's celebrated Chinatown. They were relaxing in one of the restaurants reliving the evening when four men came through the door and settled themselves at a nearby table. At first the newcomers showed little interest in their fellow diners, but one of them recognised Rotten from the newspapers and the insults began to fly. Having survived repeated barrages of sticks and stones, the five weren't about to let a few insults bother them. But as the abuse grew more and more antagonistic, Goodman made a show of going to the toilets so that he might implore the restaurant's owner to allow him to use their phone. Ten or so minutes later the restaurant's door almost came off its hinges as Fat Freddie came bursting in. Freddie grabbed up a chair and planted his eighteenstone frame between his charges and their tormentors while Rotten and the others made their escape. The evening was to have one final twist, however. Upon their arrival back at the Arosa, Rotten and co. were stunned to find everyone else was on the bus. It seemed the hotel's manager had given in to the demands of his other guests and cancelled their booking. With no hope of finding alternate lodgings at that late hour – and with a five-day lay off before the replacement Caerphilly date – Malcolm was left with little option but to order Andy to make for the M1.

Chapter Thirteen

The Damned are off the tour following the incident in Derby where they said maybe they would play, and the Buzzcocks have replaced them.

Stiff Records stand to lose a lot of money because of the group leaving the tour, and the lack of venues for them to play subsequent to the present "punk" backlash. And if Stiff Records gets in serious trouble because of the Mary Whitehouse mentality of officialdom then it would be nothing short of a real obscenity. [We] spoke to Rick Rodgers of Stiff Records and Damned management: "I don't want to get into any bitching," he said, "It's just a shame."

New Musical Express, Saturday, 18 December 1976.

Glen had been hoping against hope that Malcolm would come up with something to avoid their return to London. If only because he knew the field day the newspapers would enjoy at announcing the Sex Pistols' tour had been derailed – albeit temporarily. However, unlike most black clouds of late, this one had a silver lining thanks to Mike Thorne's suggestion the band take advantage of the enforced layoff by coming into Manchester Square to work on some demos. With it being a Saturday, they had the studio to themselves. EMI employed two engineers to work alongside Thorne, but neither had proved willing to give up their weekend. The five songs Thorne had selected were "Liar", "Problems", "No Feelings", "Pretty Vacant", and "No Future". Although he'd unwittingly been responsible for giving life to "No Future", Glen had since voiced his concerns about the potential adverse public reaction to a song about the Queen with her Silver Jubilee less than six months off. It was all well and good John and Malcolm spouting off about the establishment's using the Jubilee celebrations as a means of papering over the cracks of a crumbling empire, but Joe Public was fond of the royal family. And the grief he'd be in for didn't bear thinking about! His mum was already planning what to bake for the street party on their road; while his Nan still treasured the souvenir tin she'd kept from King George V and Queen Mary's Silver Jubilee back in 1935 or whenever the hell it was. His concerns had ultimately been proved right, because when they'd unveiled the song at Lanchester Polytechnic in Coventry at the end of November, the Student Union there had refused to pay them their booking fee and accused them of being fascists. And Malcolm's pressuring them to rename the song "God Save The Queen" could only make things worse. He was still puzzled as to why Thorne would waste time recording "No Future" as there was sod all chance of EMI releasing it. Glen already knew that EMI were working towards "Pretty Vacant" being the Pistols' follow-up single. The label had, of course, pressed for "Vacant" to be the debut single, and it would have been had Rotten not spat his dummy out. He'd come up with the idea for "Pretty Vacant" from a handbill for a Richard Hell/Television show that Malcolm had brought back with him from New York. The handbill was peppered with song titles, one of which was "(I Belong To The) Blank Generation). Glen hadn't heard the song of course, but was familiar with the nihilistic and Dadaistic aspects the title conjured up from his reading up on 20th century art as part of his foundation course at St. Martin's. Malcolm had mentioned they should look to write their own song encapsulating the "Blank Generation" theme during a band discussion.

The general consensus around that time was the emptiness pervading the UK music scene – a real "situation vacant" feeling. Thinking how "pretty" was often used as a prefix to describe certain things or situations – "pretty good", "pretty naff", "pretty basic" etc – he'd come up with "Pretty Vacant" to encapsulate the malaise. He'd quickly put a melody to the lyric,

but couldn't shake the feeling that the tune wasn't echoing what he was trying to say. He'd often found that inspiration struck when least expected, and so it had proved with "Vacant". This was long before Malcolm put them on a weekly retainer, and he'd been steadily working his way through that week's giro in Moonies on Charing Cross Road when Abba's "SOS" came on the jukebox. He'd heard the song plenty of times before, of course, but that lunchtime all he'd heard was the song's simplistic repeated octave riff. All it had taken was to alter the riff slightly be putting in a fifth. He'd then melded the riff to the chord sequence for the chorus that he'd lifted from the Small Faces' "Wham Bam, Thank You Ma'am" and "hey presto". They'd first performed "Vacant" the night they'd played with Mr. Big in Welwyn Garden City, and had quickly become a crowd pleaser.

It wasn't that Glen didn't like "Anarchy". It was just that he thought the opening couplet was so cheesy. If John couldn't find anything to rhyme with "Antichrist", then he should have sharpened his pencil and have a rethink about the song's opening salvo. Regardless of whatever else he thought about John, there was no denying he was proving a gifted lyricist. A perfect example of John's prowess came in changing the line at the end of the second verse in "Vacant". Glen had written something along the lines of "If you don't like this, shove it up your bum", but John's changing it to read "Stop your cheap comments, 'cos we know what we know we're for real" was infinitely better! But rhyming "antiChrist" with "anarchist" just simply didn't work. Glen couldn't claim to be an expert when it came to recording studios, but he couldn't for the life of him understand why Thorne had opted to record the new demos in EMI's basic eight-track studio instead of hiring Wessex or Lansdowne again? After Lansdowne's state-of-the-art sixteen-track consol, reverting back to an eight-track consol was like driving down to Brighton in a Rolls Royce and coming back to London in a Ford Cortina. Steve and Paul had also surprisingly proved receptive to Thorne's suggestion. John, however, had showed up in a surly mood. Arsenal were apparently at home to Man United, and he'd anticipated having a jolly-up with his mates. He'd argued his corner all the way back to London and had only capitulated when Malcolm threatened to withhold his wages. When Glen arrived at Manchester Square that morning, he'd been praying that John would still carry out his threat and shy off from the recording session. This would have allowed him an opportunity to sound out Steve and Paul on what he saw as John's demigodlike behaviour since getting his mug in the newspapers. Although they'd been playing together for a couple of years before John joined, he'd long-since accepted that Steve and Paul would choose John over himself. However, if he could get them to understand that John's inflated ego meant that no one was safe from his sniping line, then it might not be too late to get John to accept that he was acting like a complete twat. It sounded good in theory, but he knew there was more chance of getting Steve and Paul to include "I Wanna Hold Your Hand" in the set than there ever was of getting them to side against John. And seeing as the three of them had just swanned off to the pub over the road together, he pushed the thought from his mind and instead began running through the catchy new bass line that he'd accidentally happened upon whilst messing around with the A scale. He was running through the bass line a second time when he sensed a presence in the doorway. It was Thorne. "That sounds really interesting, Glen," he said. "Does it have a title?" "It doesn't even have a middle-eight yet," Glen shrugged. "I was just messing about with the A-scale. But I think it's definitely got potential." "I'd say it's got more than that," Thorne enthused as he walked across to the consol. "I found myself humming along to it as I was coming along the corridor. What time can we expect the others back?" he asked. "Only I'd like to run through 'No Feeling' and 'Pretty Vacant' again before we call it a day.' "Call it a day?" Glen frowned. "But it's still early." "Well, it is a Saturday, after all," Thorne nodded. "But if we can run through 'Vacant' again, and get John's vocal laid down on 'Problems', I'd say it was a good day's work all round." Glen had to agree. Thanks to Thorne, they'd been able to forget about the on-going disaster that was unfolding around them - if only for one day. And despite the grumblings from certain quarters, they'd got quite a lot done. "I suppose it all depends on whether his Highness is holding court over in the Devonshire Arms," Glen shrugged. "Running through 'Vacant' and 'No Feelings' again, I mean." "You're referring to John, I take it?" "Who else," Glen sighed wearily, placing his bass on its stand. Thorne came out from behind the consol. "Look Glen, it's no secret around here that you and John haven't – shall we say – been seeing eye-to-eye of late." He paused and glanced towards the doorway before continuing. "And while we're all hoping the two of you can sort out your differences for the good of the group, I just want you to know that should that not turn out to be the case, then EMI would be more than willing to listen to any ideas you might have on a future away from the Sex Pistols." "What are you saying, Mike?" Glen asked, glancing towards the doorway. He was sure he'd heard a door bang to somewhere in the outer offices. Thorne had obviously heard the noise as well as he was following Glen's gaze. "I'm saying that we're all aware that you're the main composer within the Pistols," he said, turning back to face Glen. "John might write the lyrics, or the majority of the lyrics, but it's you who sets them to music." "Steve and Paul do their bit," Glen said, feeling slightly disloyal. "I'm not saying they don't," Thorne conceded. "I love Steve's guitar style, and Paul is one of the steadiest drummers I've worked with. But you have to admit they always follow your lead when it comes to structuring the tunes. Chris and Bill Price both said as much from when you recorded 'Anarchy' at Wessex. Anyway," he said hurriedly, on hearing familiar voices growing louder on the corridor, "I'm sure things won't come to that." "Won't come to what?"

Glen and Thorne both turned towards the open doorway to find John eyeing them suspiciously. "Oh . . . hi, John," Thorne said, glancing at his watch. "I didn't expect you back so soon," he added disarmingly. He walked over to the consol and slipped the headphones around his neck. "I was just saying to Glen that I was hoping that I won't have to get you to redo the vocal to 'Vacant'." "I fuckin' hope so," John snarled as he removed his coat and slung it over a chair. "I'm fed up with running through old stuff like 'Vacant' just for the fuckin' sake of it. If we have to be here on a Saturday, then we should be working on 'No Future' . . . seeing as it's a definite single." "We can give it another run-through before we wrap up," Thorne nodded. "What I want to do first though is have you run through 'Vacant' again and-" "You just said that we might not have to do 'Vacant' again," John spat. "It's gettin' a bit fuckin' tedious, Mike. We did 'Vacant', 'Problems', and 'No Feelings' at fuckin' Majestic with Chris Spedding back in May. And we've done 'em since with Dave Goodman at our place." Majestic Studios was owned by Mickie Most's RAK Records. Chris Spedding was the main session guitarist at RAK, but had appeared on albums by the likes of Harry Nilsson, Sharks, and Roxy Music. He'd also enjoyed a UK Top 20 hit with "Motor Bikin'" the previous autumn. Having caught one of the Pistols' early 100 Club shows, Spedding had petitioned Most to let him bring the Pistols into Majestic with a view to signing them to RAK. Nothing had come of the session, but it had at least allowed the band the chance to work in a proper studio. It was Spedding that had dragged the reluctant Chris Thomas along to the "Midnite Special" showcase at the Screen on the Green. Glen remembered that night at the 100 Club as Spedding had brought along his German girlfriend, Nora, who he'd since learned was reputedly the heiress to a newspaper fortune. She'd also apparently gone out with Jimi Hendrix at one time. Nora had dumped Spedding soon after the Majestic session after setting her sights on Steve; turning up at show after show. Steve had taken her out a few times before losing interest.

Rumour had it that John was now sniffing around. Thorne grabbed up his notepad and began leafing through the pages. "Alright, then; how about 'Problems'? There was a slight glitch with the vocals earlier, and-"

"No," John said emphatically. "We either do 'No Future', or I'm fuckin' out of here. I might still catch the second half of the match if I'm lucky . . ." On seeing Thorne remove his headphones Glen took a step towards his bass

"Mike; I'm happy to go over 'No Future' again. I mean, the lyrics aren't right yet; are they?" "And what's that's supposed to mean exactly?" John challenged, glancing towards the doorway as Steve and Paul came in.
"Well, you sang, 'God save the queen, God save Windolene' for starters"Sowhat if I fuckin' did?" John snapped.
"It was only a guide vocal, Glen," Thorne offered, hoping to prevent another argument. Though he'd known about how John and Glen hadn't been getting along of late, but until that moment he hadn't realised the gravity of the situation. What was equally perturbing was that Steve and Paul weren't doing anything to intervene. Steve was just staring at the floor, while Paul fiddled with the hi-hat. He could also surmise that the two had grown accustomed to John and Glen's constant bickering, and preferred to wait for the latest squall to blow over. "It's got fuck all to do with you what I choose to sing," John continued. "You're just the fuckin' bass player."
"I just think you should sing the correct lyric," Glen countered, suddenly happy to stand his ground thanks to his revelatory conversation with Thorne. "Like Mike said, it was only a guide vocal," John said in a mock pedantic tone. "So I could sing what I fuckin' hell I wanted. I don't tell you what to play, do I?"
"No, but-"
"And if you don't shut your hole, I'll change the lyric to 'God Save the Queen, Glen's a complete cunt!'" "There's only one of those around here," Glen muttered to himself as he turned away from John. "What did you say?" John challenged. "Nothing; a rude word . . . next insult," Glen chuckled to himself on parodying John's retort during the *Today* interview when Grundy had tried shaming him for swearing on air. "So, Steve, are you and Paul doing anything later?" Thorne asked, hoping to diffuse the situation. "I think we're meeting up with Simmo and Roadent," Steve said, glancing across at Paul as though seeking confirmation. Without waiting for confirmation that the session was at an end, he plucked his Les Paul from its stand and put it back in its flight case. "Yeah, we'll probably start off in the Cambridge if anyone else fancies

it," Paul said, taking his cue from Steve and coming out from behind the kit. Since their relocating to Denmark Street, The Cambridge had become the Pistols' preferred West End watering hole. "That's if we can get some more money out of Malcolm," he chuckled. "The cunt had better put his hand in his fuckin' pocket, cos I'm skint again," Steve growled, grabbing up his sheepskin coat. "I'd love to join you, but I've got a prior engagement," Thorne said. "But I expect I'll see you boys at some point during the coming week."
"You're not coming to Caerphilly, then?" Glen asked Thorne. "No, I-"
"You shit yourself in Manchester," Steve cut in. "Well, there's no denying the Electric Circus show was something of an eye-opener," Thorne smiled.
"More like a head-opener," Glen said, nursing the bruise from where the Newcastle Brown Ale bottle had struck him. "I'd love to come to Caerphilly," Thorne said, turning to face Glen. "But I've got something on that night as well, I'm afraid." "Yeah, what's she called?" Steve grinned. "And more importantly, does she have a friend with big tits?" "No such luck, I'm afraid, Steve," Thorne sighed. "It's work-related. There's a group from Newcastle that Nick is interested in checking out. They're playing the Marquee, and he's badgered me and Fletch from EMI International into going along with him." "Well, you can tell them Geordies from me that they'll have to fuckin' behave themselves on stage," John chuckled. "They can be a bit touchy at the Marquee." "Ah yes, but that's only when the group is into chaos rather than the music, John," Thorne smiled, remembering Steve's tongue-in-cheek quip that Neil Spencer had tagged onto the end of his Marquee review.

♪♪♪

Following on from The Cambridge, Steve, Roadent, and the two Pauls made their way over to The Speakeasy on Margaret Street. The late-night private drinking club was regarded as the music industry's premier London watering hole. It had first opened its doors a decade earlier in 1966 when the capital was in mid-swing and on any given night the clientele might include The Beatles, The Stones, The Who, Led Zeppelin, Elton John, or David Bowie; all of whom were also known to have taken to the club's small stage on occasion. Such was the club's reputation that an end-of-tour stop-off was considered something of a prerequisite for any self-respecting American group. "How did it go today?" Simonon asked after taking the top off of his lager. He'd always got on well with the two Sex Pistols, but the tour had brought them even closer. "We got quite a bit done, as it happens," Paul replied. "Yeah,

when John and Glen weren't at each other's fuckin' throats!" Steve added, accepting a pint from Roadent. Hearing this caused Paul to almost choke on his pint. "What was that?" he spluttered. "I can't imagine Glen being at anyone's throat; let alone John's." "Steve's over-egging the pudding a bit there," his namesake chuckled. "But there's no denying Glen stood his corner." "Glen and John have never really got on," Steve shrugged. "But even I was shocked at some of the things John's said to Glen while we were out on the road." "You'll lose Glen if you're not careful," said Roadent. "Nah, never happen," Steve shook his head. "He's got it too good." "I wouldn't be too sure about that, mate," Simonon said. "I wouldn't put up with Joe or Mick saying stuff like that. They can take the piss out of my bass playin', cos I'm still learnin' while they've both been playin' for ages. But if they ever made it personal I'd give them a slap." "I can't see Glen clocking John one," Steve chuckled. "But you have to admit there's been a change in Glen since what happened on the *Today* show," Paul said. "He never used to stand up to John like he's done of late. And he was even more cock sure today." "Maybe you should swap bass players?" Roadent said. "Maybe we should," Steve nodded. "I mean, you get on alright with John, don't you?' he said to Simonon. "And that way Glen could spend even more time with his new bum chum, Mick."
"It's a good job Johnny or Jerry ain't here tonight," Roadent interjected, looking over to where the club's owner Laurie O'Leary was in conversation with Bob Harris. "Jerry would give him a good kickin' for his 'mock rock' comment." "I'm tempted to go over and give the bald-headed cunt a slap myself," Simonon said eyeing Harris. "There's a musical revolution sweepin' the country, and he can't see what's going on under his fuckin' nose!" "That's 'Bernie speak' if ever I heard it," Roadent grinned. "But 'Whispering Bob' will get what's coming to him soon enough," he added while pretending to scribble Harris' name into an imaginary black book as Harris and O'Leary came past their table heading for the restaurant. 'Whose round is it?" Steve asked, draining his glass. "Don't look at me," Roadent shrugged. "All I've had out of Bernie of late is a new pair of fuckin' socks. And that was down to Mick!" "I'll get 'em," Simonon said getting to his feet. "But you can give us a hand," he said to Roadent before making his way over to the bar. Steve waited until Simonon and Roadent were out of earshot. "Do you reckon John would go for it?" he asked Paul. "Go along with swapping Simmo for Glen, I mean." Paul glanced over to the bar. "He's still learnin' to play." "Yeah, but he'd look good in an Anarchy shirt . . ."

Chapter Fourteen

Punk rock – we don't want it either
As representatives of a variety of Christian opinion in Caerphilly, we feel bound to protest against the decision of our local Castle Cinema management to engage a "punk rock group" already notorious for its dependence on obscenity, blasphemy, and open violence.

We are saddened to think that an act which has been dropped by a Cardiff management as altogether too depraved, would be deemed quite suitable for a Caerphilly audience.

G. Edwards-Benyon Secretary, Caerphilly Free Church Council, and H Lewis Clarke (Rector)

Malcolm was lost in thought as the coach ambled along Caerphilly's main thoroughfare. With the exception of the occasional passer-by the road appeared completely deserted. And while the weather was no doubt playing its part, every shop, café, or public house they passed was closed for business. The eyrie stillness reminded him of a scene from the Sixties horror film, *Village Of The Damned*, but he suspected the reason for the apparent absence of life in the Welsh market town wasn't down to the weather. Nor was it due to it having been taken over by diminutive blonde-haired, blue-eyed aliens, but rather the imminent arrival of the Sex Pistols. That the show was going ahead at all was solely down to the determination of the Castle Cinema's owner, Pauline Uttley. The vice-chairman of Rhymney Valley District Council – a Madeline Ryland, if memory served - had been so incensed that Uttley was happy to allow the Sex Pistols across her threshold that she'd threatened to take out a high court action to stop the show from proceeding. Unfortunately for Ryland, however, the council's legal team had advised her of the futility of seeking redress in the high court owing to the show having been arranged at short notice. Over the last few days Malcolm had developed something of phobia where local councils were concerned, and before setting off from London that morning he'd called Uttley to satisfy himself that it wouldn't prove a wasted journey. Not only had she assured him that the show would go ahead come what may, she'd regaled him with an article concerning the show that had appeared in that morning's local newspaper. It seemed that having been denied legal recourse, Ms Ryland was letting it be known that she and her council colleagues intended to voice their displeasure at the "punk rock invasion of their town" by staging a protest in the car park opposite the cinema. She was calling on the people of Caerphilly to join them in their protest. She was also quoted as saying how those same people were horrified at reports of the Sex Pistols' previous concerts in Wales, and that she and her fellow councillors felt their constituents shouldn't have to be subjected to such treatment. The only politics that interested Malcolm were the politics of boredom, but he readily recognised political manoeuvrings when he saw them. Indeed, it would appear the Sex Pistols were to be used as a political pawn by every facet of Rhymney Valley's District Council as according to the article, Caerphilly's Labour and Conservative group leaders would be joining Ryland in her car park protestations.

♪♪♪

The previous Friday afternoon Malcolm had paid a visit to Manchester Square with the intention of bringing Leslie Hill up to speed with the tour. He'd also hoped to convince Hill that EMI should honour its original commitments to the tour as the two shows played to date had only brought in revenue of £1,198 against the £9,000 costing the tour itinerary had thus far incurred. Again, Hill had proved sympathetic, and had again given Malcolm his personal assurance that he would do everything within his capacity as Managing Director of EMI Records to fight the Sex Pistols' corner. Suspecting that Hill's support might not hold much sway with his bosses, Malcolm had demanded to see Sir John Read. Perhaps unsurprisingly, Hill had informed him that there was no way Read would ever design to meet with Malcolm in person. However, Hill had admitted that he himself had come to recognise that while EMI strove to behave within contemporary limits of decency and good taste, what passed for "rigid traditional conventions" within one section of society, didn't necessary transcend to other more liberal sections. With this in mind, he'd instructed EMI's Director of Public Affairs, Bryan Samain, to organise a behind-closeddoors meeting in order to explore all avenues as to where a corporation such as EMI should draw the line in regard to morals, manners, and taste. Amongst those invited to express their views at the meeting were non-executive directors former Attorney General Lord Shawcross, Conservative Shadow Cabinet Minister Geoffrey Howe, and Lord Wolfenden, who was also a part-time director of Thames TV. Thames TV was represented by Jeremy Isaacs, Howard Thomas and Verity Lambert, while Nat Cohen was there on behalf of EMI Films. Hill and Bob Mercer would be there to represent EMI Records. There were also EMI's American interests to consider. In recent years, EMI had apparently invested heavily to expand its brain scanner business – most notably the revolutionary CAT scanner. As the corporation's CEO, Read was naturally anxious that sensationalist headlines in US newspapers about the Sex Pistols might jeopardise potential sales. Hill had personally thought Read was worrying unnecessarily, because while there were those occupying the rarefied air of Manchester Square's sixth floor who would jump at the chance to point an accusatory finger at the Sex Pistols should EMI's projected sales of its new CAT scanner fall short of the mark, the American music market was showing little or no interest in either the Sex Pistols or punk rock in general. On a lighter note, Hill told Malcolm about Paul Watts' recent encounter with Cliff Richard. During a wine and dine PR exercise on the eve of Cliff's forthcoming UK tour, the holier-than-thou Cliff had voiced his displeasure at his being on the same record label as the Sex Pistols. Watts had tried shrugging the whole thing off by saying, "Okay, so they went on TV and said 'fuck', which, needless to say, had made for a rather uncomfortable evening. With personal assurances being all Malcolm had to go on of late, the previous afternoon he'd called a group meeting at Dryden Chambers in order to discuss the latest developments with EMI. Doubts about the Sex Pistols' long-term future with EMI were naturally causing some friction within the group – with Glen bearing the brunt of the infighting. Following the meeting, however, he'd been surprised to learn that the backbiting wasn't solely reserved for their long suffering bassist as his own actions were now receiving close scrutiny - and from a totally unexpected quarter. Sophie had apparently overheard Steve - whom he'd always perceived to be his strongest ally within the group - questioning his behaviour in the wake of the *Today* fiasco to John. It would seem Steve suspected him of contacting the promoters at various venues and purposely frightening them off in order to keep the headlines rolling in. Yet whilst he'd been surprised that it had been Steve and not John who'd voiced said accusations, he was secretly thrilled that Steve would think him capable of carrying out such an audacious caper. Being the manager of a pop group was certainly a lot more trouble than he had first envisaged when agreeing to help them. He could only begin to imagine how difficult it must have been for his hero, the legendary Fifties pop impresario Larry Parnes, who'd had a whole host of temperamental stars on his roster. But then again, none of Larry's acts would have dreamed of calling Richard Baker or Kenneth Kendall a "fucking rotter"; at least not whilst the cameras were rolling.

♪♪♪

Glen was oblivious to the ghostly goings-on on the other side of the window as he'd finally gotten his hands on a copy of that week's *NME* at the last service station. Given that it was the paper's first issue in the wake of the *Today* saga, they'd devoted several pages to the incident - including a full transcript of the now-infamous interview - along with reports on the devastating consequences it had had on both the Sex Pistols, and the tour. The front cover bore the banner headline: '100 SECONDS THAT P*NK ROCKED FLEET STREET', along with an image of a stand-alone television set with a photographic still taken from the interview showing on its screen. The cover also carried a caveat, which had nothing to do with the unexpurgated transcript contained within its pages, but rather because that week's issue had been forced to go to press incomplete owing to on-going industrial action at the printing plant. He'd got such a buzz from seeing the cover as it showed a true measure of support at *NME*. The *NME* usually came out on a Thursday along with the other leading music papers, but owing to an industrial dispute, it hadn't come out until today. There'd been some coverage in *Melody Maker* and *Sounds*, but nothing complimentary. And while *Record Mirror* had nailed its colours to the Pistols mast, the *NME* was the paper that truly counted. "Let's have a butcher's," Mick said, playfully snatching at the paper. "Hold your horses," Glen retorted, pulling the paper away again. Satisfied that Mick wouldn't make another grab he opened the paper; his eyes being instantly drawn to the lead article on page two: 'Chaos on the U.K. tour '76'. To his chagrin the photograph accompanying the article was of John rather than the band as a whole. He wasn't surprised to find the *NME* following the tabloids' lead because while Steve was the Sex Pistol that had caused the uproar with his colourful usage of the English vernacular, he'd been largely overlooked due to his lacking a headline-grabbing moniker. "Steve Jones" was the guy who cleaned your windows, whereas "Johnny Rotten" was the spawn of Satan. "Is there any mention of us in there?" Mick asked. "You'll have to wait and see, won't you," Glen teased. "If you were that keen to find out what's going on you should grabbed yourself a copy while we were at the services." "I would have done, but Bernie ain't paid us our wages yet." "This makes a change," Glen mused. "What, me being skint?" Mick frowned. "Nah, that's old news," Glen grinned. "Your being skint is as natural as night following day. I was referring to this" – he turned the paper so that Mick could see the article he was referring to – "It's nice to read an article which actually sticks up for us for a change." Mick leaned in to peruse the article. "Mike Mansfield's being generous, I see," he said, stabbing a finger at the paragraph in which the renowned producer - who'd directed the Sex Pistols' promo video for "Anarchy in the UK" – was comparing them to the Rolling Stones, before going on to opine how he believed the group's calculated approach to the music industry was going to make them very successful. "Well, being compared to the Stones never does anyone any harm does it?" Glen mused.

"Tell that to Johnny and Jerry," Mick grinned. "Johnny was tellin' us how the Stones had been considering signin' the Dolls to their own label. They didn't go ahead 'cos of David Johansen's lookin' a bit too much like Jagger." Glen didn't respond as he was too engrossed in reading Malcolm's refutation of his supposedly having staged the band's confrontation with Grundy for publicity purposes. It still baffled him that people could think it had been pre-planned or stage-managed. Grundy had baited Steve, and once he'd got a reaction he'd goaded him on. Sure, Steve was pissed, but if Grundy had have been sober he'd have thought twice about telling Steve to say "something outrageous. And Malcolm was right in saying that while the language Steve used might cause offence, it was nonetheless part of everyday vernacular.

"I see Genesis are getting a new drummer," Glen said, pulling the paper closer while pretending to read the article. "Who cares?" "And Tommy Brolin, the ex-Deep Purple guitarist, has died from a heart attack at twenty-five," he teased. "You'll be joinin' him on the slab if you don't get a shufty on," Mick retorted, making another playful grab for the paper. "Well tough titties, cos I wanna read about Bob Marley being shot." Glen already knew about the attempt on Marley's life, but this was the first time he'd seen anything about the incident in print. According to the article, Marley had been hit in the chest and arm when five gunmen – all apparently armed with automatic weapons – had attacked the singer's Kingston home the previous Friday. Marley's wife Rita had also been wounded in the attack, while his manager, Don Taylor, was still on the critical list having been struck by five bullets. Though no arrests had yet been made, it was assumed the attack was a politically motivated assassination attempt over Marley's decision to perform at a free concert at Kingston's National Arena on Sunday, 12 December. It seemed that Jamaica's impending general election had been dogged by political violence between the supporters of the incumbent Prime Minister, Michael Manley's PNP party, and the opposing JLP party. Manley had been quoted saying that he believed the CIA was involved in engineering the violence. Marley, although having publicly supported Manley during his successful 1972 election campaign, had as yet not done so during the current campaign; although Sunday's concert had originally been scheduled to take place on the front lawn of Manley's presidential palace. The recuperating Marley was quoted as saying that there was no political motive behind his decision to perform at the concert. And that he'd merely wanted to "play for the love of the people." "Did you know The Wailers were in the house at the time of the shootings?" Glen asked Mick, glancing up from the article. "Amazingly none of them were hurt."

"They'd have probably been too stoned to notice what was going on anyhow," Mick offered. "I mean, Bob's only gonna have top quality Ganja in his private stash." "Jesus, is that all you think about these days?"
"Aside from rock and roll and sex, it is," Mick grinned. "Speaking of good weed, I hope Goodman's replenished his stash whilst he was back in London."

♫♫♫

Glen had little need in reading the fully-transcribed *Today* interview in the *NME*'s tonguein-cheek *Thrills* section. Instead, he focused his attention on Julie Burchill's article – entitled 'And After All That, The Dear Lads Tussle With The City Fathers' - relating to the group's no-show before Derby's Leisure Committee on page six. He'd chatted briefly with the Bristol-born Burchill backstage at Leeds Polytechnic, and been slightly taken aback that she was only seventeen-years-old. He remembered her saying how she'd only recently been taken on by the *NME* after responding to the paper's call to arms for two "hip young gunslingers" to write about the emerging punk movement. She'd apparently got the gig by penning a eulogy of Patti Smith's *Horses*, and had abandoned her A-Levels on joining the paper. The *NME*'s other "gunslinger", Tony Parsons, was also covering the tour. He'd observed the two together both in Leeds as well as Manchester, and couldn't yet decide whether their relationship was strictly professional. He had to admit that he liked Julie's style of writing, even though she'd started off her article with a pronouncement about how the man on the desk at EMI House apparently thought the Sex Pistols to be "a bunch of stupid kids", whilst likening the Pistols to a dose of venereal disease – at least in the eyes of Derby's upstanding citizens. She'd then gone on to give a somewhat light-hearted account of the band's encounter with the Leisure Committee, before echoing Leslie Hill's claims about the sizeable contingent of the National Front outside the Kings Hall on the day of the aborted show, and that the ultraright-wing party was threatening to align itself with the Sex Pistols. This tidbit, when taken in context with the rest of the article, could be viewed as nothing more than an aspiring journalist's attempt to spice things up by adding a little political flavour to their piece. But to his mind it posed serious implications for the Sex Pistols. John and Steve had both worn clothing bearing Nazi imagery at the Electric Circus show, and this could be misconstrued as the group having fascist or racist leanings. And right about now this was the last thing they needed. The NME's concert-listings featured the original tour dates. Those that had bought tickets for tonight's original date at the Cardiff Top Rank would most likely know about switch to Caerphilly, but trying to keep up with the ongoing cancellations and everchanging replacement dates was like playing hopscotch blindfold on a minefield. Tomorrow night's date at the Glasgow Apollo had been one of the first to fall, with Scotland's Lord Provost declaring Scotland had enough hooligans of its own to contend with without importing them from over the border. And boy oh boy, hadn't that one tickled John! Malcolm had been quick to line up a replacement date at Lafayette's in Wolverhampton, but that had also fallen through. Thursday's show at Dundee's Caird Hall was also a no-go, as was the following evening's show at Sheffield City Hall. Malcolm's attempts to seek an alternate port in the storm at Carlisle's Market Hall had since fallen foul of local council interference. Saturday's show at Southend's Kursaal had been an early casualty, and the mooted replacement at Skindles in nearby Maidenhead had also longsince gone tits up. Glen knew that Malcolm was still intent on finding another alternate venue, but the majority of those onboard were hoping he'd fail in his task as they'd be able to take up the *NME*'s invitation to their Christmas shindig at Dingwalls. From what Tony Parsons had told him, they'd be able to gorge themselves silly as well as drink their own bodyweight in lager. They would have to be up at the crack of dawn the following morning as Malcolm had booked a second date at the Electric Circus in Manchester to replace the cancelled show at Guildford's Civic Hall. But at least they'd have plenty of time to sleep off their hangovers. With Parsons and Julie Burchill having both been in attendance at the Leeds Polytechnic show, Glen would have been surprised if there hadn't been a review. He chuckled to himself on reading Parsons' opening salvo about how Malcolm's mate Kenny Anger had once called James Dean a human ashtray. Parson's had actually approached John backstage and asked him about the burns. John had packed him off with a flea in his ear. Parsons had sought revenge in likening John to an "amphetamine corpse from a Sunday gutter press dream", before waxing lyrical about the amphetamine corpse's stage antics and his "dementoid vocal". He was pleased to see his own performance on the night hadn't gone unnoticed. He especially liked Parson's citing his and Paul's playing as being "tighter than tomorrow". "You remember that kid Tony Parsons that's working for the *NME*? Glen said, angling the paper. "He's penned a review of the Leeds show. You get a mention . . ." "Yeah, what's he say?" "That you look like 'Keith Richard's grandson'." "Fuckin' cheek!"

The *NME*'s centre pages featured an article/interview with George Harrison relating to the ex-Beatle having been found guilty of copyright infringement by a US court earlier in the year over his 1971 hit, "My Sweet Lord". Bright Tunes, which owned the copyright to The Chiffon's 1963 hit, "He's So Fine", had issued the writ claiming Harrison had lifted the melody to the latter song. Harrison had attended the trail, going so far as to bring his acoustic guitar into the court to play the tune. Despite the high-profile busking session, Harrison was deemed guilty of having "subconsciously" copied the tune owing to his being aware of the Chiffons' song. Glen chuckled to himself while pondering what his reaction would be should Abba's management company Polar Music issue a similar writ against himself for lifting the riff to "SOS". Plagiarism was a grey area. After all, there were only twelve notes on the chromatic scale, and it was therefore inevitable that some tunes would sound similar to others without the musician in question having knowingly straying into plagiaristic waters. There was also an interview with Eddie & the Hot Rods' frontman, Barry Masters. Glen had no interest in reading what Masters had to say, but before turning the page he quickly scanned the text to see whether there was any mention of the Marquee show. There wasn't. "Would you Adam and Eve it," he said on turning the page towards Mick. "Believe what?" Mick asked. "Oh yeah," he deadpanned, on seeing the full-page advert for Santana's forthcoming sell-out show at the Hammersmith Odeon. "I've asked me Nan to get me their new album for Christmas." "Oh good, you can tape it for me," Glen shot back. "But I wasn't referring to Santana, was I. I was referring . . . to . . . this . . ." he opened out the paper so that Mick could see
the opposite page and the attendant article: 'Eighteen Flight Rock, and the sound of the Westway.' Accompanying the interview was a photo of a pensive-looking Joe sporting his paint-splattered "Passion is a Fashion" shirt, with smaller postage stamp-sized images of Mick, Paul, and Rob Harper.

"Give us it!" Mick snapped, grabbing the paper from Glen. "Oi, Joe, Paul, that interview we did with Barry a few days ago is in here," he shouted without taking his eyes from the page. "I see the singer's the one hogging the limelight again," Glen said dryly, casting an eye over at John as Joe and Paul Simonon came bounding over and slid into the seats directly behind him and Mick. Instead of sitting down, the two knelt on the seats while resting their arms on the headrests. "Barry's even put some of the lyrics to our songs in here," Mick beamed. "He's also reviewed our ICA show," he added, twisting around in his seat so that he could see Joe and Paul. "He says that we sounded like the fuckin' Ramones." "And that's a compliment?" John guffawed. "Too right, it is," Joe grinned. "Only Barry thinks our songs are better; impressive, huh?"

"But your new best friend ain't all that accurate in his reporting, is he?" Glen said. "Whad'ya mean?" Joe asked. Glen stabbed a finger at the page. "Well, for starters he's not only got your name wrong," he said, glancing up at Simonon, "he's credited your photo as being Terry Chimes. And Rob, who - as you keep insisting - isn't actually a member of the band - is credited as Paul." "He got my name right at least," Mick grinned.

"Oh well, that's alright then," Joe said, leaning over and snatching the paper from Glen's hands. "I haven't finished with it yet," Glen snapped. "I always read the Lone Groover." "Fuck the 'Lone Groover'," Joe retorted. "Besides, I'm a better cartoonist than this Benyon cunt." "Then how come the only thing you were drawin' before joining up with us was the dole?" Simonon quipped. Whereas Joe and Mick had opted for Art School as it was infinitely preferable to gainful employment, Simonon's portfolio had led to his being given a grant for the prestigious Byam Shaw School of Art in Paddington.

"Fuck off," Joe said, playfully elbowing Simonon's arm. "C'mon, let's go show Roadent." With that he and Paul got to their feet and scurried down the aisle to where their roadie was sitting with Keeth Paul. "What did you think of the bit where Joe said we're 'anti-fascist, anti-violence, antiRacist, against ignorance, but pro-creative'?" Mick asked Glen. "What am I supposed to think about it?" Glen asked. "If you're supposed to be so 'antiviolent', why was Joe playing with a flick-knife throughout the interview?' "Joe was just usin' the knife to explain to Barry the difference between ordinary violence and creative violence." "Creative violence," Glen spluttered. "Twelve months ago Joe was playin' in the 101ers and calling himself 'Woody'!"

Chapter Fifteen

Chaos on the U.K. tour '76

THE SEX PISTOLS' debut tour was almost destroyed his week as a result of hostile publicity following their controversial two minute television interview.

· University, and Rank Leisure Group officials tried to hurriedly ban the four group Punk Package from appearing. At the beginning of the week no less than 12 venues scheduled to present this show refused to do so.

The Pistols' recording future was also uncertain when top EMI directors pledged to investigate the group's reported behaviour, on and off camera. Unrepentant, the Pistols and the other bands involved were determined to play a national tour, although it is certain they will suffer a financial loss, and on Monday played their first concert at Leeds Polytechnic; originally scheduled to be the fourth date of the tour.

New Musical Express, Saturday, 11 December 1976.

Upon their arrival at the Castle Cinema, Malcolm once again had everyone remain aboard the coach while he went in search of Pauline Uttley. It was a refreshing change arriving at their destination without being besieged by the media. However, if what Malcolm had told them about the proposed council protest, he suspected it wouldn't be long before the reporters came crawling out of the woodwork. They'd stopped off at their digs en route, and Glen hadn't been surprised to find that it ranked alongside the Arosa in Manchester in terms of mediocrity. With EMI having put their wallet away, the days of five-star accommodation were seemingly at an end. The cinema wasn't much to look at from the outside either. While it would suffice as a makeshift venue, its being a cinema meant it lacked the prerequisite licensed bar facilities. This meant that after completing their respective soundchecks, the three groups would be left with nothing to do other than count down the minutes until showtime. Malcolm must have sensed the potential pitfalls several hours of enforced inactivity might bring, and having spoken with Uttley he sent Nils and Dave Goodman into the town centre in search of a pub or an off-licence willing to put profit before protest. Unfortunately for all concerned the duo returned twenty or so minutes later empty-handed except for a handbill one of the locals had pressed into Goodman's hand while they were returning to the cinema.

IS ANARCHY THE ANSWER????

Does the Sex Pistols' Anarchy in the UK tour offer the real answer to the needs of Youth? What is the meaning of this latest controversial trend in the pop world? Oddly enough, this group's own reported use of the word 'antichrist' indicates the answer.

This term describes the essence of the spirit of rebellion against all that God stands for. Even though apparently just a passing fad, therefore, such trends are clearly in part fulfilment of Jesus' prophecy that before His return to earth, wickedness would multiply beyond all previous limits. The rise of such rampant evil is a direct result of national rejection of God. Scripture warns when this happens He abandons men to vile affections, dishonouring their own bodies.

So great becomes the degeneration that, although fully aware of God's righteous judgement that they who do such things deserve to die, they not only do them themselves, but actually approve and applaud others who practice them. The iniquity of this day will culminate in the worst period of judgement ever known in human history. When God arises in wrath, the very ground we stand on will shake. The Bible says it will be so terrifying that men will actually pass out at the thought of the things which are coming. But there is hope: not for the Earth, but for individuals. They who turn from their wicked ways, and experience the amazing grace which transforms the heart will escape the wrath to come. The power of Christ breaks unclean thoughts and habits. Jesus is the friend of sinners:

He died both to forgive our sin and to offer His life to overcome tyranny. 'The vilest offender who truly believes, that moment from Jesus a pardon receives.' Come and join us at the Elim Church, St Fagan's St, Caerphilly, this Sunday at 6.30 p.m. (Tel: 883007). Meet young people who can testify further of the reality of God's power to break the hold of sinful habits, and to satisfy without needing modern trends.

Malcolm ran his eyes over the handbill. "Where on earth did you get this?" he asked Goodman. "Some bible-basher shoved it in my hand as we were coming back up the rise," Goodman said. "Can't think how the guy knew we had anything to do with the tour." "Really?" Malcolm smiled to himself. Goodman's dungarees and Afghan coat attire might have allowed him to pass for one of the locals again, but Nils' spiked hair alone was a dead giveaway. "We saw a van with 'BBC Wales' written on the side," Goodman continued. "It was parked up in the town. "Can you believe they asked us for directions on how to get here?" "Well, I hope you didn't tell them!" Malcolm snapped. "What harm is it going to do, Malc?" Goodman sighed. "Come to think of it, we should have hung around and cadged a lift." Malcolm walked towards the doors and peered through the glass towards the car park where he imagined those responding to Madeleine Ryland's rallying call would shortly be gathering. "I was hoping the poor weather might deter the protests," he said, glancing up at the darkening skies. "Once the townsfolk get wind of a television camera they'll come here in their droves, if only in the hope of getting their face onscreen."

♪♪♪

With the soundchecks completed Glen wandered through into the foyer to find Malcolm in discussion with a dark-haired woman he assumed was the cinema's owner. He heard her saying something about her telling the local newspaper that she had no opinion on the Sex Pistols one way or the other; that it wasn't her job to serve as a public censor. Rather than eavesdrop on their conversation he continued over to the doors. He cupped his hands to the glass, and was surprised to find scores of people packed inside the car park opposite, with many others approaching along the road in both directions. At that moment the protesters burst into the Lutheran-hymnal "Oh, Come All Ye Faithful". He was second-guessing which hymn the protesters might offer up next when the surrealism of the situation went into overdrive. The grim-faced pastor that was leading the protesters in song through a megaphone from his makeshift podium suddenly launched into vitriolic rant about how he wanted the people of Wales to know that he'd had done everything within his power to stop the Sex Pistols coming to Caerphilly. Listening to the pastor hamming it up for the television cameras, he couldn't help wonder if the clergyman wasn't enjoying his Warholian fifteen minutes in the spotlight? Glen was turning away from the door when he spotted a familiar figure come bounding out of the car park entrance and across the road. It was Julien Temple, the rookie film maker, who'd spent the last six months or so gathering footage of the Sex Pistols both on and off stage. At Malcolm's behest, he was serving as the tour's official documenter. He'd filmed the Sex Pistols on stage at both Leeds Polytechnic and the Electric Circus, but only on Malcolm's strict proviso that he film partial clips of the group on stage. After graduating from King's College, Cambridge, Temple had enrolled at the National Film and Television School in Beaconsfield where he'd originally intended on make a film about The Kinks for his senior film thesis. After accidentally happening upon the London punk scene, however, he'd abandoned the Kinks project in favour of the Sex Pistols. Glen knew full well that the underlying factor in this arrangement wasn't due to whatever filmmaking talents Temple possessed, but rather because he had free and unlimited access to his school's equipment. Temple had filmed the Sex Pistols on stage at both Leeds Polytechnic and the Electric Circus, but only on Malcolm's strict proviso that he film partial clips of the band onstage. Malcolm had issued the caveat because while the Sex Pistols had been plastered across every newspaper in the land, he wanted to maintain an air of mystery surrounding the band. He was powerless to prevent members of the audience from making secret audio recordings to sell on the black market, but he was determined there would be very little in the way of visual footage. Limiting Temple's access was one way of ensuring this.

"Would you believe I bumped into Leee and the Heartbreakers earlier?" Temple grinned. "They'd been up to see the castle." "You don't get many castles in New York," Glen smiled. He'd caught sight of the castle's outer wall when alighting from the bus, but he'd felt no urge to go exploring. "Where's Malcolm?" Temple asked, glancing about the foyer. "Oh, you'll remember Janice, won't you?" he added, casually indicating towards the striking blonde he'd brought along to serve as his assistant. Glen smiled at Janice before responding. "He's around here some . . . there he is," he said, on seeing Malcolm emerge from Pauline Uttley's office. Malcolm had already spotted Temple and was striding towards them. "Where the hell have you been?" he growled. "I've been over in the car park," Temple said, jerking a thumb over his shoulder towards the doors. "We've got some great footage." Malcolm calmed down on hearing this. "It is all rather bizarre, isn't it," he smiled ruefully. "All this fuss over a pop concert; anyone would think it was the Salem witch trials! If it wasn't bloody freezing out there, I'd go over and challenge that idiot with the megaphone to write a sermon about the state of the country!" "Just remember to give me sufficient notice if you do, because I'll need to set up the camera," Temple grinned. "There's a BBC Wales film crew set up over there?" "So I've been informed." "I heard their anchor asking some old boy why he'd ventured out on such a cold night. You should have heard his response. It was brilliant, wasn't it, Janice?"
"Enlighten me." "He said he was here tonight because he was a 'recognised Christian'." "And what was the reporter's response?" Malcolm asked, going over to the door and peering out through the glass panels as though he might recognise this paragon of righteousness by the illuminated halo poised above his head. "He didn't get chance," Temple replied, as he and Janice joined him at the door, "because some woman burst in on them and began ranting on about this" – he swept his hand through the air – "having nothing to do with Christianity. She thought it was disgusting'-" "And 'degrading'," Janice interjected. "That it was 'disgusting' *and* 'degrading' that her children were being exposed to such things," Temple continued. "She then started harping on about if she thought one of her brood was in here, she'd come in and drag them out." "Well, there's nothing we can do about what's going on out there," Malcolm sighed wearily. "You might as well go on through into the cinema and find the best spot to set up your camera." "I also got talking to one of the local Labour councillors," Temple said. "Can you believe his name was Ray Davies? Ray Davies is the lead singer in the Kinks. It's kinda ironic that I was going to use the Kinks for my thesis, don't you think?" "You should have had

him ask the protesters if they know the words to 'Johnny Thunder'," Glen grinned.

♪♪♪

Caerphilly was the first date with a reduced billing and Malcolm had taken refuge in Pauline Utley's office to sort out the amended time slots for each band to go onstage. He'd just finished when Nils popped his head around the door. "Perfect timing for a change," he said handing the slip of paper to Nils. Nils pocketed the slip without looking at it. "There's a guy called Brian Case outside. He says he's been commissioned by The *Observer Magazine* to do a special feature on the Pistols and punk rock." "*Sex* Pistols," Malcolm chided him, coming out from behind the desk. Though he'd never met Case in person, Malcolm knew that aside from his working for the broadsheets, he was also the *NME*'s jazz critic. The tabloids had been harassing the Sex Pistols at every turn, but here was an opportunity to get the band's message across to a more discerning audience. "Brian, how nice to meet you," he beamed, extending a hand to Case on following Nils out of the office. "Nils has told me the reason you're here. Might I ask what angle you're intending to use in your article?"
"To be perfectly honest with you, Malcolm, I haven't decided yet," Case shrugged. "But I can assure you I'm not just looking to offer ubiquitous similarities between the Sex Pistols and the early Rolling Stones or the Beatles." "I'm relieved to hear it," Malcolm nodded. "Come on, I'll take you through to meet the boys." "One idea I had while driving up here was to link the Sex Pistols to other groups that have possessed a similar street gang mentality," Case said, falling in behind Malcolm and Nils. "Such as . . .?" Malcolm paused. "Well, the Ramones are a contemporary group that obviously springs to mind," Case offered. "But I thought maybe tracing a direct line through from the fifties . . . starting with Dion & the Belmonts."
"It's certainly an interesting approach," Malcolm said as they made their way through into the cinema's backstage area which was serving as a communal dressing room. "But as wonderful as Dion was, I doubt that John would ever consider himself to be a 'Doowopper'."

♪♪♪

When Malcolm brought Case through into the backstage area John and Paul were sat away from everyone else with two lads; one of whom was nervously fiddling around with a portable tape recorder. He vaguely remembered Nils having mentioned something about a couple of local kids wanting to interview the band for their fanzine. "Looks like you'll have to wait line, Brian," Malcolm told Case while pointing casually towards the two youths. "It doesn't look like they've even started their interview yet." He stepped towards the one fiddling with the tape recorder. "Are you going to be much longer getting started, lad?" he asked the rookie reporter. "This is Brian Case from the *Observer Magazine*. He's here to get an interview as well." "Right you are, Mr. McLaren; I think we're nearly there now," the one without the tape recorder said with a sheepish smile. "That's alright, son; a good reporter always takes care to make sure his equipment is in working order before starting an important interview," Case said, nodding at John and Paul before turning back to Malcolm. "I think I'll go outside and have a chat to one or two of the protesters." John watched Case and Malcolm disappear back the way they came before draining the last of his can of cola. "Can't believe there's no fuckin' beer to be had!" he said to Paul while casually tossed it over his shoulder. "What's the name of your fanzine again?" he asked his would-be interrogators. The more he watched the pair, the more they reminded him of Bert and Ernie from *Sesame Street*. "It's called 'Buzz'," said Bert, the taller of the two. "We haven't been doing it very long. And we've not seen anything like what's going on round here today . . . other than Christmas Day, of course." "'Buzz', eh. Is that as in 'bumble bee', or 'the number thirty-nine'?" John smirked, glancing sideways at Paul. "As in 'bumble bee'," Bert smiled. "We haven't been doing it very long." "I'd never of guessed," John chuckled. "We really do need to get this going, lads; cos I've heard a rumour the pub next door will be opening for business tonight. And I can feel a thirst coming on."We're ready," Ernie said, speaking for the first time. Bert looked away and coughed into his cupped hand before turning back to face John. "I'd like to start off, John, by asking you how you feel about what's going on over in the car park?" "Well, I'm just surprised that so many grown-up adults can behave so ludicrously childish," John responded. "Don't they know their papers tell lies? I don't think they do. They live in a twilight zone." He shifted in his seat before continuing. "That's alright, they can be happy in their own way, but I don't think they've got the right to interrupt my way; each to his own, God loves all kinds." "That's the only reason that these council officials want to stop this," Bert shrugged. "I mean, they just don't know." "No, it's probably because they don't offer the young generation of Caerphilly anything," John nodded. "They offer them nothing and along comes an alternative and it makes them look foolish. While they've been in office they've done sweet FA for anybody except themselves. There are people getting blown up and they have the nerve to come and complain about this – ridiculous." "How do you feel about the reaction you've had from the national and musical press?" Bert asked while glancing at the tape recorder nestled on his colleague's lap as though assuring himself the spools were turning.

"I don't really care what they get up to," John said, toying with the safety pin dangling from his left earlobe. "I mean, I've known for years that the national press is squalid and that any cheap rumour – they just love it. And the music press is even worse. Hypocrisy? They live for it. Well good luck to them, that's fine," he spat before the interviewer could respond. "They can play their games all day and night. It's when people start taking notice of them it becomes offensive." Bert wasn't sure if John had finished. On realising he had he hurriedly blurted out his next question "How about the Bill Grundy affair?" John took a breath while mentally composing his answer, but to his surprise, Paul jumped in and beat him to the punch. "We just done it on the spur of the moment," Paul said. "It wasn't premeditated or anything it just happened, you know? We forgot about it the next day, but I couldn't believe it when I woke up." "Does the fact that a lot of universities who are supposedly open-minded people, pulled out of dates surprise you?" The question was initially greeted with silence as John had assumed Paul would offer a response. But Paul had been distracted by something Steve was doing. "Oh no, universities have proved to be the worst,' John offered. "They went on about us being fascist and rubbish like that. Students have proved that they're not open-minded, they've got closed minds; they're a closed shop." Bert swallowed hard, as though he unsure about whether to pose his next question. "Do you think of yourselves as part of a passing phase?" he said at last. John was immediately taken aback, but before he could respond Paul stepped in to diffuse the situation. "People can say that," he shrugged. "We're not worried; we're not in it to make thousands of pounds-" "Speak for yourself," John interjected.

"We're just in it cos we wanna do it," Paul continued. "And we're doin' what we wanna do." "Where do you get your roots from . . . as a rock group?" Ernie asked, glancing up from the tape recorder. "Just basic honesty," John said, relaxing again. "There's been no honest bands for years. It's all big moguls and twenty thousand tons of equipment." Ernie nodded, but continued his line of questioning. "What do you think of Clapton and Townshend?" "They're finished," Paul said dryly. "Some bands are doing things by Townshend," Ernie fired back. 'Things like 'Substitute' for instance."

"Yeah, it was alright then," Paul shrugged again, purposely ignoring the sarcasm. Ernie, however, was on something of a roll. "You think they should have packed it in, then?" he asked. "No, they could have carried on but they just covered it up in bullshit and hype," John said, narrowing his eyes at Ernie. "They became out of touch, and you can't like go up to

Pete Townshend and say, 'Hello Pete'. He's become distant. He's not even a human being anymore. I doubt if it's him on stage. He's like a puppet in the distance." "Do you think there's a lot of snobbery in rock music?" Bert asked, retaking control. "Yeah, there has been for centuries," John nodded. "Some of the biggest snobs are rock musicians."

"Is it all that important that you can play really good music?" "No, I don't think it's essential," John said guardedly. "It's your attitude that counts." He paused while glancing at his watch. "If you can express something to someone, that's it; you've got it," he added. Bert took the hint. "I think we've got everything we need," he smiled. "So thank you both."

"No, thank you," John said, getting to his feet. "And if you're in the pub later I'll allow you to buy me a Guinness."

Chapter Sixteen

Court bid on Sex Pistols ruled out

LEGAL ADVISORS told Rhymney Valley District Council yesterday that it could not take any court action to stop next week's concert appearance at Caerphilly by the punk-rock group Sex Pistols.

But publicans in the area have said they are considering closing their doors until after the concert.

The vice-chairman of the council, Mrs. Madeleine Ryland, said last night that the public outcry against the group's appearance had forced the council into considering a high court action.

"But we have been told that there is nothing we can do legally to stop the event because it had been arranged at such short notice after the concert had been cancelled in Cardiff," she said.

The Guardian, Thursday, 9 December 1976.

Malcolm was in the foyer chatting with Brian Case. They'd moved on from the car park protest and were now discussing a recent article in the *London Evening Standard* in which Bill Haley had given his thoughts on punk rock. Speaking with reporters at Heathrow while awaiting a flight to New York after completing a brief UK tour, the 51-year-old rock'n'roll legend said how he felt punk was "carrying things too far," and that while he was all for entertainment he wouldn't want his teenage daughter listening to punk bands – namely the Sex Pistols – because of the "language some of these fellas use." "I don't remember Bill complaining much when Teddy boys were slashing cinema seats while watching *Rock Around The Clock*, Malcolm said, idly toying with a loose thread on his gold and pink string mohair sweater.

"From what I hear, there was some trouble on his current tour," Case grinned. "Aging Teds going at each other with their Zimmer frames and walking sticks." "I saw Bill play the London Rock and Roll Show at Wembley the other year," Malcolm said. "August '72, I think. There was something like fifty thousand people there, but it was quite a billing. Aside from Bill and his Comets, there was Bo Diddley, Jerry Lee Lewis, Little Richard, as well as the Platters, Drifters, and the Coasters." "Didn't Billy Fury appear as well?" Case asked. "He did indeed," Malcolm smiled. "Billy was the highlight of the show for my money. We had a stall there that day – to promote the shop. We printed up hundreds of T-shirts with our own 'Vive le Rock design. "Did you sell many?" "Let's just say we'd have done better setting up a hot dog stand." Malcolm was about to say something else, but paused on seeing John at his shoulder. "What is it, John?" "Got any cash on you? The pub next door will be open in" - John paused to look at his watch – "in five . . . no, four minutes."

"No one's to go outside," Malcolm replied, glancing towards the doors as the protesters suddenly burst into 'The Old Rugged Cross'. "We don't want to give those do-gooders over the road further cause for antagonism, do we?" He paused again and indicated towards Case. "Besides, Brian's here to interview you. The band, that is. Brian's with the *Observer Magazine*." "Pleased to meet'cha," John said, smiling at case's reaction to the bondage suit he was wearing. "Likewise," Case nodded, unable to take his gaze from the bondage suit. "Does that strap go between the knees?" he asked, stooping slightly to get a better look. "It stops him running away," Malcolm smiled. "Where are the others?" he asked John. "Where I fuckin' left 'em most likely," John said, lifting an arm to scratch his armpit. He smiled again on seeing Case's bemusement as the straps across the bondage top constricted across the chest in tandem with John's movements. "It can be murder if you get caught fuckin' short," he chuckled. "Kindly take Brian through with you," Malcolm said. "I'll be through in a few minutes." "At least send someone next door for a fuckin' carry-out," John sighed, turning on his heel and heading for the door through to the backstage area.

♪ ♪ ♪

Case positioned himself by the window with his portable tape recorder resting on a chair. He plucked a cassette tape from the recorder's carrying case, slipped it into the machine, and depressed the start button. "I think we're good to go," he smiled at John who was sitting to his left. Steve, Glen and Paul were sat facing Case. "Fire away, mate," John said. "Do you think it's fair to say that those people gathered outside have taken the opening line to 'Anarchy in the UK' a bit too literally?" Case asked, holding the microphone towards John.

"How do you mean?" "Well, it's almost as though they believe their hymns and Christmas carols will somehow drive the 'antichrist' away from their door." "I feel sorry them really," John shrugged. "But only for allowing themselves to be so easily misinformed." "I feel sorry for them cos it's freezing out there," Glen offered. "They must be-" "It's like I told that other reporter,"

Steve interjected. "We're in here, so we're alright. It's fuckin' brass monkeys outside!" "When I arrived here this evening and saw what was happening across the road I was reminded of the religious protests over screenings of *The Exorcist* from a couple of years back," said Case. "Perhaps I should go out there and start speaking in tongues," John grinned. "Or with a fuckin' crucifix shoved up your arse," Steve quipped as Malcolm came across to join them. "This venue wasn't on the original tour schedule was it?" Case asked looking up at Malcolm. "No, the original show was scheduled for the Top Rank in Cardiff," Malcolm said. "But this will suffice. There are enough seats for six hundred or so." "But Caerphilly is quite a ways off the circuit," Case said pointedly, remembering his own lengthy journey up from London. "What sort of following do you have in this neck of the woods? After all, it's a long way for your fans in London to come for a one-off show." "That's what's been worrying me," Glen said. "But I did see a few punk types outside. And some of them were even wearing gear from the shop," he said, turning to Malcolm. "Ah yes, that will probably be Christopher and his friends," Malcolm nodded to himself. "They've become regulars at the shop in recent weeks." "What's your view on the dates that have been cancelled so far?" Case asked John. "It's diabolical, really," John said, shifting in his chair. "Because when it comes down to it, we're being denied the right to fuckin' work. Now how does that work - if you'll excuse the pun - in a supposed democracy?" "Has the tour incurred serious losses?' Case asked Malcolm.

"Yes," Malcolm winced; "several thousand pounds." "It's a piss-off, but we're not gonna give up," John spat defiantly. "Although the tour will probably bankrupt us. Fuckin' hell, about time!" he yelled on seeing Nils and Keith Paul coming through carrying trays loaded with pints of beer. "Over here, Nils!" "So it's a matter of principle then?" Case asked. "Absofuckinlutely," John said, while nodding to Nils as he grabbed two pints from the tray . "Cos if we give up now then no new band will get the chance to play again. Ever." "Have you stopped to consider that the Sex Pistols are simply being used as political pawns here in Caerphilly?" "The thought had crossed my mind," Malcolm nodded. "While I was other in the car park I spoke with a Labour councillor-" "That would be Councillor Ray Davies," Malcolm said, remembering his earlier conversation with Julien Temple.

"Yes, that's the chap. He certainly had a lot to say. He ranted on about how the Sex Pistols are 'vandalising and prostituting children's minds'. And that apart from using obscenities on stage you'll also be responsible for the dope and filth-peddlers that will descend upon Caerphilly in your wake." "I fuckin' hope so," John said. "Dave's supplier let him down at the weekend." "I'm sorry?" case frowned. "Ignore him, Brian," Malcolm sighed, shaking his head at John. "I also spoke with the leader of the local Conservative group," Case continued. "It seems to me that he and Councillor Davis are only here tonight to gain some political kudos for the forthcoming local elections." "Sounds about right," John sneered. "I think they're very bored people who just need something to entertain their drab lives, and we're the excuse. It's pathetic the way people can be swayed like that. How places can have their licenses revoked by some sod who's never seen us – just goes by what the papers say. Everybody knows the nationals are liars," he said, fixing his gaze on Case.

"The music industry needed an injection, they just didn't know what," Malcolm cut in. "They'd tried to create bands to fill the vacuum, but it didn't happen because it was coming from them and not the streets. If they weren't playing rock and roll, they'd be on the dole or in prison, or working in a factory. Most kids don't have a lot of future. If we're violent, all I can say is people don't know what violence is all about," Malcolm continued. "The violence of the Sex Pistols is basically in celebration of themselves and of whatever reaction occurs in the audience to that fact. Rock and roll is a violent music – assertive. But it's violent to see those guys over there trying to prevent young kids from making their choice. Violence is kids being out of work on the streets with nothing to do – that's society being violent." "And violence can also be about havin' to go without a beer when there's a fuckin' pub next door," John said mischievously.

♪♪♪

With *The Observer* regarded as one of Middle England's preferred broadsheets, Case knew he couldn't return to London without interviewing the Sex Pistols' colourful menagerie of fans that were sat huddled together in the front rows. Although rock music wasn't his thing, he'd kept a finger on the rock'n'roll pulse-beat. He'd come to believe that nothing could shock him in terms of fashion fads, yet here were these kids looking like characters from a dystopian nightmare. He snapped a shot of a girl with a safety-pin through her nose; the angry-red welt where the pin protruded evidence enough that the pin was a recent adornment. "Does that not hurt?' he asked, setting his tape recorder down on the seat next to the girl and holding the microphone in front of her. The girl in question eyed the recorder as if expecting it to leap up and bite her. "No, no, not really," she stammered into the microphone while fingering her paint-splattered tie as her friends looked on in eager anticipation of their being interviewed. "What's your name?" Case asked. "Jill, Jill Taylor." "How old are you, Jill?" "Eighteen.' "Do you live here in Caerphilly?" "No, Cwmbran. It's about twenty miles away." "Do your parents know you're here?" "Course they do." Case could feel his left leg beginning to seize up so shifted position. "What was it that made you latch onto the Sex Pistols, Jill?" he asked, looking up as several other colourfullydressed kids - their ensembles a mixture of black leather, paint-daubed jackets, ripped Tshirts festooned with chains and safety-pins, dog-collars and various other accoutrements - came bounding down the central aisle and took their seats in the row directly behind Jill and her friends. Several of the girls were sporting fishnet stockings and skirts that that left little to the imagination, and Case had to remind himself that he was old enough to be their father. Jill paused to wave at one of the new arrivals before turning back to face Case. "They face the realities of life. They understand people on the dole, and they play especially for us. We feel closer to them than to people like Rod Stewart and famous stars with all their swimming pools and things. The Sex Pistols don't treat us like dirt like top stars do." Case shifted position again. "Thank you very much for your time, Jill; I hope you enjoy the show. And what's your name?" he asked, holding the microphone to the girl in the next seat. "Josie Rafferty." "Can I ask you why you've drawn swastikas on your shirt, Josie?" "Just to look unusual," Josie shrugged. "We don't follow fascism or anything like that. We just like the gear. I've got pictures of Hitler in my bedroom. It's not that I admire him," she said hurriedly on seeing Case's reaction. "I just like the way he shows all his wickedness and that." Case knew that had he been in the employ of either The *Sun* or the *Daily Mirror*, then the girl's comments about appreciating Hitler's "wickedness" might well have ended up on the following morning's front pages. "What about you . . .?" he asked the dark-haired youth sporting a studded leather jacket sat perched on the seat directly behind Josie. "My name's Chris Sullivan," the lad in question replied, leaning forward in his seat so that he was closer to the microphone. "I live over in Merthyr Tydfil." "And when did you first discover the Sex Pistols?" "Me and my mates" – he jerked his thumb along the row – "caught one of their early shows at the El Paradise. It's a strip club in Soho," he added for Case's benefit. "When was that?" Chris turned to the lad sitting next to him. "Must have been around April time, wasn't it, Jonathan?" Jonathan gave a nod of confirmation. "We saw them quite regularly after that," he said, turning back to face case. "And we were at the 100 Club on Oxford Street the night the Clash supported them as well." Case was aiming the microphone towards Jonathan when he suddenly paused. "Wait a minute. Would you be the same Chris that Malcolm told me about?" "What did Malcolm say?" Chris asked, grinning from ear to ear. "I was interviewing the band in the backstage area and Glen said something about seeing some fans wearing clothing from Malcolm's shop," Jonathan opened his jacket. "This is from the shop," he said tugging at his T-shirt. Case leaned in closer. "Is that . . . is that a naked boy?" he gasped, taking in the image of a prepubescent youth smoking a cigarette. "It's great isn't it," Jonathan grinned. "But aren't you worried about getting arrested?" Case asked, his eyes still riveted on the shirt. "I keeps my jacket fastened when I'm outside," Jonathan smiled "What did you think when you heard the Sex Pistols were coming here to play tonight?" Case asked.

"We couldn't believe it, could we," Jonathan beamed. "When we heard the original date at the Top Rank in Cardiff had been cancelled, we thought, 'Well, that's that, then.'" "I thought they were pulling my leg when they told me the Pistols were coming to Caerphilly," Chris added. "I said, 'Don't be so ridiculous, man. The Sex Pistols won't come to bloody Caerphilly.'"

"What's your name?" Case asked the pimply-faced youth sat behind Chris, taking in the lad's hacked-off ginger hair and studded dog-collar. "Noddy?"

"And how long have you been following the Sex Pistols, Noddy?" "About six months. In the past, I've been into soul, reggae, Bowie, Roxy Music. I was also into the New York Dolls-" "Was you fuck as like!" someone along the row shouted. "I was too!" Noddy challenged, twisting round to find the culprit. "It was through the Dolls that I heard about the Pistols," he said, turning back towards Case, "because Malcolm McLaren used to manage them before, like." "What impresses you about their lyrics?" "Well, to be honest, I don't find much meaning in all that myself," Noddy confessed. "Because they're new bands, and they're singing all this . . . and we don't know the words ourselves really. Only what we can just about pick up." "Speak for yourself you daft twat," the same wag shouted to everyone else's obvious amusement. "We know really from the write-ups in the press what they're on about," Noddy continued, refusing to rise to the bait this time. "The words of 'Anarchy In The UK' they don't give you no clear view." "Where did you get your dog-collar?" Case asked him. "From a dog," Noddy grinned.

"Your dog?" Case asked "I haven't got a dog, I-" "What about that bird I saw you with the other week?" someone shouted, causing another burst of laughter. "You mean your sister," Noddy shot back without looking away from Case. "I got it off of a dog I came upon in the street one night."

"You're saying you stole it?" Case gasped. "But the dog could have been picked up by the local dog warden for not having a collar." "Well the owner shouldn't have let the dog out on its own then, should they?" Noddy countered "But what about germs?" Case grimaced. "It's alright, the dog doesn't want it back after Nod," the first wag said, causing more merriment. Noddy twisted round in his seat again. "I'll come over there and give you a thump, so I will," he snarled. "Or the smell?" Case continued. "Oh, it stunk something terrible it did, but I soaked it in Domestos overnight," Noddy grinned. "It was alright after that, cos the man on the telly says Domestos kills ninety-nine per cent of germs dead."

♪♪♪

Owing to the truncated bill The Clash come onstage later than they had in either Leeds or Manchester. The cinema was barely a quarter full, but unlike the previous two dates the hundred and fifty or so souls that have braved the weather - while also having to run the God-squad gauntlet outside the venue - are all converts to the cause. These kids are here to dress up and mess up and have the time of their lives. Having hit a couple of chords to ensure his Gibson SG hadn't strayed out of tune since the soundcheck, Mick stepped up to the mic. "All you whose mummy and daddy didn't make you stay at home, well done." His salutation receives a thunderous burst of applause, but this is drowned out as the band thunder into "White Riot". The sound is slightly hollow owing to the acoustics, but there's little Goodman and Micky Foote can do to rectify the problem other than add a little reverb The positive reaction received at the Electric Circus had further galvanised The Clash, and Joe, Mick, and Paul exude a renewed confidence as they plough through their set. This is the first time The Clash have ventured into Wales, but the brouhaha surrounding the tour means their burgeoning reputation has at least preceded them. The energy emanating from the stage isn't reciprocated from the audience, however. The underlying reason for this, of course, is that a cinema setting isn't the most conducive setting for high-energy rock'n'roll, and the rows of empty seats make the fans feel all the more self-conscious. The vast majority of the audience are also unfamiliar with The Clash, other than their name. However, Chris and his chums had caught their performance supporting the Pistols at the 100 Club at the end of August, and they heartily applaud each number.

When Mick stepped across to tune Paul's bass, Joe took the opportunity to engage the audience. He'd lived in nearby Newport for a time while playing with Flaming Youth, the band consisting of kids from Newport College of Art's students' union. It was at his insistence that they'd changed their name to The Vultures. To make ends meet, he'd worked as a gravedigger at St. Woolos Cemetery. He told them about his smoking sneaky spliffs by the Newport Docks Disaster Memorial, the granite obelisk erected in memory of the victims of the Newport Docks disaster of July 1909. The set is in a near-identical running order as those of the previous shows, with "Hate and War" and "Protex Blue" following "London's Burning", and "I'm So Bored With The USA". They again close with "1977"; the song's apocryphal mantra of "No Elvis, Beatles, or the Rolling Stones . . ." receiving an added cheer. The excitement level has cranked up several notches by the time The Heartbreakers emerge from stage left, because compared to The Clash who – as indeed were the Sex Pistols – were still honing their craft, the Americans were seasoned pros. True, they'd hitched their reins to the Bowery bandwagon, but with The Ramones, Television, and the other CBGBs groups all citing the New York Dolls as a major influence, Thunders and Nolan were regarded as rock'n'roll royalty on the Lower East Side. The Clash's threechord thrash may have been in keeping with what was going down across the Atlantic, but with all four Heartbreakers' roots being solidly steeped in old fashioned rhythm & blues; they soon had everyone on their feet.The anticipation was almost tangible when the Sex Pistols took to the stage, and at the back of the hall a film crew from Border Television is hurriedly setting up to capture the spectacle of the bondage-suit-bedecked Johnny Rotten for the viewers at home. What Malcolm didn't seem to have taken into consideration when inviting The Heartbreakers onto the tour, however, was that they were always going to be a hard act to follow – regardless of their offstage antics – and the Sex Pistols would have to be at the top of their game. Tonight, however, they appear languid before a note has even been played. And although the audience immediately responds to John's barbed challenge for them to "get off their fuckin' arses and fuckin' dance!" as Steve, Glen, and Paul launch into "Anarchy In The UK", they cannot help but pick up the group's subdued mood. Midway through "I Wanna Be Me" a couple of kids leap to their feet and start spitting at each other, but the unconvincing gob fight fails to elicit much of a response from their friends and they quickly sit down again.

Chapter Seventeen

PUNK and PROTEST ... AND VICTORY GOES TO THE CAROLLERS

FIVE HUNDRED AND SEVENTY empty seats out of 630 showed what South Wales teenagers thought of Punk Rock last night. And across the road Christmas carols were sung by a packed protest in the open. **group failed to produce the expected capacity crowd All the ballyhoo about the Sex Pistols rock for the first live concert at the Castle Cinema, Caerphilly, and only 60 fans turned up.**

The big snub went further – the police said their only problem was preventing interested onlookers blocking the pavement.

South Wales Echo & Western Mail, Wednesday, 15 December 1976.

The NME's Camden Christmas party was in full swing with the San Franciscan rockers, The Flamin' Groovies, up on the Dingwalls stage – or the raised platform that passed for a stage - entertaining the assembled musicians, journalists, and music industry types with their version of Eddie Cochran's 1959 hit, "Somethin' Else" from their debut album, Supersnazz. The self-confessed sixties fetishists were signed to Seymour Stein's Sire Records, the same label as The Ramones. They'd released Shake Some Action, their first album for Sire – their fourth long-player overall - back in June. The album had failed to crack the Billboard 100, but had received positive reviews upon its release in the UK. Dingwalls, situated adjacent to Camden Lock, was enjoying its third year as a music venue. Like many of the Victorian-era buildings within the locale it had stood derelict while the world moved on before being given a new lease of life. The name of its previous owner – a T. E Dingwall – was still prominent on the outside wall, and as the new owners couldn't think of anything better they kept the name. The club's' manager, Dave "The Boss" Goodman had banned the Pistols from performing there owing to their supposed reputation for violence at their London shows. Conversely, the ban didn't extend to Sex Pistols themselves.

This was the first time Glen had been to Dingwalls since The Ramones had played the second show of their two-date sortie to London at the beginning of July, which had of course, coincided with America's bicentennial celebrations. Though why the Ramones had elected to celebrate their country's 200th birthday some three thousand miles from home was still a mystery to him. Of course, they would have been in attendance at their opening show at the nearby Roundhouse the previous evening had they not been otherwise engaged in Sheffield. He – - as indeed had John, Steve, and Paul - had been flattered to learn that the Ramones were familiar with the Sex Pistols thanks to their mutual friend, Bob Gruen.

The New York-based photographer knew Malcolm from his mis-managing the New York Dolls, and would always pay a visit to 430 King's Road whenever he was in town. By fortuitous happenstance, Gruen had been at Denmark Street taking some photographs of the group rehearsing when the call had come through from Malcolm that they were set to sign with EMI. Indeed, it was Gruen who'd snapped the celebratory publicity photo in Bob Mercer's office that had been sent to the media. They'd chatted with Joey, Johnny, Dee Dee, and Tommy, backstage both before and after the show. The evening, however, had ended on something of a sour note as Paul Simonon had unwittingly gotten himself into a situation with The Stranglers' bassist, Jean Jacques Burnel, outside in the cobbled courtyard. The Stranglers had been one of the support acts at the Roundhouse along with The Flamin' Groovies, and both groups had been at Dingwalls as the headliners' guests. Paul had apparently spat on the floor, but Burnel had thought Paul had spat at him. It had largely been Paul's refusal to apologise for spitting anyway that had led to the Mexican standoff. A simmering rivalry of sorts already existed between their two camps as many of those within the Sex Pistols inner-circle believing The Stranglers – who'd been treading the boards on London's pub-rock circuit for several years - had grabbed onto punk's shirttails to further their career; their securing a support slot with The Ramones had only served to exacerbate the grumblings. Thankfully, the matter had been resolved without their coming to blows, which was rather fortuitous for Paul seeing as the French-born Burnel was a black belt in karate. Christmas may have been a week away, but the festive mood didn't extend to every corner of the room. Not only were the guys from Eddie and the Hot Rods in attendance, but so were The Damned. On seeing their erstwhile tour mates come through the door Glen had initially feared another square up, but Rat, Dave, Brian, and the Captain were purposely maintaining a healthy distance. John had deigned not to attend the bash, but Steve, Paul, and Nils were there, along with Joe, Mick, and Paul from The Clash.

The Heartbreakers were also expected to put in an appearance at some point during the evening, but although the food and drink were free, Glen suspected the Americans had more pressing habits to feed. And with the Anarchy Tour being the hottest industry talking point in years, the three Sex Pistols found themselves the centre of everyone's attention; such was the extent of their new-found popularity that Joe, Mick, and Paul were able to bask within their reflected glory. Unsurprisingly, everyone had their opinion on what was going to happen once the tour came to an end. The overriding view from those supposedly "in the know" was that EMI were set on ditching the Sex Pistols in the new year, so Glen had taken great pleasure in telling those same know-it-alls that since returning to London after the Caerphilly date EMI had confirmed a promotional visit to Holland early in the coming year to promote the release of "Anarchy In The UK" via EMI Holland. From what Malcolm had told him, Glen knew the trip had been arranged by Hilary Walker, who was the second in command at EMI International. What Glen had kept to himself, of course, was that when Malcolm had asked whether the promotional trip was confirmation that EMI would be keeping the Sex Pistols on its roster, Walker had responded by saying that rather than allow herself to be influenced by the in-house rumour mill regarding the Sex Pistols, she'd chose to get on with the job of promoting the group overseas. Needless to say, thanks to Fleet Street's continued public flaying of Sex Pistols the heads of EMI's overseas offices were all wary of bringing the group over to their respective territories. Walker's first obstacle had involved convincing each of them that the Sex Pistols were still very much a viable commodity. With her own department slowly winding down for the Christmas break she wasn't wholly surprised on being politely asked to defer any decisions until after the holidays. However, seeing as her opposite number in Amsterdam had been the most receptive to the idea, she'd set the ball rolling with a promotional visit to Holland in the first week of January to kick-start the European campaign. And while this would be the group's first overseas promotional trip since signing with EMI, he knew enough to know that such trips usually involved a couple of live dates.

♪♪♪

The four Heartbreakers, closely followed by Leee Black Childers and Keeth Paul, emerged from the tube station out onto Camden High Street. As they stepped out onto the pavement a wino hurriedly shuffled out of his dirt-smeared sleeping bag and came scurrying towards them. Upon seeing their collective dishevelled state, however, he reluctantly withdrew his hand and retreated back into the shadows. What the old boy didn't know, however, was that the Americans in his befuddled mist were flush with cash after playing The Roxy; the newly-opened music venue on Neal Street in Covent Garden, three nights earlier. The Roxy, which would be specialising in punk rock, had opened its doors for the first time the previous evening whilst the Sex Pistols, The Clash, and The Heartbreakers had been in Caerphilly. The headliners were Mick Jones' mate and former London SS collaborator, Tony James's new outfit Generation X, with Siouxsie and the Banshees serving as support. The club's leaseholders, Andy Czezowski and Barry Jones were already known on the nascent scene. Czezowski was acquainted with both Malcolm and Bernard, and had witnessed the Sex Pistols' live debut at St. Martin's College of Art some thirteen months earlier, while Jones was good friends with Glen and Mick. Glen's girlfriend Celia was also helping out with the paperwork. The Roxy may have been highly unsuited for live music owing to the stage and bar area being on two separate levels, but Czezowski and Jones were hoping the former gay bar would take over from the 100 Club as London's premier punk venue. Having secured The Heartbreakers' services, the entrepreneurial duo had printed up flyers and handed them out to the hundred and twenty punters that had attended the opening night. It had proved a savvy move, because although a hundred and twenty was pretty much the club's fire-safety capacity, the flyers – coupled with the resultant word of mouth – had brought three hundred through the door the second night. "Hey, Leee; I hope you remembered to bring the invites for this thing?" Thunders said, tugging at the collar of his motorcycle jacket to offer some protection from the biting wind. Compared to New York, a British winter was a walk in the park, but while their leather jacket, jeans, and winkle-picker boots combo looked great on a stage, it was woefully unsuited for outdoor hikes and he could already feel his fingers going numb. "I'd kinda hate for us to get turned away, ya know." "Relax, Johnny," Leee smiled. "We didn't receive any invitations, but yesterday I rang the *NME*'s offices to make sure our names were on the guest list." "Which way is it?" Nolan asked, plucking an apple from his pocket. "Apparently we just have to follow our noses towards the canal," Leee said. "I wouldn't mind getting refused," Nolan chuckled. "That way we could go back to the apartment and have ourselves a real good time." "It's a flat, Jerry," Leee corrected him. "New York and Paris have apartments, but in London they have flats." "Whatever." "Right with you on that one, Niggs," Thunders said, stepping into a shop doorway out of the wind so that he could light his cigarette. "But it's been a while since we ate anything proper, you know." "And I'm with you on that one, Johnny," Keeth Paul nodded. "I'm so hungry I could eat a fuckin' horse with a side order of saddle. And the jockey better watch his ass in case I need dessert!" "D'ya wanna bite of my apple, Keeth?' Nolan asked him, plucking an apple from his jacket pocket. "Uh, no thanks, Niggs," Paul shook his head. "How many of them things you got, anyway?" "This is my last one," Nolan said, stuffing the apple back into his pocket. "You know what they say about an apple a day . . . I'm gonna need some more, Leee," he said, turning to Childers. "You've got your own money now, Jerry," Childers chided him. "Yeah, but most of it went on our favourite cure-all," Nolan said with a knowing smile. "I still can't believe you managed to score," Childers said. "I mean, I'm glad you did, because we can't afford for any of you to be sick. But still . . ." he shrugged, letting his voice trail off "Ah, we kinda met a guy that knows a guy, if you know what I mean," Thunders shrugged. "Hey, is this it, Leee?" he asked, as they approached a brightly-lit entrance. Childers pointed up to the neon-lit sign above the doors. "This is the Electric Ballroom, Johnny. It's a club, just not the one we want." "We should-a got a cab," Billy Rath sulked.

"That would be a waste of money, Billy," Childers sighed. "It's just a little ways further." "You know what I heard today?" Nolan said, shucking a cigarette from the packet and slipping it into his mouth as they waited at the kerb at the junction of Jamestown Road. "What's that, Jerry?" Childers asked him. "I heard the Sex Pistols and the Clash are playing the Roxy's official opening night on New Year's Day." "I don't think it's been confirmed yet, Jerry," Childers nodded. "Malcolm mentioned something about it when I saw him the other day." "What about us?" Thunders grumbled. "We could wipe the floor with those bozos." "That may be so, Johnny," Childers smiled. "But we'll be back in New York by then." Childers stood waiting until a car had done past, and was about to cross the road when Thunders grabbed him by the arm. "What if we didn't go home, Leee? What if we stayed here?" "We've been through this already, Johnny," Childers sighed. "We can't stay here because we don't have necessary work permits.""We could get them." "What are you saying, Johnny?" "Me and the boys have been talking," Thunders continued, glancing briefly at the others as though assuring himself he had their support. "We don't wanna go back . . . we wanna stay here in London." "Yeah, we got nothing going on back home," Nolan said. "What about Nancy?" Rath chuckled. "There ain't nothin' going on with me and Nancy, Billy," Nolan snapped. "She's just a friend, is all." "We're sick and fed up hauling our asses between CBGBs and Max's, Leee," Thunders said, steering the conversation back to their plight. "But you said you hated it here, Johnny," said Childers. "You said Earl's Court made the Bowery look like Fifth Avenue." "Well, I guess I've had a rethink since then." "I don't suppose you're rethink has anything to do with you finding a dealer?" "Not entirely," Thunders chuckled. "Look, Leee; you're our manager and we love you," Nolan said. "You can go home if you want to . . . but we're stayin' put." "And that's your final decision?" Childers asked, glancing at each of them in turn. "What say you, Keeth?' Childers asked Paul. "I ain't got nothing back home, either," Paul shrugged. "Well, you know I love you boys," Childers smiled. "And where my boys go, I go." "This calls for a celebration!" Thunders yelled, punching the air in delight as they made their way over the canal.

♪♪♪

Glen was standing close to the stage watching The Flamin' Groovies' balding and bespectacled bass player, George Alexander, as the American outfit played the title track from the new album. He didn't think much of the song per se, but it had a great middle eight, and he thought he might be able to work the riff that Alexander was playing into the melody he'd played for Mike Thorn the previous Saturday. He was still watching Alexander's fancy fret play when he noticed Joe standing next to him. "Food's fuckin' great, innit," Joe grinned, shoving another sandwich into his mouth. The Clash frontman had particular reason to appreciate the free gratis frolics as on their return from Wales he'd gone back to the disused ice-cream factory on Foscote Mews in Maida Vale, where he'd been squatting for the past few months, to find the renovators had moved in and dumped his meagre clutch of possessions in a skip. He'd since been forced to seek refuge in the upstairs room at The Clash's rehearsal space where Paul and Roadent were already living.

Mick had returned from the bar. "We should have looked at playin' tonight," he said, helping himself to one of Joe's sandwiches. "This lot are dismissed the Mancunians as little more than a "provincial copy of the Sex Pistols" that he understood Malcolm's reasoning. Another reason, of course, could have been the paltry £240 the promoter was offering. He could understand Malcolm's reasoning for agreeing to a return to the Electric Circus in order to keep the bandwagon rolling, but he'd known in his heart of hearts that it would backfire on them. And so it had proved . . . if only because the Pistols bombed on the night. According to the original tour itinerary, Monday night's show should have been at Birmingham Town Hall. He and the rest of the group had been particularly looking forward to that date as they'd built up a sizeable following thanks to several previous forays to the UK's second city. A mooted replacement show in nearby Bingley had also long-since fallen through. Rather than return to London again Malcolm accepted an offer from Jimmy Jackson, the manager of the Winter Gardens in Cleethorpes. Somewhat unbelievably, Jackson claimed to be unaware of the media shit-storm surrounding Pistols' appearance on *Today*. The fee was £40 less than what they'd been paid in Manchester, but Malcolm was desperate to recoup as much of the losses as he could from wherever he could. This resulted in a cross-country foray from Manchester up to north Humberside. Talk about bleak! Indeed, there were times during the three-hour journey that he'd felt he was looking out on a lunar landscape. Prior to their arrival in the windswept seaside town, he doubted he'd have been able to locate Cleethorpes on a map of the British Isles if his life depended on it. Despite its dark-side-of-the-moon remoteness, he'd been astounded to learn that the Winter Gardens was a renowned live music venue, with dozens of established acts having trod its boards including Hawkwind, Roxy Music, Thin Lizzy, Queen, and Genesis to name but a few. On the afternoon of the Cleethorpes show Glen had broken the heel on one of his boots – the only footwear he'd brought with him on the trip. He'd gone to Malcolm to explain his predicament fully expecting him to put his hand in his pocket so that he could go into town and get the necessary repairs done. Malcolm, however, had been in one of his moods, which meant the boot didn't get repaired, and he'd had to stand rooted in front of his amplifier for fear that he might go arse over tit if he went walkabout. Steve had been equally inactive throughout the performance, but his unwillingness to throw his customary "guitar hero" shapes was due to his being shit-faced as he and Paul had spent the day helping Paul Simonon belatedly celebrate his twenty-first birthday. The Clash bassist had celebrated his coming of age five days earlier by hitting every pub in Camden with Mick and Joe, but when Steve and Paul heard about the birthday boy they'd insisted on a pub crawl. The trio had barely made it back to the Winter Gardens in time for the curtain fuckin' rubbish." "They're not that bad," said Glen. "But in case you're forgetting" - he suddenly had to raise his voice mid-sentence as The Flamin' Groovies burst into another number – "the *NME* booked their Christmas party before our going on the Today show threw a spanner in the works, and one of us would have been on stage at the Kursaal in Southend right about now. And seeing as we're barred from playing here, you lot are probably barred as well." "Guilty by association, an' all that," Joe nodded. "Yeah, but-" Mick suddenly fell silent on seeing Thunders, Nolan, and Billy Rath coming towards them.

"Hey, those fucks from the Damned are here," Thunders said, jerking his thumb over his shoulder towards the bar without turning around. "D'ya think they wanna rumble, Johnny?" Nolan chuckled. "We're ready for 'em if they do, Niggs." "Well, don't come running to me if you get yourselves arrested, Jerry," Caroline Coon said, suddenly appearing at the drummer's elbow.

"Well, hello Doll," said Nolan, turning to face Caroline and absent-mindedly running a hand through his hair. "Can I get you a drink?" "You can knock off the charm, Jerry," Joe grinned. "Caroline's with Paul," he said as Simonon came sidling across and slipped his arm around Caroline's waist. "Sorry, brother," Nolan apologised. "I didn't know she was with you. Boy, I really need a drink now!" he added glancing over at the bar. "I could use one myself," Simonon said, following Nolan's gaze. "But they must be fuckin' three deep over there." "What do you expect; it's fuckin' free booze!" said Joe. "Then allow me, boys," Caroline said, linking arms with Paul and Nolan. "I may not work for the *NME*, but my press card means I won't have to queue like you mere mortals." "Paul's sure a lucky guy, cos that's one classy broad," Thunders said, watching the three making their way towards the bar. "Wish I could find me a woman like that," Rath said. "Well, there's plenty of crumpet here tonight, Billy," Mick told him. "Uh, no thanks, Mick; I've already ate." "He means the birds, Billy,' Joe grinned. "And there's more to Caroline than meets the eye," he added. "In what way?" "She's a co-founder of Release." "What do they do?" Thunders asked. "It's a charity organisation that provides assistance for those nicked on drug-related charges," Joe explained, as Steve and Paul came over to join them. The two Sex Pistols had been queuing at the other end of the bar, but had rushed across on seeing Caroline. "I'd better get her number, cos we've decided to stick around after the tour," said Thunders. "That's great, Johnny," Steve beamed. "You can play with us anytime." "Thanks," Thunders nodded. "But we'll have to ah . . . sort out the running order," he smiled, accepting a bottle of lager from Nolan. Caroline and Paul had now also rejoined the group. "Before I forget," Caroline said, "I'm inviting you all to a party on Christmas Day."

"What kind of party would that be?" Steve asked her, flashing a lecherous grin. "You've got a one-track mind, Steve Jones," Caroline said, rolling her eyes in mock annoyance. "It'll be a traditional Christmas party, with turkey and all the trimmings. Jonh and I" - she indicated over to the bar where her opposite number at *Sounds*, Jonh Ingham was in conversation with Nils – "are looking after a friend's house in Cambridge Gardens." Ingham had nailed his colours to the Sex Pistols' mast after giving the group their first major interview back in April, and had been something of an ever-present at their shows ever since. He'd also accompanied Caroline to Paris to watch them play the opening night of a new nightclub. "That's not too far from The Elgin as I remember," Joe said, referring to the pub where The 101ers had cut their musical teeth. "And I expect you all to be there," said Caroline. "I think we might be able to fit it in before we start packing for Holland," said Steve. "What's this about you going to Holland?" Caroline gasped, anxiously glancing over at Ingham. Though she'd come to regard her fellow journalist as a friend, she never let sentiment stand in the way of a by-line. And aside from being a good story, the scoop would be one in the eye for her peers at *Melody Maker*, all of whom were convinced that EMI was set to drop the Sex Pistols. "We're going over there sometime in the New Year to promote 'Anarchy'," Glen told her. "Apparently, it's part of EMI's European promotional campaign for the single." "Will you be playing any shows while you're over there?" Caroline asked, already seeing the by-line taking shape in her mind's eye. "Maybe we can come along for the ride?" Nolan asked hopefully. "I remember Arthur sayin' you can order drugs from a fuckin' menu card over there." "Nothing's been said but it would make sense to play some dates whilst we're there," Glen replied, ignoring Nolan's comment. "I'd love to play the Paradiso in Amsterdam." "Hopefully, I'll be able to persuade my boss to let me come along to cover the trip," said Caroline. "Well, I'd bring along an extra pair of knickers if I was you, Coony, because Holland's just for starters," Steve grinned. "From there we'll be going on to France, Germany, and loads of other places." "Are you talking about a full European tour?" Caroline asked, salivating at the prospect of traversing the continent with the Sex Pistols. "With the Clash and the Heartbreakers?" "If they play their cards right," Steve smirked. At that moment Rat Scabies and Dave Vanian came past on their way to the bar. "What about the Damned; will they be coming?" Joe asked Caroline. "To the Christmas party, I mean." "I think John's already invited them," Caroline nodded. "So I'll expect you all to show a little festive spirit and behave yourselves."

Chapter Eighteen

SEX PISTOLS LATEST

London gigs are off
- only 4 dates left
THE SEX PISTOLS'decimated by more cancellations, and now only four gigs package tour has been further remain in their itinerary. Biggest blow is the scrapping of their two major London concerts, which should have opened at the new Roxy Theatre in Harlesden on December 26 and 27.

And with The Damned now out of the package, the current bill consists of the Pistols, The Clash and Johnny Thunder's Heartbreakers. Remaining dates are at Birmingham Bingley Hall (December 20), Plymouth Woods Leisure Centre (21 and 23) and Paignton Penelope's (22).

However, at press-time there was still some doubt as to whether the Heartbreakers would fulfil these bookings, as Thunder told NME at the weekend that he is "thinking of going home."

New Musical Express, Saturday, 18 December 1976.

The enforced tour layoffs might have hamstrung the Sex Pistols, but the breaks between dates had at least enabled McLaren to focus his energies on overseeing the latest renovations at 430 King's Road; the fourth incarnation in as many years. When McLaren and Vivienne Westwood had first taken over the lease back in October 1971 they'd begun trading as Let It Rock. They'd soon established themselves by cashing in on the early Seventies Teddy boy revival, selling vintage clothing such as pegged pants, scarlet shirts, and flecked jackets. In keeping with the merchandise, the shop's interior had had an authentic Fifties theme - replete with Odeon wallpaper, furniture of the period, and a trompl'oeil window; the retro look being completed with McLaren's collection of rock'n'roll 45s, coupled with original handbills for films such as *Rock Around The Clock*, *Vive Le Rock*, and *The Damned*. By the spring of 1973, however, drapes and suede had given way to studded-leather. In keeping with the shop's new Sixties Americana biker culture theme, Malcolm and Vivienne changed the shop's name to Too Fast Too Live Too Young To Die in homage to the actor James Dean who'd died behind the wheel of his Porsche Spyder sports car in September 1955. By April 1974, having become hopelessly enamoured with the New York Dolls, Malcolm had decided upon the infinitely more radical makeover to "SEX"; the name spelt out in four-feet-high pink foam rubber letters. The interior was decked out in pink Lurex and rubber gauze giving it a womb-like feel, new features included foam-covered wall bars and a surgical bed, while the studded leather apparel gave way to S&M fetish wear that was hitherto the reserve of the back pages of porn magazines. Aided and abetted by Bernard, Malcolm and Vivienne began conjuring up ever more provocative designs incorporating sexual taboos and Situationist slogans, which they printed onto the sleeveless T-shirts already on sale in the shop. Glen, of course, had already been working at the shop for a couple of years by this juncture, and it was the risqué Tshirts that had first attracted Steve, Paul, and John to the World's End. They brought in 26-year-old designer David Connor, who'd just received his MA from the Royal College of Art. The interior of Seditionaries was to be high tech, more pristine, and more Spartan. The surgical bed had been consigned to the scrapheap, to be replaced with more modern fittings such as sixties-style futurist nuclear chairs made from fluorescent-orange plastic, while the floor was fitted with a rugged-grey industrial carpet. The wall bars had escaped the overhaul, but they were now polished and placed in the centre of the shop. Three walls were now adorned with floor-to-ceiling black and white photographs of Dresden being bombed during World War II, while the remaining wall – the one directly behind the new counter – was an upside print of Piccadilly Circus. To complete the bombed-out look, he'd smashed several holes in the centre of the ceiling through which the light-fittings protruded. The most radical idea, however, came not from Malcolm or Vivienne, but rather Connor himself – a pet rat that would live in a cage mounted upon a table that the designer had constructed with his own hands. The shop's exterior would undergo an equally radical makeover. Just as he had when insisting that EMI issue "Anarchy In The UK" in a plain black bag so that only those looking for the record would know to find it, Malcolm was adamant that only those seeking out the shop would cross its threshold. The SEX lettering that had stood above the lintel was gone, as indeed was the seventeenth century philosopher Jean-Jacques Rousseau's aphorism, "craft must have clothes but the truth loves to run naked". The windows and door were to be fitted with milked glass that allowed in daylight, but prevented people from looking in, while a fluorescent strip would sit above the door. Whereas SEX had been obvious from a distance, the only giveaway to the shop's new identity was a solitary brass plaque that bore the new name.

♪♪♪

There had also been a flurry of activity regarding the tour, as after two weeks of stop-start uncertainty, the groups had played four consecutive dates. The first of these had been the return to the Electric Circus in Manchester the previous Sunday. Just as Glen suspected, however, the occasion proved a case of déjà vu for all concerned - including the local yobs who had returned in even greater numbers. With the violence at the previous show making both local and national newspapers, the police were out in force – the majority of them on horseback. Despite their hard-pressed efforts, the police failed to keep the mob at bay, and Collyhurst Street once again resembled a war zone. Gazing out on the carnage from the safety of the dressing room, Glen was astounded to see that some of the thugs had set up shop on the roofs of the nearby council blocks with a seemingly endless supply of bricks and bottles and were hurling their arsenal of weaponry at anyone who strayed into range. Glen had initially been surprised to find that Malcolm didn't extend another helping hand to Buzzcocks to flesh out the bill. Paul had echoed his surprise, whereas all Steve and John were interested in about the return to Manchester was that it allowed them to while away another afternoon at Tommy Duck's. It was only upon reading *Sounds* journalist, Pete Silverton's subsequent review of Buzzcocks' performance on the original date in which he'd dismissed the Mancunians as little more than a "provincial copy of the Sex Pistols" that he understood Malcolm's reasoning. Another reason, of course, could have been the paltry £240 the promoter was offering. He could understand Malcolm's reasoning for agreeing to a return to the Electric Circus in order to keep the bandwagon rolling, but he'd known in his heart of hearts that it would backfire on them. And so it had proved . . . if only because the Pistols bombed on the night. According to the original tour itinerary, Monday night's show should have been at Birmingham Town Hall. He and the rest of the group had been particularly looking forward to that date as they'd built up a sizeable following thanks to several previous forays to the UK's second city. A mooted replacement show in nearby Bingley had also long-since fallen through. Rather than return to London again Malcolm accepted an offer from Jimmy Jackson, the manager of the Winter Gardens in Cleethorpes. Somewhat unbelievably, Jackson claimed to be unaware of the media shit-storm surrounding Pistols' appearance on *Today*. The fee was £40 less than what they'd been paid in Manchester, but Malcolm was desperate to recoup as much of the losses as he could from wherever he could. This resulted in a cross-country foray from Manchester up to north Humberside. Talk about bleak! Indeed, there were times during the three-hour journey that he'd felt he was looking out on a lunar landscape. Prior to their arrival in the windswept seaside town, he doubted he'd have been able to locate Cleethorpes on a map of the British Isles if his life depended on it. Despite its dark-side-of-the-moon remoteness, he'd been astounded to learn that the Winter Gardens was a renowned live music venue, with dozens of established acts having trod its boards including Hawkwind, Roxy Music, Thin Lizzy, Queen, and Genesis to name but a few. On the afternoon of the Cleethorpes show Glen had broken the heel on one of his boots – the only footwear he'd brought with him on the trip. He'd gone to Malcolm to explain his predicament fully expecting him to put his hand in his pocket so that he could go into town and get the necessary repairs done. Malcolm, however, had been in one of his moods, which meant the boot didn't get repaired, and he'd had to stand rooted in front of his amplifier for fear that he might go arse over tit if he went walkabout. Steve had been equally inactive throughout the performance, but his unwillingness to throw his customary "guitar hero" shapes was due to his being shit-faced as he and Paul had spent the day helping Paul Simonon belatedly celebrate his twenty-first birthday. The Clash bassist had celebrated his coming of age five days earlier by hitting every pub in Camden with Mick and Joe, but when Steve and Paul heard about the birthday boy they'd insisted on a pub crawl. The trio had barely made it back to the Winter Gardens in time for the curtain going up. Simonon had staggered out on stage so out of it that he'd struggled to decipher the notes he'd stuck onto the neck of his bass guitar to help him remember where to place his fingers. Steve and Paul were in just as bad a state, and he was still surprised that they'd made it through the show. Thankfully, the onstage lethargy hadn't transmuted to the audience, and what the Cleethorpes crowd had lacked in numbers they'd more than made up for in volume. There'd been the odd scuffle here and there, and a couple of windows were smashed outside after the show. But there'd been no mass brawls, and no arrests, and the amiable Jackson had told Malcolm that he'd happily rebook the Sex Pistols for the Winter Gardens. It was also at Cleethorpes that the new *Anarchy In The UK* fanzine had gone on sale. Of course, the idea was to have the fanzine ready in time for the tour, but as with the ladies at EMI's Hayes pressing plant, the printer had seemingly taken umbrage at the foulmouthed Sex Pistols and had deliberately delayed delivery. At Malcolm's behest, Debbie Juvenile and Tracie O'Keefe – both of whom were occasional workers at SEX - had travelled up from London with a batch of the fanzine's inaugural issue. The fanzine was priced at 20p, and bore Ray Stevenson's photograph of Sue Lucas – or "Soo Catwoman", as she called herself - in her full feline regalia on the front cover. Like Soo, Debbie and Tracie were fully paid up members of the so-called "Bromley Contingent", the name Vivienne had bestowed on the colourful clique that had latched onto the Sex Pistols at the beginning of the year; several of whom had since formed their own groups. The majority of the fanzine was give over to the 100 Club Punk Festival back in September, and featured several pages of black and white photographs taken by Stevenson during the two-day event. On a lighter side, the fanzine also included a full-page feature on "the luscious Paul Cook." Not everything was quite so rosy of the literary front; however, as the December issue of EMI's monthly in-house magazine, EMI News, featured plenty of internal grumblings about the corporation's association with the Sex Pistols; the most vociferous complaint coming from those employed at EMI's Radar and Equipment Accounts Department, which was part of EMI Defence Weapons & Systems. Glen didn't have a problem with people expressing their opinion, but he couldn't fathom how these same people could attack the Sex Pistols for muttering a few expletives on tea-time television whilst spending their working week perfecting weapons systems that were ultimately sold to questionable regimes around the world? The Pistols also came under attack from the American music journalist Lisa Robinson, who'd apparently rubbished them in one of her columns. Malcolm hadn't thought this to be all that big a deal, but Glen knew that Robinson's column was syndicated in 187 papers across America and Australia, which meant that her disparaging remarks about the Sex Pistols would reach a significant audience. Malcolm might not be paying much heed to what was being written about his charges, but he'd been sufficiently outraged by Capital Radio DJ Roger Scott's accusation that the Sex Pistols had called in session musicians to help record their debut single, that he'd called the station and forced Scott into making an on-the-air retraction.

♪♪♪

The Woods Centre was only the third of the original nineteen dates to proceed as planned. Despite having endured an eight-hour journey from north Humberside, they'd arrived in Plymouth in good spirits. It had been a great show with all three groups putting in good, solid performances before a packed and enthusiastic crowd. Indeed, the promoter was so enthused by how things had gone that he hurriedly booked a return date for the twentythird to replace an additional date that Malcolm had provisionally booked at the Manor Ballroom in Ipswich. This, however, was where things began to unravel as the replacement show at Penelope's Ballroom in Paignton for the long-since cancelled booking at Torquay's 400 Ballroom for the following night had also fallen through. Glen was never one for finger-pointing, but while town councils, leisure committees, high-handed university authoritarians, and Rank Leisure officials, had all undoubtedly played their respective part in derailing the tour, the Torquay's 400 Ballroom cancellation proved the most bizarre. Devon County Council had initially raised no objections to allowing the Sex Pistols play the date, but a self-righteous local housewife called Sheila Hardaway who'd called upon the council to have a rethink. Two years earlier - as part of her one-woman "Clean Up Torquay" campaign – the English Riviera's answer to Mary Whitehouse had unsuccessfully fought to get a bill -passed which would have obligated male holidaymakers to keep their shirts fastened whilst out and about the coastal resort's cobbled streets. In a bid to avoid any further unnecessary expenditure, Malcolm instructed the Plymouth promoter to bring the second Woods Centre date forward. However, what had seemed like a sound solution in theory was never going to work on a practical level as Malcolm hadn't stopped to take into account that the switch would leave the promoter with little or no time to advertise the second Plymouth show. As a result of Malcolm's non-lateral thinking, they'd been obliged to play to a near-empty hall.

Malcolm, of course, wasn't around to see the folly of his ways as immediately after the first Woods Centre date he'd dashed off to catch the last train to London. The hapless promoter may have been left out of sorts – not to mention out of pocket - but the tour party was so relieved that an end to their suffering was in sight that they refused to allow the lack of an audience to dampen their collective spirit. In fact, the mood was so relaxed that none of the musicians bothered changing into their stage gear, and had happily handed their instruments over to the next band up onstage. Unfortunately, for the Pistols, by the time they took to the stage Goodman was completely off his head on pills and they suffered as a result. Despite a nine-month on-going involvement with the group, Goodman was still a hippy at heart, and had chosen to start his Winter Solstice celebrations a tad too early. Nils, in a fit of pique at Goodman's lack of professionalism, had replaced him with Keeth Paul. The switch failed to bring about much of an improvement, however, as the happy-go-lucky American had spent the evening dipping into Goodman's goody bag.

Chapter Nineteen

Pistols, Clash etc.: What Did You Do On
The Punk Tour, Daddy?

TO TURN up to a Sex Pistols' show nowadays is to make a statement to the world that you care about rock 'n' roll and don't give a Bill Grundy what the yellow press thinks. And enough kids in Manchester, God bless 'em, were prepared to do just that, almost filling the Electric Circus.However, once there, they weren't quite sure what to do.

When Johnny, Glen, Steve and Paul sliced through the crowd (no folding lotus stages for them...yet), bounded up the steps and roared straight into 'Anarchy In The U.K.', the kids knew just what to do because they knew the song. They sang along and jumped and bumped me back into the unreceptive arms of the national daily press photographers, one of whom was trying to take his pix with his hands over his ears (try it sometime).
Sounds, Saturday, 18 December 1976

It was just after midday when McLaren arrived at Manchester Square. He'd spent most of the morning on the phone speaking with the music papers. The papers would be going to press that day, and he wanted to ensure each had his version of the ongoing events surrounding the Sex Pistols' relationship with EMI. He paid a quick visit to Hilary Walker's office to get the latest update on the proposed Holland trip before seeking out an empty office to make a couple of quick phone calls. He was having a coffee with Nick Mobbs bringing the latter up to speed on the tour when one of girls from the typing pool popped her head through the door to say Leslie Hill was now free to see him. Malcolm made his way up to Hill's office where Hill made some perfunctory comments about the weather before enquiring about the previous night's show in Plymouth. "It went rather well," said Malcolm. "So well in fact, that I booked a second show there tonight." "The Woods Centre, is that right?" "It's situated above a Montague Burtons store," Malcolm replied. "But I didn't come here to discuss the tour. At least not the performance side of things." "I didn't think you had," Hill said with a wry smile. "By Stephen's calculations the tour is set to incur losses of around ten thousand pounds," Malcolm continued. "And I really don't see how you – EMI that is - can expect us to shoulder those losses alone." "Yes, that's the figure I've heard being bandied about," Hill nodded. "From whom?" Hill leaned back in his chair, absentmindedly rubbing at the corner of his left eye. "Come on, Malcolm; we do have a press office. Whenever you speak to the music press, the first thing they do is call us in the hope of getting a response." He leaned forward again. "Look, Malcolm, I'm as sorry as anyone about what has happened, but we

have fulfilled our obligations in regard to the contract. The contract states that you - i.e. Glitterbest - are responsible for all tour costings . . . as Mr Fisher well knows." "You're missing the point here, Leslie," Malcolm pressed on. "This has been the most talked about tour in the history of rock'n'roll. We're making the nine o'clock news most evenings. You can't buy this amount of exposure." "Yes, but it's your being on the news most evenings that's casing all the problems upstairs," Hill retorted.

"You still have friends here, Malcolm; and I count myself as one of them. But there's only so much Nick, Bob, and I can do." "All I'm asking for here, Leslie, is affirmation that the Sex Pistols are to remain an EMI act," Malcolm said matter-of-factly. "You simply can't keep us dangling like this. It's all very well sending us a Fortnum and Mason Christmas hamper, and talking about promotional trips to your overseas territories, but I'm fielding calls left, right, and centre from the music press about the rumours that EMI intends to drop the Sex Pistols from your roster." "I can assure you no one here at EMI Records is talking about dropping the Sex Pistols," Hill countered. "Mike is focusing on the follow-up single to 'Anarchy', and he and I had a meeting the other day to discuss a schedule for the album. In fact, I'm due to speak with Bob later this afternoon about the situation. We're just as frustrated as you are. It's become a matter of principle for us. How are we expected to function if corporate continues to dictate policy?" Malcolm jabbed a finger towards the ceiling. "The problem with that lot up there is they have no concept of what it's like out there in the real world. How can they condemn something they haven't the slightest understanding of? If they came to a Sex Pistols concert, they would see how much the band means to the kids that come to see them." "I'd certainly pay to see that," Hill smiled. "Have you spoken with Hilary about the proposed Holland trip?" he asked. "She's proposed a meeting with the boys," Malcolm nodded. "I said they'd be over sometime tomorrow afternoon." Hill stood up and came around his desk. "You won't be coming in with them?" Recognising the meeting was over Malcolm got to his feet. "It's difficult to say," he said, following Hill to the door. "We've got major renovations going on at the shop, but I'll try. Oh, that reminds me. I forgot to ask Hilary if she'll be accompanying the group on the Holland trip." "Well, she doesn't normally accompany the artists . . . unless she happens to be a fan of their music," Hill smiled. "I should think she'll have Fletch accompany the group. That's Graham Fletcher. But don't worry; the group will be good hands. Fletch is an old hand at this sort of thing."

"But it would be seen as an indicator to EMI's intent if Hilary were to go over with them." Malcolm countered.

"I would have thought the fact that Hilary is arranging the Holland trip is indicative as to our intent," Hill reasoned. "Look, I can't give you any cast-iron assurances, but with the tour coming to an end the tabloids will have nothing to write about. Everyone here is winding down for Christmas, and with a bit of luck the whole Grundy fiasco will have blown over by the time we come back after the holidays. All that's required is for the group to avoid any repeat of what happened on the *Today* show."

♫♫♫

A commotion in the outside corridor wrenched Glen from his slumber. He was so disorientated that it took several seconds to familiarise himself with his nondescript surroundings. The exertions of the last few days had exacted a wearying toll; his lethargic state stemmed from stringing four consecutive shows together. If this was how he felt after just four shows, imagine how exhausted he'd have been had they actually completed the scheduled nineteen dates. He sluggishly rolled off the bed got to his feet and made his way over to the door. On stepping outside he discovered the strange thumping noise that woke him was due to some prankster slapping a trifle on every door along the corridor. He stood watching the paper plate sliding down the door, leaving a snail-trail of jelly, cream and custard. He was reminded of the Great Plague when people had marked their door with a cross to warn others that those within were infected. For a heartbeat he wondered whether the hotel manager was responsible for the trifles; that he was warning his other guests that these rooms housed those vile punk rockers they might have read about. He stepped back into the room and was closing the door when he heard what sounded like muffled giggling. As he stepped out to investigate, the door to the room directly opposite burst open and Dave Goodman and Sophie Richmond came charging out to attack him with water pistols. "What the hell are you doing here, Soph?" he yelled, struggling to fend them off. "I'd wrapped things up at the office so I thought I'd make the trip down here," Sophie said, giving him another squirt. "Corkie and the rest of the crew got really excited on seeing her," Goodman grinned. "They thought Soph had brought their wages." "You brought ours though, right?" Glen asked. "Sorry," Sophie giggled. She gave Glen another soaking before fleeing along the corridor. Glen set off in pursuit and easily caught up with her. He grappled Sophie to the floor and was wrestle the water pistol from her grasp when Mick and Ray Stevenson emerged from the lift. Mick merely stepped over Glen's outstretched leg and continued along the corridor, but Stevenson unslung his camera.

"What was that, two knock-downs and a submission?" Mick grinned as Glen came through the door. "It wasn't what it looked like," said Glen. "Ray took a bleedin' photograph!" he grumbled. "What if Celia sees it?" "Ray's been in this game long enough to know what happens on tour stays on tour," Mick grinned. "I brought you a present," he added, tossing a copy of the previous week's *Record Mirror* onto Glen's bed. "Besides, Ray's too cock-a-fuckin' hoop about havin' one his shots on the *Mirror*'s front cover to bother about much of anythin'. The fuckin' drinks on Ray tonight, that's for sure." Glen picked the paper and opened it out and instantly recognised the shot of John as being from the session Stevenson had taken at Dryden Chambers a few weeks back. "Johnny Rotten wants you dead," he said, reading aloud the subtext accompanying the photograph. "In my case, they're not far wrong, either. Where did you find this?" he asked. "There's a Co-op around the corner," said Mick. I managed to sponge a few quid off of Bernie cos I needed some fags. The girl on the desk gave me directions.""What about this week's?" "Dunno," Mick shrugged. "I was on my out again when I spotted John's mush starin' out at me. They've got 'Anarchy' as a new entry at number 43 on their Top 50. And the editorial makes for interesting reading. It's on page three, I think," he said, walking across to check his hair in the mirror Glen settled himself down on his head and opened the paper. Under the heading 'Press Is A Five-Letter Word', the *Record Mirror*'s editorial kicked off by borrowing The *Sun*'s 2 December headline 'We're The Pistols Loaded?', before going on to question why Fleet Street had got itself all hot and bothered over a few fourletter words when there were far more important issues currently going on in the world; going so far as to suggest the media triumvirate of Press, Radio, and TV - with its collective power to make or break a "cult" such as punk rock - had purposely given the Sex Pistols maximum exposure to ensure that punk would become the music industry's biggest money spinner for the coming year. The editorial also accused Bill Grundy of having deliberately encouraged the Sex Pistols to swear on live television as there could be no other reason for his churlish insistence that John repeat the word "shit", which had been barely audible the first time round. The editorial concluded by posing the question: why was it that Grundy had been suspended after supposedly being deemed blameless by the powers-that-be at LWT? On turning the page Glen was shocked to find another article relating to the Pistols: this one mooting the possibility that EMI were set to drop the band.

Mick ran his fingers through his hair again before turning away from the mirror. "You reached the piece where-" "Where is says EMI are set to dump us," Glen cut in. "I wouldn't pay much attention to that if I was you," Mick offered. "It's just paper talk. Have you seen the photo of Billy Broad?" he asked in reference to the postage stamp-sized photo of Broad that accompanied the article. In the photo, Broad was sporting a SEX Tshirt fitted with two strategically placed zips that allowed the wearer to expose their nipples. "The article's supposed to be about us!" Glen harrumphed. "Billy's fronting Generation X now with Tony," said Mick. "You remember Tony, don't you? He was with me the night we came over to Denmark Street . . ."

"They played the opening night at the Roxy the other night," said Mick. "I'd have gone along if we hadn't been in Wales." "Have you seen where it says the owners are hoping to have us playing there on New year's Eve with the Damned?" "I can't see that happenin' somehow," Mick grinned. "You'll know Andy, won't you? Andy Czezowski . . ." "He's a mate of Malcolm's," Glen nodded, dabbing his fingertips against his tongue before turning the page. "He was at St. Martin's when we made our debut. Wow, you kept this quiet," he gasped on arriving at a full-page interview the *Mirror*'s Barry Cain had conducted with John at Manchester Square a week or so before the band's ill-feted appearance on *Today*. The interview - under the heading: 'Johnny knows he's not mad. Can you say that?'- was accompanied by two more of Stevenson's photographs of John from the same photo-shoot as the one adorning the paper's front cover. "Have you noticed how small the shots are of me, Steve, Paul compared to ones they used of John?" Glen said sourly. "It's like we've been reduced to sidemen. "I like the bit where it says the Pistols are as 'subtle as a sawn-off shotgun'," Mick said coming across. "You should use that on one of your flyers." "I vaguely remember John saying something about doing the interview," said Glen. "How come you, Steve, and Paul weren't there?" "I can't remember now," Glen shrugged. "I think I spoke with Cain on the phone, but that could have been another interview. It all seems like a lifetime ago now" "Well at least they've used a decent photograph of you," said Mick. "Steve and Paul look like a couple of fuckin' barrow boys off of Smithfield Market." "Well, Paul did used to be an electrician." "Yeah, but John's the one who looks like he's just stuck his knob in the power socket," Mick grinned "I see they're harping on about how I went to a grammar school," Glen said dismissively. "It's hardly a crime, is it?" "Steve and Paul don't get a mention in the whole article," said Mick. "But they've got your quote about the Bay City Rollers havin' spotty fuckin' arses. I'd have kept that one to myself, if I was you," he chuckled. "Anyway, you'd best be getting' your own arse in gear, hadn't you." "Why, what's happening?" "The aftershow, remember?" "I don't think I'll bother," Glen said, plumping up the pillows before sprawling across his bed. "I'm gonna get my head down."

"Suit yourself," Mick shrugged, heading for the door. "Don't wait up."

CHAPTER TWENTY

PISTOLS
Episode 93.

THE FACT that ninety-nine per cent of their critics have never even seen a live Sex Pistols gig doesn't really matter anymore. What does matter is that the storm of self-righteous indignation that swept the nation after the episode with Bill Grundy has resulted in Town Hall, local council, University and Rank Leisure officials exercising their virtual monopoly of potential rock venues in this country, and, by doing so, taking away the right of certain young rock bands to play for the people who want to see them.

Don't bother with the old Any Publicity Is Good Publicity line; never before has there been a situation where rock bands have been so severely restricted in the right to play their music.

New Musical Express, Saturday, 18 December 1976.

The Holiday Inn's residents bar was decorated throughout with framed sketches celebrating Plymouth's historical past: Sir Francis Drake's ships sailing out to give battle to the invading Spanish Armada in 1588, the Pilgrim Fathers setting sail for the New World in 1620, and the siege of Plymouth during the English Civil War. The hotel usually catered for sailing enthusiasts, sales reps, and the occasional American tourist keen to trace the family lineage to the place where their ancestors departed on the *Mayflower*. It was totally unsuited for boisterous end-of-tour shenanigans. "Where's your boyfriend?" John shouted on seeing Mick approaching their table. "He'll be washin' his fuckin' feet again, I expect," Steve chimed in. "He's havin' an early night as it happens," Mick said, squeezing himself between Thunders and Walter Lure. "What time did you lot start?" he asked, taking note of the array of empty glasses and bottles on the table. "You could have given us a knock." "This is the VIP party, Mick," John said, accepting a cigarette from Debbie Juvenile sitting next to him. "Not sure where the riff-raff are havin' theirs . . ." "Have you seen last week's *Record Mirror*?" Mick asked John. "You're on the front cover. Glen thinks you're hauntin' him." "In his dreams," John chuckled dryly. "It's one of the shots I took at Dryden Chambers," Ray Stevenson beamed. "And they've used a couple more with the interview. That's next month's rent sorted." John drained his glass and put it down on the table. "What interview's that, then?" "The reporter's name was Barry Cain, I think," said Mick. "Yeah, I remember now," John nodded. "He grew up in Islington so we had some common ground. We did the interview at Manchester Square. Can't think why, as their offices are on Holloway Road. We could have done it there and I could have popped round to see mum." "Get the fuckin beers in, Ray," Steve shouted over. "I haven't been paid for the photos yet, Steve," Stevenson said, patting the front pockets of his jeans. "Best make sure," Steve grinned, giving the photographer a playful shove to send him tumbling onto his brother. "Get his keks off!" Stevenson was fending off Steve when the manager came hurrying out from behind reception. "What on earth is going on here?" he demanded. "This is the third time I've had to warn you about your behaviour. This is a respectable hotel, and I simply won't tolerate it! And if I find out it was one of you lot that desecrated the doors with trifle you'll be out on the street. One more peep out of you and I'm closing the bar. He then turned on his heel and retreated towards his office, choosing to ignore the catcalls and questioning of his parentage that trailed in his wake. Paul was returning from the bar when he espied Steve standing waiting for the lift to descend. "Where you goin', you closet?" he shouted across. "To see a man about a dog," Steve said, giving Paul a sly wink. "He's up to somethin'," Paul chuckled, as Steve disappeared inside the lift. "What did you think of tonight's show?" Mick asked the group. "Apart from us outnumbering the crowd you mean?" John sneered. "Typical fuckin' Malcolm; couldn't arrange an orgy in a fuckin' brothel!" "It's over now though, ain't it," Mick sighed. "Back to London tomorrow." John was about to respond but was distracted on seeing the lift doors open to reveal a pair of beetle crushers resting upon a chair. "They look like Steve's," Paul frowned as the doors closed and the lift began its ascent. "What's he up to now?" Two minutes later the lift descended again and the doors pinged open to reveal a neatly folded pair of jeans had been added to the brothel creepers. "What's it gonna be next?" Mick chuckled; his eyes riveted on the lift doors. "What else was he wearin'?" "I'll be his mohair jumper," Nils said, seeing the floor numbers mounted above the lift doors light up in turn as the lift made its decent. "Should have put a bet on it, bro," Ray Stevenson grinned as the doors opened to reveal Steve's mohair draped over the back of the chair. By now, everyone in the room was fixated with Steve's antics; even the barmaid was enthralled as the lift slowly made its descent. "By my reckonin' he's only got his undercrackers left," Paul howled on seeing Steve's Two Cowboys T-shirts nestled on top of the mohair. As the doors closed again Ray Stevenson jumped up and dashed across to the lift. "Let's chuck his clobber in the sea," He fell silent on seeing the lift returning. The doors opened and Steve came bursting out stark naked; one hand cupped about his privates. The raucous laughter brought the manager at a run, but Steve had already made good his escape. The manager was gazing about the bar area when the lift began yet another descent. All heads turned towards the door assuming Steve was returning for an encore. It wasn't Steve that emerged, however, but a visibly-shaken Bernie Rhodes. On seeing the manager he demanded he be given another room as someone had shit on his bed.

It was an open secret amongst the musicians that the road crew had long been plotting their revenge on The Clash's manager over his high-handedness and demeaning attitude towards them throughout the tour. Rhodes' revelations proved the final straw for the manager and he ordered the bar closed.

♪♪♪

The revellers had retreated upstairs to the lighting crew's room; the door of which was also smeared with trifle. A pillow-fight was in full swing with John playfully jumping around on one of the beds swinging his pillow above his head challenging all-comers for a shot at the title. Steve, having got dressed again, simply wrenched the mattress to send John crashing against the bedside table dislodging a dozen or so empty cans and bottles. Mick was helping John to his feet when Sophie and Dave Goodman came charging in dousing Steve with their water pistols. Steve grabbed hold of Goodman, and after wrestling the water pistol from the engineer's grasp, he chased Sophie out into the corridor. Steve was returning from giving Sophie a soaking when Goodman announced he'd found the door to the hotel's swimming pool unlocked. The chance to continue the party poolside was too good to pass up. The mischievous revellers were making their way down the emergency stairwell when Paul realised Steve was missing. At that moment Steve was conducting his own commando-style raid on Ray Stevenson's room. He'd spotted Stevenson sneaking off with Jo Faul, who'd accompanied Sophie on the journey up from London. His reputation as the group's Lothario was seriously on the line as the tour was all but over and he'd yet to get his end away. He was hoping his being a Sex Pistol would give him a higher ranking in the bedding stakes than a mere photographer. Should that not prove to be the case, he was perfectly willing to settle for sloppy seconds. Of course, with Stevenson having put in all the legwork he was reluctant to share his prize and continued to ignore Steve's pleas to be allowed in. When the corridor fell silent he'd assumed Steve had given up the ghost, but he and Jo got the shock of their lives a short while later when Steve came through the door. It seemed Steve had headed downstairs and beguiled the receptionist into believing he was sharing with Stevenson and had mislaid his key. Steve's ingenuity would count for nought, however, and after conducting a search of the room for some non-existent item he'd finally conceded defeat and retreated from the room.

When Steve arrived poolside the sulphate-fuelled frolics had gone into overdrive with everyone stripped down to their undies. He was still smarting at having lost out to Ray Stevenson, but was still hoping to get his ticket stamped by one of the other girls. Tracie was looking particularly tasty with her clinging wet T-shirt emphasising her shapely form. He'd flirted with Tracie often enough in the shop, and had marked her down as a "possibility" when she'd turned up at the Winter Gardens in Cleethorpes. He'd no sooner set off towards Tracie, however, when Roadent came staggering across and slipped his arm about her waist. He had to admire Roadent's taste, but he wasn't about to let his last remaining hope of a shag slip from his grasp. Deciding all was fair in love and war, he set out to knobble the opposition. Roadent and Tracie had their backs to him so he jumped in the pool and quickly swam across to the shallow end. Having sunk down onto his knees, he then shouted for Roadent to join him. Roadent was too pissed to realise what was going on and threw himself head first into the water, splitting his head open on the tile floor. He broke the surface moments later with a nasty gash to his forehead. It was obvious to all that the wound would require stitches. After giving Steve a dressing down Tracie rushed out in search of a payphone to call an ambulance while Sophie and Micky Foote gingerly guided the concussed Roadent in her wake.

♪♪♪

The journey from Plymouth had been in total contrast to the outbound journey up to Derby. There'd certainly been no high-jinx or service-station raids. The after-effects of the previous evening's merriment were no doubt playing their part, but Glen couldn't help thinking a collective uncertainty about what the future held for all onboard was also proving a factor. The impending Holland trip was proof enough that EMI Records was intent on maintaining their working relationship with the Pistols, but of course, the final decision as to whether they would remain an EMI act rested higher up the corporation's food chain. Had it not been for his conversation with Mike Thorne, he'd have spent Christmas walking on eggshells dreading the call confirming his worst fears. Now, however, he could make merry with Celia and make a decision on his future in the New Year. It was all dependent on the Holland trip. If that went without a hitch, promo visits to EMI's other territories would surely follow. There'd be a follow-up single and an album, and they'd be off touring in support of the album. John and Steve didn't seem particularly perturbed about what was happening. He could only assume they'd fallen for Malcolm's patter about his having spoken with several record labels that were supposedly keen

to take on the Pistols should EMI swing the axe. Paul was quieter than usual owing to a recent interview his mum Sylvie had given to the *Daily Mail*. According to the article, Paul's dad had left the family home on account of his struggling to cope with family name being dragged through the newspapers. After everything the media had accused them of doing, the only thing he'd take at face value in a newspaper was the date. He'd met Paul's parents several times, and had always found them to be fully supportive of what Paul was doing. They hadn't put up much of an argument when he packed in his apprenticeship at Watney's. Mick had the hump as Rob Harper had apparently given Bernie notice that he had no interest in joining The Clash and unless they woke up to find a drummer in their Christmas stocking, they were in for a miserable winter. The Heartbreakers had even more reason to feel despondent. If Childers didn't have any luck at the Home Office they'd be up the creek without the proverbial paddle. They didn't even have return tickets to the states. And while they were insisting their having sold out the Roxy was behind their decision to seek permission to remain in London, Glen suspected the availability of Methadone on free prescription had featured in their reasoning. Glen turned away from watching the shoppers braving the elements on the Old Kent Road. "Well we managed to pass 'Go', but there's sod all chance of us getting our twohundred quid. I still haven't bought Celia's Christmas present yet." Mick lifted his head and fixed Glen with bloodshot eyes. "Did you say somethin'?" he asked drowsily. "Jesus, your eyes are redder than Rudolph's hooter!" Mick offered a wane smile. "Yeah, but it was a great night. What was about going some place?" "Were on the Old Kent Road," Glen said, pointing out the window. "You know, like in Monopoly?" "I can't fuckin' stand board games," Mick shrugged. "Monopoly always reminds me of Christmas," said Glen. "Can't stand fuckin' Christmas, either," Mick groaned, without bothering to open his eyes. "Well, it's alright if *Zulu*'s on I s'pose. But it ain't on this year. It's just gonna be the same old shit as usual: 'Morecambe & Wise; the Two Ronnies, and James fuckin' Bond."
"What are you prattling on about?" "*Zulu*'s the best film ever made," Mick said, suddenly becoming more animated. "It's a fuckin' classic!" "Don't think I've seen it," Glen shrugged. "Who's in it?" "Michael Caine and Stanley Baker. It's based on a true story; the Battle of Rorke's Drift," Mick continued. "Can you believe less than a hundred British soldiers successfully defended the mission station against four-thousand fuckin' Zulus? They handed out something like twelve Victoria Crosses that day." "Thanks for the history lesson," Glen chuckled. "When we get signed," Mick continued as though Glen hadn't spoken, "the first thing I'm gonna do is buy one of these new

video machines that Bernie's been bangin' on about." He suddenly fell silent, sniffing the air. At that moment Joe popped his head over the backrest of Mick's seat "Can I tempt you with a spliff, Brother Michael?" "Too right, you can," Mick grinned, accepting the spliff and taking a toke. "Where are we now?" he asked blowing a plume of smoke against the window. "Just coming up to the Strand," Glen said, peering out the window." "Fuck," Mick grimaced, taking another toke. "This is it then, boys, home sweet fuckin' home." The coach parked up at the corner of Denmark Street and everyone set about gathering their belongings. "Do you fancy nipping over to The Cambridge for a quick one?" Glen asked Mick as he pulled his bag out from the overhead storage rack. "If you're buyin'," Mick smiled, following Glen off the bus. Paul Simonon reached over and plucked the spliff from Mick's mouth before leaping down onto the pavement. "Not with this, you fuckin' don't," he shouted taking a satisfying toke as he raced down Denmark Street to catch up with Joe.

Chapter Twenty One

MORE PISTOLS

The Sex Pistols have added another date to their chaos-stricken British tour. The group, with support acts the Clash and Johnny Thunders' Heartbreakers, now end the tour at IPSWICH Manor Ballroom on Thursday, December 23. and have criticised their record company, EMI, for The group claim they have lost £10,000 on the tour allegedly not supporting them during the shows.

An EMI spokesman commented: "We are having regular meetings with Malcolm McLaren and the Sex Pistols and if they are in need of money then I am sure the question has been raised and discussed.

"We have certainly fulfilled our obligation as far as an advance on their contract is concerned so there is no question on that account. Whether we pay them any more is a matter between EMI and the group."

Melody Maker, Saturday, 25 December 1976.

Getting to Cambridge Gardens from Chiswick on a Christmas Day had proved no easy task, but Glen thought it only fair that he show his face. Steve and Paul had been here all afternoon, as had Joe, Mick, and Paul. Nils, Sid, and Soo Catwoman were also in attendance. The three-storey Victorian stucco house was a tasty piece of real estate, and he still couldn't figure out what had possessed Jonh Ingham to acquiesce to Caroline's wishes to throw a party for a bunch of reprobates. He surely wouldn't have been so accommodating had it been his name on the deeds. Caroline's underlying motive for throwing the party was so she could ensure spending Christmas Day with her Clash lover boy, and she was also no doubt hoping the occasion might serve to engender a little punk harmony. However, with Captain Sensible, and Rat Scabies having taken up Caroline's invitation for turkey and trimmings, the atmosphere around the yuletide log proved far from festive. From what Paul had told him, even Steve's grabbing one of Soo's breasts and shouting out that he'd found the "thrupenny bit" during the dessert had failed to lift the strained ambiance. Glen had no sooner stepped through the door when John and Caroline both pounced on him demanding to know the latest on the EMI situation. It seemed that either Steve or Paul had blabbed about his having been at the shop the previous afternoon when Hill had called to speak with Malcolm. He'd only called in to get a sub from Sophie, but had ended up spending the afternoon helping her and Malcolm lighten the Fortnum and Mason hamper that EMI had sent over. He'd been astounded that Hill was still at Manchester Square, as most MDs would have long-since left the office. It seemed Hill had been enmeshed in lastminute discussions about the Sex Pistols with Sir John Read, and Sir Leonard Wood, EMI's Group Director of Music. Before retiring to Gerard's Cross for the holidays Hill had called to give Malcolm the latest update

The thrust of Hill's main argument was that Read or Wood could walk into W.H. Smith's, John Menzies, or any other leading book store and probably purchase up to a hundred books containing the word "fuck" within its contents. He'd also argued that although the F-word might not be in common use within the world of corporate boardrooms, it was most definitely part of the public vernacular. Unfortunately for Hill, neither Read nor Wood appeared willing to accept this as a valid argument. Hill had then tried a different tack by focusing on the Sex Pistols' marketability, claiming that if EMI dropped the group from their roster they would be missing out on somewhere in the region of £1million in record sales. Whether losing out on a six-figure return over a couple of four-letter expletives had altered Read and Wood's perspective remained to be seen . . .

♪♪♪

Ingham and Coon's music writer pals Jon Savage and Steve Walsh arrived twenty or so minutes after Glen, but whatever bonhomie the two brought with them was soon shattered with the arrival of The Heartbreakers. Childers was grateful for the opportunity to spend an evening amongst friends but Thunders and co. showed scant respect for either their hosts or their surroundings. Caroline continued being the gracious host, of course, but Ingham sought sanctuary from the Americans in guiding Jon and Steve upstairs to the second living room. Glen had no desire to suffer the Heartbreakers' rude and unruly antics and instead followed the three writers upstairs. He didn't much fancy making journalistic small talk either, and so grabbed the Christmas issue of the *NME* from off the coffee table and went and sat over the window. Malcolm had said something about Neil Spencer calling the shop looking for a response to an "open letter" that would feature in the paper's festive edition in which The Pat Travers Band was issuing a direct challenge to the Pistols to a musical playoff with all proceeds going to charity, and how they would outplay the Pistols using defective instruments. Ignoring the photo of John on the cover he flicked through the pages until arriving at the article in question. He was reading the piece when he noticed Walsh coming over. "Alright, Glen; Merry Christmas an' all that." "Yeah, same to you." "Wasn't it the *NME* that said punk would be over by Christmas?" Walsh grinned, indicating to the cover. "The Christmas issue of *Glue*'s got John on the cover as well." "Are you still writing stuff for *Glue* then?" Glen asked, closing the *NME* and dropping it to the carpet. "Occasionally," Walsh nodded. "Jon's also asked me to help him with his new fanzine," he said, looking over at Savage. "He's called it '*London's Outrage*'. It's not bad as it goes. It's made up of stuff he's cut out of the *NME* and his collection of sixties pop annuals. He says he shifted a few copies of the first issue at the Damned's gig at the Hope & Anchor the other night. You know, the one Jake Riviera apparently organised as a "fuck you" to Malcolm." "Yeah, I heard about that one," Glen nodded.

"Course, I've been busy helping Sid and Viv in that band of theirs," Walsh continued. "They've got Keith Levene jamming with 'em now."

Glen was about to respond when Jerry Nolan came through the door; his face the pallor of a dead carp. "Help me out would you, brother," Nolan mumbled approaching Glen and Walsh. "I'm a dude in real need of a lude." "It's upstairs, first door on your left," Walsh smiled. Nolan automatically glanced up at the ceiling. "What? No," he shook his head "I don't need a dump. I just need a fuckin' lude!" "Sorry, Jerry; can't help you there," Glen shrugged. "We've ah . . . We've celebrated Christmas a bit too much today, if you catch my meaning," Nolan said, tapping the side of his nose. "I just need to come down a little, is all . . . What you bozos lookin' at!" He challenged Ingham and Savage. At that moment Thunders appeared in the doorway. "Jerry, whad'ya doin' up here?" he asked. "I'm lookin' for ludes, Johnny; but nobody's holdin'." "Do you know where we can get a little somethin'?" Thunders asked Glen, stepping into the room as Roadent appeared at his shoulder. "Merry fuckin' Christmas, Johnny!" Roadent grinned. "Who wants a drink?" he asked, offering up his can of Heineken. "I'll take a hit," Nolan nodded, failing to see the look of expectant glee in Roadent's eyes. "Man, I fuckin' hate' warm beer!" he grimaced. "I call it 'Roadent's Special Brew'," Roadent giggled, retreating towards the door. "Do you know where we might get a couple of ludes?" Thunders asked, catching hold of Roadent's arm.

"Sorry, Johnny; can't help you," Roadent shook his head. "It's Christmas Day! You got as much chance of findin' a virgin in a brothel than you have a dealer." Thunders remained silent for a moment. "You boys should get to know your town a little better. If we was back in New York right now, Jerry an' me would know exactly where to go."

♪♪♪

It was going on midnight, and while the more considerate guests such as Savage and Walsh had taken their leave, the party was still in full swing. Sid had spent most of the day holed up in one of the bedrooms listening to Jim Reeves albums, but had at last come down to join the party. He sat cradling a clockwork doll with a safety-pin through its nose and a Durex tied about its neck. The doll was a gift from John, who'd also playfully scrawled "Auntie Sue" on the doll's forehead in mock-reference to Sid having adopted Sue Catwoman as his latest female role model. "What's this I hear about you losin' another drummer?" he asked Mick. "What is it with you lot and drummers?" Paul grinned. "I don't know why you guys didn't try harder to keep Rob Harper," said Glen. "Rob could play well enough, I s'pose," Joe said begrudgingly. "But he'd never have fitted in." "Why's that?" Glen asked. He knew that no one within The Clash camp had made any real effort in befriending Harper. He suspected that Harper's not "fitting in" stemmed from his surname being "Harper-Milne". Having a university-educated drummer with a doublebarrelled surname certainly didn't fit in with The Clash's working class "street fighting man" ethos. Harper's being 27 would have also proved problematic, if only because it might have led to awkward questions being raised about Joe's true age. Joe was so obsessed with fermenting the Clash's street-gang credibility that he'd gone so far as to suggest they give Roadent a try-out on drums. Mick, of course, had been quick to nip that one in the bud. "He was a fuckin' Bob Dylan fan for a start," Joe sneered. "I caught him listenin' to Dylan tapes on the coach!" "So what're you gonna do for the Roxy date on New Year's Day?" Glen asked. The Roxy's management had wanted a Sex Pistols/Clash double headliner to mark the club's official opening, but Malcolm declined the invitation. "We'll see if Terry'll help us out until we can find someone else," Mick shrugged. "Not if I can fuckin' help it, we won't!" Joe growled. "Joe's got a problem with Terry's ideology," Mick grinned, dropping his spent fag into an empty beer can. "What do you expect?" Joe snapped. "All he wants out of life is a fuckin' flash car!" "Andy Czezowski's asked us to do some gigs there," said Scabies. "Only so we can pay him back the money we owe him from when he was our manager," Sensible chuckled. "But once we've settled what we owe, he's gonna give us a Monday night residency," Scabies nodded. Steve leaned back in his chair idly toying with the damaged lamp stand he'd used as a makeshift microphone earlier to amuse everyone with his Rod Stewart impression. "Fuck the Roxy," he said, letting go of the stand. "We're goin' on a promotional trip to Holland."

"Remember to bring some good hash back with you," said Mick. "If I bring anything back with me, Mikey boy; it'll be the fuckin' clap." Ingham walked over to the record player. "Any requests?" he asked. "Yeah, put 'Anarchy' on," Steve said, grabbing hold of the lamp stand again and dropping into his Rod Stewart impersonation. "I am an anti-Christ . . . I am an *anarchist!*" "*Harold, feed the horses!*" Sensible yelled. "What was that?" Steve asked.

"Oh, don't me wrong, Steve; you boys do the song right enough on stage," Sensible said. "But on vinyl it sounds like a Bad Company outtake with Old man Steptoe on vocals. "You're still pissed off 'cos you got chucked off the tour?" Steve sneered. "We didn't give a fuck about being kicked off the tour," Scabies retorted. "We're just pissed off about what happened in Derby."
"Yeah, we were made to look like tossers," Sensible nodded. "I mean, we are tossers. But not in that sense." Ingham was anxious to avoid the frisson of earlier. "What would you like on, Sid?" Go on, anything you like. I can't keep playing the Faces, Dolls or Stooges . . ." Sid got up and headed for the door without responding. Caroline came over and replenished Ingham's glass. "What a year this has been," she said, settling herself cross-legged on the rug. "It's certainly the most exciting year since I started at *Melody Maker*; the latter half especially. And I suspect next year's going to be even more exciting."
"Why do you say that?" Glen asked. Caroline took a sip from her glass. "This time last year, you - the Pistols - were just starting out. July saw the Clash and the Damned make their debuts. We've also got Suzi and the Banshees, Buzzcocks, Generation X. And from what I'm hearing, more and more bands are forming up and down the country. Punk is a genuine movement now; with its own '*raison d'etre*'." "How many of them have you had?" Glen smiled.

"You could have called it somethin' else though, Coony," said Steve. "Somethin' other than 'punk' . . ." "I still say '? Rock' would have worked," Ingham offered. "You would, wouldn't you seeing as it was your idea," Caroline smiled. "'Punk' derives from the sixties garage scene," she said, turning to Steve. "Yeah, but in the states a 'punk' is a bloke that takes it up the shitter in jail!" Steve fired back. "That's just one of the connotations," Caroline said with a dismissive wave. "And Jimmy Cagney always calls someone a 'punk' in his films. Like I said, punk is a movement now. And while I can't seem to get Ray - my editor at *Melody Maker* - to understand this, I've started writing about punk in my own time. I'm focusing on how punk has broken down the barriers in the hitherto male-dominated world of rock.. Even as little as five years ago women were either solo artists, or backing singers. You never saw a girl fronting a rock group. Punk has done away with the misogynistic barriers, and allowed girls like Suzi Ballion to take centre stage. And that's why people will still be talking about what punk has achieved in a hundred years." "You should get yourself down to Hyde Park Corner on a Sunday morning, Caroline,'" Joe smiled. The room fell silent as the sound of Jim Reeves crooning "Welcome To My World" drifted down from upstairs. "What the fuckin' hell's that?" Steve gasped. "It'll be Sid," Caroline smiled. "He was playing it earlier. And before you ask, no, it's not mine."

♪♪♪

Steve and Paul made their way downstairs to the kitchen where the four Heartbreakers and Keeth Paul were sat huddled around the table. Thunders had the telephone clutched in one hand, the receiver nestled in the crook of his shoulder. Steve was grabbing a couple of beers from the fridge when Roadent came in bursting in singing the chorus to Slade's "Merry Christmas Everybody". "Keep it down!" Thunders snapped. "I'm tryin'," he broke off upon being connected. "Hi, Baby . . . Jules? . . . Who the fuck is this . . . Nancy . . . Nancy Spungen? . . . What the fuck are you doin' there, Nancy? . . . What? . . . Yeah, Jerry's fine." He twisted round as Nolan grabbed his shoulder. "What . . . No, Jerry's not . . . he's ah . . . he's ah indisposed right now . . . Sure, I'll tell him you said 'hello' . . . Yeah, Billy and Waldo are fine too . . . What, what was that? . . . What's that you say? It's a lousy line . . . 'What? . . . Yeah, London's great . . . the Sex Pistols are great . . . I don't know when . . . What? What was that you said? . . . You're coming over here? . . . When? . . . Wow, that's great, Nancy . . . Course, I'll be sure to tell Jerry . . . Now, will you get off the fuckin' phone, cos I need to speak to Julie . . . Oh, hi, Baby . . . Yeah, I miss you too . . ." "Who's Nancy?" Steve asked Billy Rath.
"Uh, she's Niggs' girlfriend," Rath said, looking over at Nolan. "How many times do I have to tell you, Billy; Nancy was never my fuckin' girlfriend!" Nolan snapped. "She's just a girl I know," he said to Steve. "Does she put out?" Steve asked using one of the American euphemisms he'd picked up from The Heartbreakers during the tour. "Nancy's legs spread like butter," Rath chuckled. "Where's she live?" Steve asked. "Greenwich," Nolan said.
"That's not too far," Steve said, as Jonh Ingham entered. "That's Greenwich, as in Greenwich Village, NYC," Nolan corrected him.
"Too bad," Steve shrugged as Ingham appeared in the doorway. "Hold me beer, John; I'm just goin' for a dump." "Jesus, please tell me he reversed the charges" Ingham said as Steve pushed past him. There was a loud commotion out on the stairwell. "Christ, that's all I need," he groaned. A

heartbeat later Marc Zermati, the owner of the independent French punk label Skydog came charging down the stairwell, ranting and raving in his native tongue; his diatribe interspersed with the occasional English swearword. Before anyone could react Zermati pulled a knife from the waistband of his jeans and stabbed it into the door, demanding the return of his fur coat. Ingham tried placating the Frenchman. "I told you earlier, Marc; no one has seen your coat." "I am not leaving here without my fucking coat!" Zermati yelled. "One of you bastards has it!" Ingham was yelling at Thunders to get off the line and dial 999 when Nolan sprang up and blindsided Zermati with a right hook before bundling him up the stairs. The atmosphere was magically transformed as everyone relived the excitement of the last few minutes. Ingham was explaining how he knew Zermati when Steve came swanning through the door with Zermati's coat draped over his shoulders.

Epilogue

Heathrow Airport: Saturday, 8 January 1977

Paul was sporting Zermati's purloined fur coat. While no one had said anything at Caroline Coon's Christmas party, Glen suspected Keeth Paul's staying in the dressing room while The Heartbreakers were out onstage at eachof the three Dutch dates had to be more than coincidental. The Pistols had been on the cusp of something great, he'd felt it in his water. "Anarchy" had been selling well, and who knows how well it might have faired had they not gone on *Today*? While awaiting their flight at Schiphol Malcolm had said how several other companies were already expressing an interest in signing the Pistols. Glen wasn't sure whether John, Steve, or Paul had believed their manager's spiel, but thanks to Mike Thorne's revelations about the possibility of a solo deal at EMI he no longer cared. He'd no intention of going it alone of course, as he liked being part of something. He already had a guitarist in mind. He could hardly ask Malcolm if he still had Steve New's number, but he remembered someone mentioning how he was working as a postal clerk at Warner Bros.' London offices. He was imagining what John's reaction might be if EMI did sign him up as a solo artist when he heard someone shout out his name. He looked round to find everyone looking at him. "Sorry, what was that?" he asked Nils who was standing the closest to him, "I was miles away." "We should be so fuckin' lucky," John scowled as he sidled past with Debbie Juvenile. "Ignore him, mate," Nils said. "You know what he's like when he's in one of his moods." "I don't to be honest," Glen sighed wearily. "I've never seen him when he's not in one of his moods. Malcolm keeps telling me how John's got 'many sides'. Well, from where I'm standing none of them are good! And do you know what, if I ever bump into Bill Grundy again I'll buy him a pint because he's done me a favour. " The cab pulled up in front of them and Glen opened the rear door and slid his bass onto the back seat. All he could think about now was getting "Rich Kids" worked up so that he could present it to Thorne at the earliest opportunity. It had been slow in coming, but he knew in his heart that he'd had enough of being a Sex Pistol. It simply just wasn't worth the aggravation anymore. And if Malcolm, or John was in any doubt as to how he was feeling, his refusal to go back onstage for the encore after the second Paradiso show should serve as his letter of resignation.